"I was enthralled from start to finish. *Remember to Forget* took me to deep places of the heart and touched the spot where we all long for unconditional love. I wanted to stay in Clayburn, Kansas, forever. Raney's best book yet!"

Colleen Coble—Author of *Midnight Sea*

"Deborah Raney has done it again! *Remember to Forget* is a wonderful, heartwarming story about learning to trust . . . and love. Yes, I loved it."

Roxanne Henke—Author of *After Anne,* and other books in the Coming Home to Brewster series, and *The Secret of Us*

"Wow. *Remember to Forget* has it all: a gentle love story that won't let go, with crosscurrents pulling way deeper than you expect. Pack your bags, because your heart is going to Clayburn, Kansas!"

Robert Elmer—Author of *The Recital* and *Like Always*

"An enthralling, realistic depiction of lives in need of God. Another unforgettable story from an excellent writer."

Yvonne Lehman—Author of forty-three novels; director, Blue Ridge Writers Conference

"Only Deb Raney can blend the story of a woman who struggles with deceit and survival into one of love and redemption. Grab your tissues as you cheer for a woman who fights her way into the hands of God and unconditional love."

DiAnn Mills—Author of *Nebraska Legacy, Leather and Lace, When the Shadow Falls,* and more

"*Remember to Forget* is an emotional ride that eloquently reminds us of God's promise to make all things new."

Carolyne Aarsen—Author of *The Only Best Place*

"Two broken souls from different worlds. Somehow, some way, you're praying Deborah Raney brings them together. A heartwarming tale, with a pulse-pounding finish."

Creston Mapes—Author of *Dark Star* and *Full Tilt*

"Deborah Raney's *Remember to Forget* is a tender, emotional story of second chances. A real blessing."

Lyn Cote—Author of The Women of Ivy Manor series.

"Deborah Raney's *Remember to Forget* is a nicely crafted allegory wrapped in a sweet love story that entertains from start to finish."

DeAnna Julie Dodson—Author of *In Honor Bound, By Love Redeemed,* and *To Grace Surrendered*

"From the opening page of *Remember to Forget,* I was swept into the idyllic town of Clayburn, Kansas. Yet even in this beautiful town, the story reveals deep heartache; but, thankfully, Deb Raney shows that within every heartache is an opportunity for hope."

Tricia Goyer—Award-winning author of *From Dust and Ashes* and *Arms of Deliverance*
www.triciagoyer.com

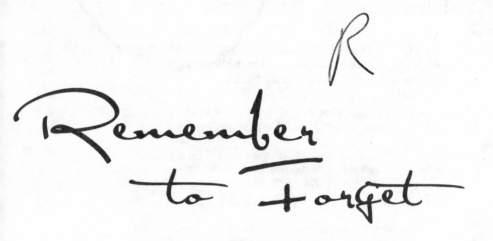

Remember to Forget

a clayburn novel

Award-Winning Author

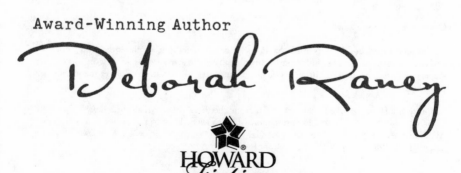

Deborah Raney

HOWARD
Fiction
A DIVISION OF SIMON & SCHUSTER
New York   London   Toronto   Sydney

Our purpose at Howard Books is to:
- *Increase faith* in the hearts of growing Christians
- *Inspire holiness* in the lives of believers
- *Instill hope* in the hearts of struggling people everywhere

Because He's coming again!

Published by Howard Books, a division of Simon & Schuster
1230 Avenue of the Americas, New York, NY 10020
www.howardpublishing.com

Remember to Forget © 2007 by Deborah Raney

In association with the Steve Laube Agency

Library of Congress Cataloging-in-Publication Data
Raney, Deborah.
   Remember to forget / Deborah Raney.
   p. cm.
   ISBN 10: 1-58229-643-X; ISBN 13: 978-1-58229-643-2
   I. Title.

PS3568.A562R46 2007
813'.54—dc22

2006052569

10 9 8 7 6 5 4 3 2 1

HOWARD colophon is a registered trademark of Simon & Schuster, Inc.

Manufactured in the United States of America

For information regarding special discounts for bulk purchases, please contact Simon & Schuster Special Sales at 1-800-456-6798 or business@simonandschuster.com.

Edited by Ramona Cramer Tucker
Interior design by Tennille Paden
Cover design by Terry Dugan

To Reed,

precious grandson,

with love

Acknowledgments

I wish to offer sincere thanks and deep appreciation to the following people for their part in bringing this story to life:

For help with research and editorial direction: Tamera Alexander; Ken Raney; Terry Stucky; Max and Winifred Teeter; my authors' groups, ChiLibris and ACFW, who are always ready with expert assistance; and the kind folks at the Swedish Country Inn in Lindsborg, Kansas, which served as a model for Wren's Nest, and where the idea for this story was born.

I also wish to thank the ChiLibris Midwest contingent for help in brainstorming this story: Dr. Mel and Cheryl Hodde, Dave and Colleen Coble, Till Fell, Judy Miller, Nancy Moser, and Steph Whitson.

Special thanks to my ace critique partner Tamera Alexander, my talented editors Ramona Cramer Tucker, and Philis Boultinghouse and Terry Whalin at Howard Books; and to my agent extraordinaire, Steve Laube. As always, all of your names deserve to be on the cover alongside mine.

To my wonderful husband, our children, and extended family: what a gift from the Lord you each are. You make it all worthwhile.

One thing I do: Forgetting what is behind
and straining toward what is ahead,
I press on toward the goal to win the prize
for which God has called me heavenward in Christ Jesus.
Philippians 3:13–14 NIV

"Get out! Get out of the car!" He spit the words like machine-gun fire.

Chapter One

A lofty full moon painted a jagged swathe of light across Lafayette Avenue. Maggie Anderson glanced at the digital numbers on the dashboard. *Four o'clock in the morning.*

An eerie calm hovered over New York, the street absent its typical bumper-to-bumper congestion. At least she would make it back to the apartment in good time. Maybe for once she wouldn't have to give him a play-by-play to justify every minute she'd been out of his sight.

A vagrant staggered into the crosswalk ahead of her, beckoning her with a leer. She averted her eyes and reached across the console of the Honda Civic to pat the brown paper bag buckled into the passenger seat beside her, testing again to make sure it was secure. Before driving away from the liquor store, she'd tightened the seat belt around Kevin's precious bottle as if it were a child. It might as well be. She would pay dearly if she slammed on the brakes and sent his next fix flying through the windshield. For a split second the thought caused a cynical smile to tug at her mouth . . . until an image of the probable aftermath came into focus.

She rubbed her left wrist, remembering his last tantrum, and forced her mind to blank out the scene. No use spoiling these brief minutes of freedom with a dose of reality.

Crossing Clinton Street, she changed lanes and reached to adjust the air-conditioner vent. The cool air caressed her face, a balm for early June temperatures that had barely dropped during the night. She leaned back against the headrest and let out a slow breath, willing her thoughts to carry her to the one place that never failed to bring her peace. She'd become adept at conjuring the scene. The city streets receded to the periphery of her vision, and there it was . . .

The riverbank, soft beneath her bare feet. Cool water lapping at her toes. And overhead, towering trees that whispered in the breeze, calling her to step deeper into the river's flow. She lowered her eyelids to half-mast, letting herself drift.

Behind her eyelids, a moon like the one that hung over New York tonight cast a yellow glow over the countryside. Except the moon of her imagination was far, far from the city. Where, she didn't know. It only mattered that it was far away from where she was now.

Opening her eyes, she reoriented herself to the road. But the scene remained, warming her from the inside out—in a way that had nothing to do with the sticky summer heat.

She tried to go deeper into the daydream, but ahead, a traffic light turned from green to amber. Hers was the only vehicle in the intersection. She could run the light and probably get away with it. Instead she tapped the brakes and prepared to stop. The light meant she could spend another ninety seconds in her tranquil fantasy world.

She could truthfully tell her boyfriend it was just the traffic. No help for that. He couldn't blame her. She rehearsed her excuse and touched the paper bag once more to reassure herself that her cargo was safe.

Closing her eyes again, she counted out the seconds before the light would turn green and returned to the riverbank in her mind.

The cool water, lapping at her—

Boom-boom-boom! A series of sharp thuds vibrated the hood of the car. Hot air and acrid exhaust fumes rushed over her, carrying with them the city's distinctive music of distant sirens and taxi horns.

Maggie jerked to attention. A blurry image loomed in her driver's side window. A man dressed in gray sweats . . . a hooded jacket over his head. A fleece-clad knee held her driver's door open.

He pounded again—louder—on the roof of her car. "Get out! Get out of the car!" He spit the words like machine-gun fire.

Heart racing, Maggie tried to yank the door shut on his knee. But his leg pried it open wider. Fingers of steel reached through the opening and clamped around her arm, wrenching her sideways from the seat.

She flailed at the steering wheel, trying in vain to sound the horn. Would anyone pay attention, even if she could? The street was deserted.

"Get out of the car!" the man screamed again, his voice as shrill as a woman's.

She jerked her head from side to side, trying to make things come into focus in the moonlight. Then she saw his hand. His left hand was hidden inside the wide center pouch of his jacket. The shape of a blunt object was outlined against the fabric. A gun?

Panic clawed at her throat. "What do you want?"

"Shut up and get out of the car!"

Her eyes fell on the brown bag beside her. If she went home without the precious Jack Daniel's . . . She shuddered, knowing that whatever this guy might do to her couldn't be much worse than what she'd have coming at home.

She checked her rearview mirror. Traffic whizzed by on the freeway in the distance, but no other vehicles were stopped at the light. Could this guy be bluffing about having a weapon? She wasn't about to get out of the car in this part of the city in the middle of the night.

When the light turned green, another car eased to a stop at the intersection on her left. The man in the hood opened her door wider. He hissed a curse and wedged himself through the opening. In one smooth motion, he undid her seat belt and, with a meaty hip, shoved her across into the passenger seat. The momentum left her sprawled between the seat and the floor.

He slammed the door and gunned the engine. The car lurched through the intersection.

Maggie cowered from her precarious half-prone perch on the edge of the seat, clawing at the dashboard to regain her balance. "What do you wa—"

"Shut up, I said!" He raised a sharp elbow and used it like a weapon.

She dodged his aim with a practiced bob and clung to the car door. The whiskey bottle dug into the small of her back. "Here." She reached behind her. "Take this. It's the good stuff. Just, please . . . let me go."

The man glared at her, meeting her eyes for the first time. He snorted, then trained a laser stare on the road as if he wouldn't dignify the likes of her with a response.

She dug in the pocket of her khaki slacks and took out the change from the fifty-dollar bill Kevin had given her for the liquor store. "Here." She thrust the money at him.

"Keep your money," he barked. "And keep your mouth shut."

Cowed, she returned the cash to her pocket and sat in silence beside him. She gripped the sides of her seat, bouncing at every bump in the road, her mind accelerating to match the engine as the car flew over the city streets. If booze and cash didn't interest him, she hoped the use of her car—Kevin's car—was the only thing he was after.

As they reached the end of Lafayette, the traffic picked up a little with early-morning commuters. With one glance in the rearview mirror, the man merged into the flow of vehicles.

Maggie was in unfamiliar territory now. No matter what happened from this point on, it was a safe bet she wasn't going to be delivering anything to Kevin. At least not anytime soon. And maybe never. She stared at the digital clock on the dashboard, watching the numbers flick forward. They'd driven at least half an hour in the opposite direction from the apartment. Kevin would be pacing the foyer and cursing her by now.

She eyed her captor before she angled her body back to attempt a glimpse at the gas gauge. Even so, her view was skewed. But she was pretty certain there wasn't enough gas in the Civic to get her back home.

What would this guy do if the car ran out of gas? A flash of memory took her back to another day on another highway. Kevin had been late for a job interview—and he'd called her at the office and coerced her into picking him up and driving him to the interview. The car had run out of gas, fueling a rage in Kevin like she'd never seen before. In the end he didn't get the job and pinned the blame on her for not filling up the tank. It was the first time his verbal lashings had threatened to turn physical.

Now her mouth twisted at the irony of finding herself a literal captive to this stranger when, in truth, she'd lived as a virtual hostage to Kevin Bryson for almost two years.

If she felt any fear, it was in imagining Kevin's accusations when she told him about her abduction.

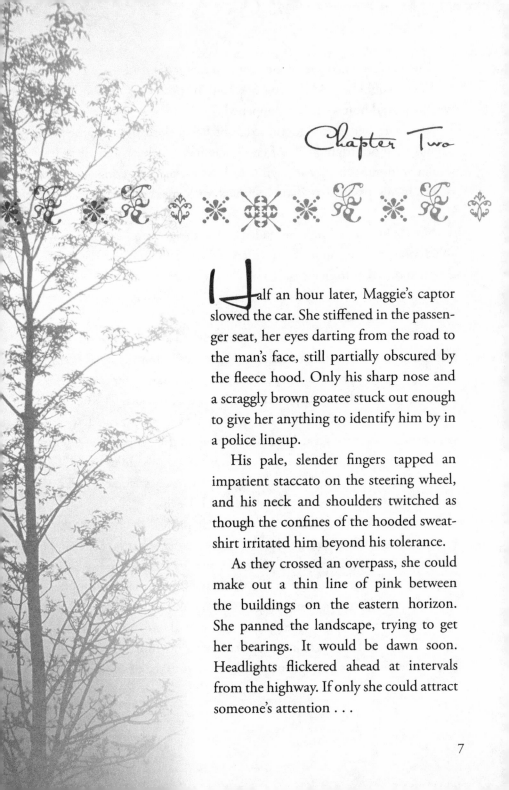

Chapter Two

Half an hour later, Maggie's captor slowed the car. She stiffened in the passenger seat, her eyes darting from the road to the man's face, still partially obscured by the fleece hood. Only his sharp nose and a scraggly brown goatee stuck out enough to give her anything to identify him by in a police lineup.

His pale, slender fingers tapped an impatient staccato on the steering wheel, and his neck and shoulders twitched as though the confines of the hooded sweatshirt irritated him beyond his tolerance.

As they crossed an overpass, she could make out a thin line of pink between the buildings on the eastern horizon. She panned the landscape, trying to get her bearings. It would be dawn soon. Headlights flickered ahead at intervals from the highway. If only she could attract someone's attention . . .

The man punched the accelerator and merged onto I-287.

Kevin would be livid by now. She couldn't even guess how he'd react when she told him what had happened.

Watching her captor in the edge of her vision, she supposed she should be more frightened. After all, she had just been kidnapped by a man who most likely had a gun. At least he kept fingering the bulky object in his pocket, as if preoccupied with making sure it was still there.

No doubt her abductor intended to use the gun on her. A quiver of some strange emotion—was it relief?—skittered down her spine. She didn't know what to make of her odd calm.

If she felt any fear, it was in imagining Kevin's accusations when she told him about her abduction.

He would never believe her. But maybe when he found out the truth, he'd finally see the value in letting her have a cell phone.

But as the road signs sailed past outside her window, her genuine fear returned and escalated. They were headed out of the city. The Civic ate up the expressway at a speed faster than she'd ever driven. In a few minutes they were crossing the Hudson, driving on the Tappan Zee Bridge. Soon after they got off the bridge, she saw a sign for Saddle River. She'd only been to Jersey once, but she was pretty sure they were now well over an hour from the apartment she shared with Kevin.

Her abductor seemed to relax a little. He pushed the hood back off his forehead to reveal stringy blond hair. As if sensing her perception, he glanced over, then quickly into the rearview mirror. Tapping the brakes, he pulled onto the shoulder of the thruway. They bumped along for a full minute with the rumble strips grinding and buzzing beneath the tires. Finally, still hugging the shoulder, he veered onto an off-ramp and brought the car to a complete stop. He made no effort to exit the car but leaned over the steering wheel and peered into the dusky light at the other traffic on the knot of intersecting roads.

Maggie studied him . . . the way his steely gray eyes darted in every direction. Was he watching for a ride, waiting for someone to pick him up? But when his gaze came to rest on her again, her heart stuttered. She edged toward her door and crossed her arms over her midsection.

Her captor's eyes seemed to pierce her thoughts. Her stomach knotted, and a bitter taste rose in the back of her throat. She had feared pain in the past, but she'd never been afraid to die. In fact, on another night not so long ago she had prayed for death. Prayed to a God she wasn't even sure existed. It shamed her to think of it now, but at the time, she'd only wanted to escape the agony Kevin had inflicted.

It hadn't been physical in nature—not that time anyway.

No, that night, *words* were his weapon of choice. And they had inflicted far deeper wounds than his fists would in the months that followed. She was still nursing those wounds. And unlike bruises that eventually faded and scabs that fell away, she suspected those words would leave her with scars that might never heal.

Again she turned to the stranger behind the wheel. He stared straight ahead, waiting for something. *For what?* she wondered.

Then, swiveling abruptly in his seat, he drilled his gaze through her and ordered, "Get out."

"But there's—"

"Get. Out. *Now.*" He rationed the words through clenched teeth, as if every syllable were in danger of extinction.

She moved her hand to the door handle, purposely fumbling with the lock. Stalling. She couldn't give up this car. Kevin would kill her for sure.

A sudden movement to her left jolted her as her captor withdrew something from the pouch of his sweatshirt. The flash of metal revealed a small handgun.

He leveled it at her. The violent shaking of his hands assured her it was loaded. But it told her something else: this man wasn't accustomed to doing things like this. Either that, or he was high on something.

"I said get out. Get out, or you are one dead chick." His face showed he meant it.

She opened the door and scrambled out. Then she remembered Kevin's bottle. If she had the whiskey, at least she could prove to Kevin that she'd been where she was supposed to be—where he'd told her to go.

She grabbed the Civic's door handle, but a sudden *screak* of tires caused her to let loose of the door handle as if it were alive with high voltage. The car lurched forward, pelting her with a spray of fine gravel.

The impact sent Maggie tumbling backward off the road's narrowing shoulder. She clutched at a fistful of weeds on the way down, but it barely broke her fall. She landed with a thud in a spongy drainage ditch.

Rubbing her eyes, she waited for the dizziness to subside. When she'd regained her bearings, she tied a loose shoestring and scrambled up the steep incline back onto the roadway. She swiped in vain at a grass stain on her white blouse and dusted the sand from her khakis. Brushing her hands together, she saw that her palms were imprinted with specks of sand and asphalt. They stung as if they'd been burned.

Now what?

Before she had time to think, a pickup veered off the ramp and whizzed past her going at least twice as fast as the 25 mph speed limit sign suggested. Two young men inside rubbernecked, taunting and blowing wolf whistles.

The bare-chested passenger hung out the window and shouted, "Hey, blondie, whatcha sellin' there?"

The truck slowed, and Maggie's heart thumped in her throat. But the pickup sped up again when a midnight blue sedan came down the ramp behind it. The truck turned on the city street as the sedan came to a halt at the bottom of the hill. But instead of turning, the blue sedan pitched into reverse and rolled back up the ramp toward her.

Maggie froze. For all she knew, she might have been safer in the Civic with a deranged gunman than with the driver of this car. The sedan came to a stop a few yards in front of her. Maggie frantically rehearsed what she would say to the driver as the dark glass of the passenger's side window rolled down smoothly.

"Do you need a ride, honey?" a squawky feminine voice called out.

Maggie stooped to peer in the window and almost laughed. The monster of her imagination was a petite, gray-haired woman. When Maggie's own reflection stared back at her in the sedan's tinted window, it struck her that the old woman was probably as frightened at her disheveled appearance as Maggie was at the unknown.

"No, that's okay," she told the woman. "I . . . I'm waiting for a ride."

"This is no place for a young girl," the driver scolded. "Why don't you let me take you wherever it is you're going?"

Maggie hesitated, then reached for the door. She wasn't going to get a safer offer than this.

Maggie settled into the passenger seat. The woman reached a diamond-spangled arm to adjust her rearview mirror. In the side mirror, Maggie spotted a car coming up behind them on the ramp. She jerked her door shut and searched for the seat belt.

A heavy, sweet perfume clung to the interior of the sedan. The driver trained her eyes on the road and swiftly merged into traffic on the one-way street that by now was teeming with morning commuters.

Maggie watched the woman from the fringe of her vision, taking in the ice blue jogging suit that was a perfect match to the neat French twist of her hair. Sparkly earrings and matching bracelets and rings seemed somehow to complement the casual outfit perfectly.

Two blocks later the woman pressed a spotless white tennis shoe to the brake at a red light and stretched a frail, veined hand toward Maggie.

"My name is Opal Sanchez. Call me Opal."

"Hi. I'm Maggie Anderson." She forced a smile. "Thanks for the ride."

Opal eyed the grass-stained knees of Maggie's pants. "Are you okay?"

"I'm fine." She would have to report the car stolen to the police, but she was hesitant to tell this woman what had happened. She'd learned long ago not to trust too easily.

"If you say so. Now where can I take you? You headed to work this early?"

Maggie shook her head. "My apartm—"

Something stopped her. Kevin would be fuming when she got there. And he'd probably send her right back to the liquor store—after he slapped her around a little.

Opal drove on, one ear inclined toward Maggie, waiting for her directions. Maggie wished she could keep going. Drive until the road ended, wherever that might be. Just disappear.

Her breath caught. The fragile seed of the idea hovered there, tempting her. She stared out her window at the blur of highway guardrail. The roadsides were overgrown with weeds.

Why not disappear?

Kevin had no clue where she was right now. What was to stop her? He might search every cranny of the city for her, but this time she had a chance. This time, he wouldn't find her. Not the way he'd followed her to the refuge of her sister's apartment in Baltimore on her twenty-fourth birthday. Not the way he'd tracked her to the women's shelter a year later. They wouldn't have let her stay anyway. Kevin's abuse hadn't yet turned physical then, and the shelter had a policy on that. Besides, he managed to say the words that charmed the folks at the shelter . . . then charmed her right back into his arms, right back into his lair.

But now . . .

Maybe she had finally stumbled on a haven that Kevin Bryson couldn't breach. And one that would protect her from her own foolishness.

Maggie's thoughts leapfrogged over themselves. "I need to get to—" She remembered the sign she'd seen after they crossed the Tappan Zee. "I need to get to Saddle River."

The furrows in Opal's forehead deepened. "We're going the wrong way for Saddle River, honey. Are you sure?"

Was she sure about this? If she disappeared, she would have to leave everything behind. But the few possessions she owned paled compared to this chance to escape the horror her life had become. Still, she wouldn't be able to go back. Not for her drawings and the arsenal of art supplies she'd paid a small fortune for. Not even for Buttons. She swallowed hard. The big green-eyed tabby had been her confidant when she had no one else to talk to. Many a night she'd soaked the big tomcat's fur with her tears. It almost made her weep now to think of never seeing him again.

At least she didn't have to worry about Kevin hurting the cat. In truth, the man had offered Buttons more respect and kindness than he'd ever granted her. For the thousandth time, she asked herself why she hadn't seen Kevin Bryson for what he was. Before it was too late.

Sadly, she'd known for months now—ever since the night he finally made good on his threats—that Kevin wasn't anything she thought him to be when she fell for him. That night, the bruises and wrenched muscles he inflicted were nothing compared to the pain in her heart. But she'd been a coward. Too terrified to do anything about her situation.

But now, freedom was hers for the asking.

Opal parked at a curb. "Do you want to go back?"

"I . . . are you sure you have time?"

Opal Sanchez had a musical laugh. "Honey, time is one possession I have in spades. Your wish is my command." She held out a hand Vanna White style.

Maggie laughed too. "Okay. Yes. Please take me to Saddle River."

The words were there before she thought about all they meant. But as soon as she breathed them into the close air of the sedan, they filled her with an elation she hadn't felt in a long time.

They also filled her with something she barely recognized.

Something all but forgotten.

Hope.

"And where in Saddle River do you live?"

Did suspicion lurk in the wavering voice? Maggie sneaked a glance at Opal. The doubt in the woman's eyes matched that in her voice.

Maggie took a deep breath. This was her moment of truth. If she did this, she couldn't tell anyone. Kevin was too smart. And he'd tracked her down too many times before. No, if she made this happen, no one could know. Not even Jennifer.

The thought of her sister's sweet face made her hesitate. What if Kevin looked for her at Jenn's? What if he thought Jennifer was lying? He might just be angry enough to hurt her. To try to make her tell him something she couldn't possibly know. Of course, Jenn had Mark to protect her. Jenn's burly, six-foot-three husband had always intimidated Kevin. But what if he waited until he knew Mark was away?

Maybe she could warn her sister somehow. Or throw Kevin off the track. But she'd worry about that later. Right now she had to make a decision. Either she was doing this, or she was going back to the life that had become unbearable. And going back to face whatever judgment Kevin decided to dole out.

"I have friends in Saddle River." The words poured out in a torrent. "They're meeting me downtown. You can drop me off anywhere there. I know my way around."

For an instant, Opal Sanchez looked as if she might challenge Maggie. But then, with a little shake of her head, she worked the gearshift on the steering column and eased back into traffic.

Maggie's senses went on alert. Had Kevin sent them looking for her already?

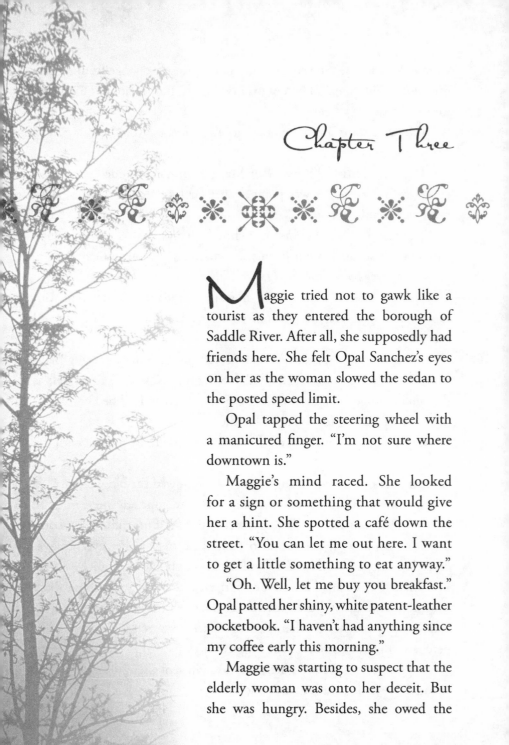

Chapter Three

Maggie tried not to gawk like a tourist as they entered the borough of Saddle River. After all, she supposedly had friends here. She felt Opal Sanchez's eyes on her as the woman slowed the sedan to the posted speed limit.

Opal tapped the steering wheel with a manicured finger. "I'm not sure where downtown is."

Maggie's mind raced. She looked for a sign or something that would give her a hint. She spotted a café down the street. "You can let me out here. I want to get a little something to eat anyway."

"Oh. Well, let me buy you breakfast." Opal patted her shiny, white patent-leather pocketbook. "I haven't had anything since my coffee early this morning."

Maggie was starting to suspect that the elderly woman was onto her deceit. But she was hungry. Besides, she owed the woman for the ride. She checked her pocket for the change from Kevin's fifty-dollar bill. She had barely twenty dollars, but it should be enough for breakfast. "My treat."

"Oh, you don't need to do that. Let me buy you breakfast. I've enjoyed your company."

"I . . . wouldn't feel right." But Maggie's protest sounded weak even to her own ears. If she was going to get far from Kevin Bryson, she'd need every dime in her pocket.

"Nonsense." Opal bobbed her chin for emphasis. "I've got plenty, and you're just starting out in this world. You keep your money."

Just starting out in this world.

Opal Sanchez couldn't know how profound her words were. But they encouraged Maggie. "Thank you. I really appreciate the ride and everything."

"Don't mention it again." Opal steered the car into a parking place in front of the café and set the brake. She fumbled with her seat belt as though her fingers might be arthritic. She winced and rubbed her shoulder before reaching for the door handle.

Maggie jumped out of the car and ran around to help Opal with the door.

Exhilaration surged through her as she followed the old woman into the restaurant. How long had it been since she'd gone anywhere or done anything without Kevin's first approving it? And if for some rare reason he didn't come with her for an occasion, he tracked her every move, dictating who she could talk to and when she should be home.

When they opened the door to the café, a bell rang somewhere overhead, announcing their arrival. Two law-enforcement officers with Saddle River patches on their sleeves turned to watch them from their perches on padded stools at the long counter.

Maggie's senses went on alert. Had Kevin sent them looking for her already? He hadn't wasted any time.

When the younger policeman turned to speak to his partner in low tones, Maggie murmured to Opal, "I have to go." She brushed past her and made for the door.

"Wait, honey," Opal said. "Wait! Just a—"

But the closing door cut off her words. Maggie jogged half a block before she stopped on the sidewalk, panning the street, calculating where she might hide if the officers pursued her.

"Maggie? Wait!" Opal's voice called from behind her.

Maggie spun around. Opal hurried along the sidewalk toward her.

The policemen were nowhere in sight.

She waited for Opal to catch up. The old woman was wheezing and breathless.

Maggie felt a stab of guilt. "I need to go." She glanced over Opal's shoulder to make sure the officers weren't following. "I-I just remembered I have to meet my friends."

"Well, here." Opal rummaged in her pocketbook. "I want to give you something."

Maggie fidgeted, anxious to get away from the diner. But she was curious too.

Opal thrust a wad of rolled-up bills at her.

"What's this?"

"I want you to have it."

"But why?"

Opal chuckled and looked toward the sky. "Honey, when the Man upstairs tells you to do something, you don't turn Him down and you don't ask questions."

"The man up—" Maggie stopped. "Oh, you mean . . . ?" She let her gaze travel up to follow Opal's.

The woman smiled and patted Maggie's hand—the one holding the cash. "Whatever you're running from, whatever you're searching for . . . maybe this will help you on your journey."

"But—"

"Shhh. Just accept it. Maybe you can do the same for someone else when you're an old woman like me."

Maggie didn't know what to think. She needed the money. It might be the only thing that kept her from running back to Kevin. But she didn't feel right accepting cash from a stranger. Besides, Opal had already given her a ride and offered to buy her breakfast.

She let her gaze meet the woman's rheumy brown eyes, questioning.

"Please," Opal said, "if it makes you feel better, I have plenty where that came from. My father left me well off."

Maggie made up her mind. She touched Opal's veined hand. "Thank you so much. You don't know what this means to me."

"I think I have some idea." Opal smiled. "You go on now. And God bless you."

Maggie wanted to hug her, but somehow she couldn't make herself reach out and embrace the frail woman. Too many times she'd made herself vulnerable, only to be rejected. "Thank you, Opal. God bless you too."

Maggie turned and ran up the street, not slowing until she veered into a side alley. She pivoted and started to jog backward, hoping to spot Opal. When a flash of ice blue disappeared into the café, Maggie stopped on the corner of the street and held up one hand in a useless wave.

"Thank you," she whispered. Reluctantly, she jogged around the corner. She ran for six blocks, careful to pace herself, so she would appear to be an ordinary morning jogger. But she took a circuitous route, going a block north, turning west for another block and a half, then zigzagging north again through a wide commercial alleyway. If the cops were looking for her, she wouldn't make it easy for them.

Now fairly certain she wasn't being followed, she stopped at a bench in front of a post office, exhausted and out of breath. Glancing around to make sure no one was watching, she plucked the wad of cash Opal

Sanchez had given her from the pocket of her khakis and unrolled the bills. She fanned them out enough to read the denominations. Her breath caught at the sight of two hundred-dollar bills along with some smaller bills. She took a quick count. With her change from the liquor store, she had almost three hundred dollars. Except for making out the checks to pay the apartment bills, she hadn't had that much money at her disposal since the day she quit her job at the design firm and moved in with Kevin.

Three hundred dollars wouldn't last long, but maybe long enough to get her far, far away from New York.

The sleepy little town of Saddle River was starting to wake up. The digital clock atop a savings and loan down the street flashed back and forth between 78 degrees and 6:15 a.m. She was in New Jersey. Probably a couple of hours from the apartment.

She'd already gotten farther away than she ever dared to dream. Strangest of all, after all the nights she'd lain awake in bed beside Kevin, planning an escape she knew would never happen—staring at the ceiling, terrified to move, lest she awaken him and provoke his ire—now, without one moment of planning, she found herself miles away and him none the wiser. She shook her head in disbelief. It was as if she'd been handed a gift beyond anything she could have wished for.

But what next? Where could she go on three hundred dollars? More importantly, if she managed to find a job and a place to live, she'd have to prove her identity, go on record. And he would find her. She knew him too well not to believe that.

The sun slanted between the buildings and warmed her face. Beads of perspiration sprung up on her forehead. She'd better decide something soon.

When her stomach growled, she remembered she hadn't eaten since yesterday evening. She stood and shoved the cash deeper into her pocket. The most important thing she could do now was to put as many miles as possible between her and Kevin Bryson.

Had he gone to the office yet? Would he stay home and worry about her, or would he go on as usual? Would he fix his own lunch, or would he have to buy something from the cafeteria at the firm? She was going to be in so much trouble when he—

She shook the thought away, wagging her head so hard her hair grazed her cheeks. Never again was she going to be in trouble with him. It was time to wash his controlling, brainwashing messages out of her mind.

She was free. *Free.*

With new resolve, she headed down the street. But after walking aimlessly for ten minutes, she realized she didn't know where she was going. She couldn't just wander around this town looking lost.

When she passed a café, a pretty hostess waved and smiled from the window. Somehow that small acknowledgment gave her courage. Backtracking, she stepped inside. The aromas of cinnamon and vanilla and strong coffee assailed her nostrils. Her stomach rumbled again.

"Good morning. Just one this morning?"

Maggie froze for a second.

The hostess waited expectantly, still wearing that welcoming grin.

Maggie inspected the merchandise in the glass case beneath the cash register while she gathered her wits. "I just need a pack of gum and—" Gulping in a deep breath, she made a decision. "I was wondering where I could buy a bus ticket."

our hours later and ninety-nine dollars poorer, every joint sore from the long hike to the bus station in Ridgewood, Maggie stared out the window of a Greyhound bus headed for Columbus, Ohio. She would have been sunk without Mrs. Sanchez's cash. As it was, she was lucky they'd let her on without a photo ID. She told them the truth— if not the whole truth and nothing but the truth—that she'd left her license in the glove compartment of her car.

She stared at the telephone poles jutting up along the railroad running parallel to the highway. They had a hypnotic effect on her as they flashed past the windows of the bus.

She had never been to Columbus. Never been farther west than Philadelphia. But Ohio was as far as she could go for less than one hundred dollars. It felt like leaping off a cliff to purchase that ticket.

Now she only hoped she could fly.

Wren's laughter
drowned out the ghost
of Amy's voice.
The relief of it eased
Trevor's pulse.

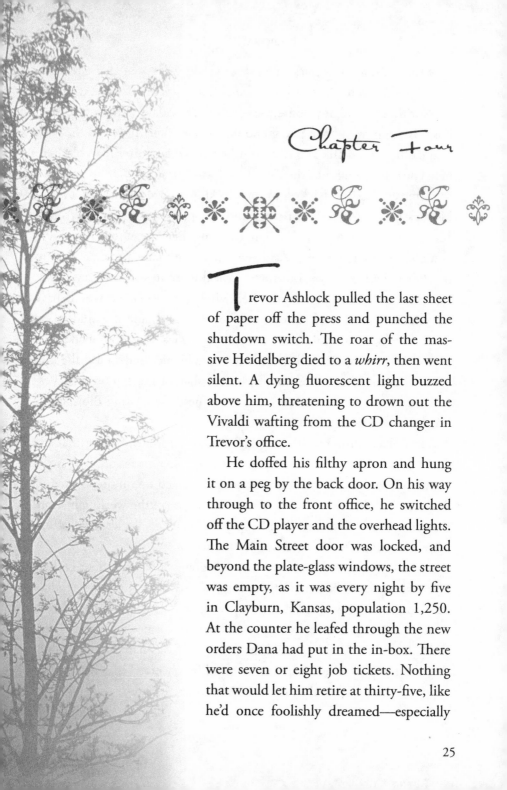

Chapter Four

Trevor Ashlock pulled the last sheet of paper off the press and punched the shutdown switch. The roar of the massive Heidelberg died to a *whirr*, then went silent. A dying fluorescent light buzzed above him, threatening to drown out the Vivaldi wafting from the CD changer in Trevor's office.

He doffed his filthy apron and hung it on a peg by the back door. On his way through to the front office, he switched off the CD player and the overhead lights. The Main Street door was locked, and beyond the plate-glass windows, the street was empty, as it was every night by five in Clayburn, Kansas, population 1,250. At the counter he leafed through the new orders Dana had put in the in-box. There were seven or eight job tickets. Nothing that would let him retire at thirty-five, like he'd once foolishly dreamed—especially now that thirty-five was less than three years away—but that advertisement they'd run in the *Clayburn Courier* had apparently done its job.

Not that he had any desire to *ever* retire nowadays. No. Best to keep busy. To keep from having to go home too soon. He moved to the back of the office and cranked the thermostat up. It'd be hotter than blazes in here come morning, but the electric bill was eating up half his profits.

After exiting the back door and locking it, Trevor headed toward his pickup. He tossed his briefcase into the passenger seat, then trotted across the alley to the inn. The sign declaring the place Wren's Nest hung at a cockeyed angle over the side entrance. He made a mental note to fix it first chance he got. But the electrical work in the kitchenette was top priority tonight. He'd promised Wren Johannsen he would have the electricity back on before he quit for the night, and it would take a good three hours to finish rewiring the tiny room. He also hoped to get a good start on the drywall. At least it would be nice and cool at the inn. And if he was lucky, Wren might have a slice of her famous peaches-and-cream cheesecake left over from the Tuesday-morning Bible study. Working on Tuesdays had its advantages.

He walked through the long hallway to the lobby, noting that the doors to all the rooms were open, meaning there was, unfortunately, plenty of room in the inn. Business usually picked up on the weekends. But if they didn't fill at least a couple of rooms on the weeknights too, Bart and Wren Johannsen couldn't pay the regular bills, let alone afford the remodeling Trevor was doing for them.

He admired the Johannsens for not giving up. But there came a point where they'd be better off cutting their losses and getting out while they could. He was afraid that point wasn't far off. Bart was surely old enough to retire, but Trevor respected the man for not taking that step. He'd already decided he would never retire. It was hard enough filling that hour or two at home before he could finally crawl into bed and let sleep dull his senses and shut off the memories.

"That you, Trevor?"

At Wren's shrill call, he shook off the voices and images that had started to play in his head—Amy's musical laughter, little Trev's pudgy arms reaching out to him . . .

"Yeah, it's me, Wren. Hey, is that cheesecake I smell?"

Wren's laughter drowned out the ghost of Amy's voice. The relief of it eased Trevor's pulse.

Wren appeared in the doorway of the little dining area adjacent to the kitchen, hands propped on her ample hips, stretching to her full five-foot-two stature. She attempted an aggravated expression but couldn't quite succeed over the twinkle in her eye. "Now how am I supposed to bake anything when my oven is sitting in the middle of the kitchen?"

"I don't know"—he inhaled deeply—"but that doesn't smell like anything that came from the Wal-Mart bakery."

Wren chuckled and shook her head. "Ooh, you're good, Mr. Ashlock. I'll give you that. Clara let me use her oven, but she was none too happy about it, I can tell you. I'll be hearing about it for umpteen weeks."

He grimaced, exaggerating his expression, in an effort to take the blame for Wren being on the outside of Clara Berger's good graces.

Her smile forgave him. "You get my kitchen back in working order before you leave tonight, and I'll send the whole bloomin' cheesecake home with you."

"The whole thing?"

She expelled a breath and tucked a strand of white hair into her frowsy bun. "Bible study got cancelled. And you know Bart. The man will eat every last slice of that thing if I leave it sitting here. And there's not enough insulin in Coyote County to counteract that much sugar."

Trevor grinned. "Well, in the interest of Bart's health, I guess I can take it off your hands."

Wren waved off his joke and bustled past him to the broom closet behind the check-in desk.

He helped himself to a couple of day-old snickerdoodles from the antique cookie jar on the desk and ducked under the ladder leaning against the arched dining-room doorway. He stood there, chewing and surveying the space.

Last month he and Bart had knocked out the back wall of the kitchenette, appropriating six feet from an unused side entry to enlarge the tiny galley kitchen and turn the dining alcove into an L-shaped room.

Brushing the cookie crumbs from his fingers, Trevor grabbed his toolbox from under the sawhorse. Why they were going to all this trouble and expense, he didn't know. They rarely filled the dining room as it was. But he admired the hope reflected in this remodeling project. And it gave him a way to fill his time. A way to forget.

She watched in horror as the bus rolled out of the parking lot.

Chapter Five

"You want half of my sandwich?"

Maggie's head jerked against the back of her seat. She fought to hold on to the fading image of her dream. To keep that flicker of hope kindled inside her.

But like a gust of wind, slumber slipped away, snuffing out a fragile memory she'd all but forgotten. The river lapping gently at her feet, cooling her calves . . .

She rubbed her eyes and blinked. Where was she? *Ah, the bus.* Outside, the western sky matched the tinted windows of the Greyhound, and the interstate spooled out before them like a never-ending silver ribbon.

Her seatmate, a toothless old man, held out a limp triangle wrapped in clear plastic. "Want half my sandwich?" he asked again. "You're welcome to it."

She made herself return his smile. "No thank you. You go ahead."

She was hungry, but not *that* hungry. *Yet,* she told herself wryly. This time tomorrow she might be kicking herself for turning down that soggy wad of bread and cheese.

The man shrugged. "Suit yourself."

She turned in her seat and rested her forehead on the cool window glass. It vibrated with the rhythmic *thump* of the highway beneath the wheels, and a childhood song her mother had sung came back to her. It played over and over in her head.

The wheels on the bus go round and round, round and round, round and round . . .

They'd been on the road for hours, and with each mile she breathed a little easier. She dozed off again briefly, but the vacuum-pressured wheeze of the bus's brakes roused her. Passengers rustled around her, gathering their possessions in preparation for the stop.

After pulling off the interstate, the driver parked at an all-night diner. Maggie followed the other passengers off the bus. The stench of diesel made her cough, and she jogged away from the fumes and toward the building.

Once inside, she waited in line to use the rest room, then washed her face and neck in the grimy sink. She tried to do something with her hair, but without a hairbrush, her efforts were wasted. She ended up slicking the limp strands behind her ears. Maybe she could pick up a few toiletries in the store adjacent to the restaurant. She wandered into the shop and selected a wide-toothed comb that would fit in her pocket, along with a toothbrush and a tube of ChapStick. Her stomach tried to remind her of its empty state as she walked by a display of candy and potato chips, but she ignored it. She didn't know how far the wad of cash in her pocket would have to stretch, but she could hold off at least until they got to Columbus.

She turned toward the checkout and stopped short as a row of pay phones outside the windows caught her eye. She paid for her items and took the bag outside. The bus was idling in front of the building, but several passengers were still inside the store. She had a few minutes.

Slipping two quarters into the far pay phone, she dialed the apartment.

The phone rang half a dozen times before a voice croaked, "Hello?"

Maggie's heart thudded at hearing Kevin's voice. Was it possible that she actually missed him? He sounded strangely subdued and, for a minute, she felt a little sorry for him.

But she pushed away the unwelcome thought when he barked, "Who's there?" into the phone.

She heard the all-too-familiar tone of agitation in his voice, heard him rattle the lamp on the nightstand. If Kevin was in bed, it must be after ten. Or else he'd gone to bed with a bottle. She peered through the window at the clock in the rest stop. *Twenty minutes after nine.* Whatever concern she'd felt seconds earlier vanished on the breeze.

"What the . . . ?" The voice in her ear spewed a curse and confirmed her suspicions. He was drunk. She heard his breathing, could feel the tension.

"Maggie? Is that you, Maggie? Where are you?" In a few seconds his terseness would turn into a string of curse words and he'd start kicking things around the apartment. Her resolve stiffened. If she were there, if she went back, how long would it be before *she* was the thing he was kicking around?

"Where's my car? Where's my fifty bucks? And where's my Jack Daniel's?" His voice gathered venom. "I don't have time for this. I have to work in the morning, you know. So help me, Maggie, you lousy little—"

She dropped the receiver back in place. Had she really thought for a minute that he might be worried about her? That he might miss her or be concerned that something had happened to her?

She was a fool.

Again.

The grinding *hiss* of compression brakes made her look back to the bus that sat idling at the edge of the parking lot. A terrifying thought struck her. What if Kevin could somehow trace her call? Did pay phone numbers show up on caller ID? Kevin was good with the computer. If there were a way to trace where a call came from, he would figure it out. Had she blown her cover before she'd tasted even twenty-four hours of freedom?

Her gaze flicked around the parking lot as she made her way through two rows of parked cars. She was being ridiculous. She'd ridden the bus for hours. Even if Kevin left New York right now, he'd never catch up with her. She should feel relief that he was at the apartment, that he'd answered the phone. Besides, he would never believe she could get this far away without him knowing it.

But she'd been stupid to call him. For all she knew, when he picked up the phone, the caller ID had spelled it out for him: *Maggie is calling from this particular bus stop. Come to Pennsylvania* (or wherever in the world she was) *and get her.*

A new thought struck terror in her chest. What if Kevin saw her location on caller ID and called the local police? They could be here within minutes. He wouldn't be above telling them that she'd stolen his car, and in that case they would have the authority to take her in—or worse, hold her until Kevin came for her.

The passengers were now waiting in queue to get back on the bus. The engine revved and diesel puffed from the exhaust. Panic seized her. If she got on that bus, she'd be a sitting duck. It wouldn't take much for the cops to discover where the bus had originated. They'd arrest her and haul her back to New York.

But if she didn't get back on the bus, she might never make it past this little spot in the road. She hadn't put nearly enough miles between her and Kevin Bryson yet. And besides, she'd paid fare all the way to Columbus. She couldn't afford to buy another bus ticket.

The bus horn blared, and the behemoth inched forward. Kevin's cursing echoed in her head. She felt like the rope in a vicious tug of war.

Finally the bus won and she broke into a run.

But even as she ran toward it, the bus crawled away. She broke into a sprint, her breath coming in sharp, painful gasps. "Stop! Wait! Stop!"

Her plea was carried away on an acrid belch of diesel fuel, and she watched in horror as the bus rolled out of the parking lot. The engine puffed and groaned, shifting gears and gathering speed. When the Greyhound finally eased down the ramp onto the interstate, Maggie slumped to the ground, burying her face in her hands.

What would she do? Her money was dwindling fast and, like an idiot, she'd convinced Kevin that she had run away. If she'd stayed away from the stupid telephone, he might think she was dead.

Now he probably assumed she was still in the Civic. If he had the police hunting for her, that's the vehicle they'd be searching for. The thought caused her to relax a little. She smiled to think how surprised he'd be when the police tracked down the car. Of course, the carjacker had probably abandoned the Civic long ago.

None of that mattered now. The bus wasn't an option anymore.

Leftover heat from the afternoon sun seeped up through the asphalt. Maggie wiped the perspiration from her forehead with the tail of her blouse and trudged back toward the convenience store.

If there was an ounce of comfort in losing them both on the same day, it was that they'd gone together.

Chapter Six

Trevor stood at the curb and looked west. The sun rode low in the sky. It would be dark in half an hour. He stepped into the street but turned back to see Bart Johannsen waving from the doorway of the inn, as Trevor knew he would be. The old man's yellow white beard nearly reached the bib of his engineer overalls.

Trevor smiled to himself. Wren would be nagging her husband to trim his shaggy mane soon.

Bart dropped his hands to clasp cigar-thick fingers over a belly that had seen too many of Wren's homemade cream pies. "See ya tomorrow, Trev."

Trevor waved back but winced at the nickname. He'd never gone by Trev. At least not after his son was born. He turned away and hurried across the alley to his pickup. Bart couldn't know how much it hurt to hear Trev's name.

It was only one of a million reminders every single day. The empty swing set in his backyard. The tricycle that sat abandoned in a corner of the garage. The day-care kids traipsing behind Miss Valdez on a field trip up Main Street—kids Trev would have started kindergarten with this fall.

Trev. It was his given name. *Trev Alex.* Trevor hadn't been crazy about the idea when Amy first brought it up, but she was adamant. "I want to name him after you, but this way nobody will saddle the poor kid with Junior." She'd wrinkled her nose then—that goofy expression that always made him think of a Chinese pug puppy.

He'd pretended to be reluctant to go along with her idea for naming their baby after him, but secretly, he'd felt honored. And when their little boy was born, nobody could have been a prouder dad than Trevor Ashlock.

The pickup was hotter than Wren's oven, but the smell that blasted him when he opened the door was more like a junior-high gymnasium on game day than one of Wren's savory offerings. He tucked the cheese-cake she'd sent with him in the jump seat. In spite of the layers of news-paper she'd swaddled the dessert in, it'd be a miracle if the whole thing wasn't a warm pool of cream and peach juice by the time he got home.

He climbed in and leaned across the seat to roll down the passen-ger side window. With his air conditioner on the fritz, it was a choice between dust and heat this time of year. He didn't handle the latter well. Dust would wash off.

He decided to forgo his usual drive-thru burger in the interest of get-ting the cheesecake home sooner. Besides, a couple of thick slices of the delicacy would make a more-than-decent dinner.

The truck bumped along the dusty road, and Trevor let the miles and the mellow tune on the radio work the kinks out of him. As promised, he'd gotten Wren's electricity back on before he left. He didn't tell her he'd probably have to turn it off for a couple of hours each evening for the next few nights. She would stew for nothing. Once he got the wiring finished, the remodeling job would move quickly. Though if he knew Wren, she'd have another project lined up for him before the paint was dry on this one.

Ten minutes later he turned up the lane to the old farmhouse he rented. Every time he wrote out that check for seven hundred dollars, he swore he'd talk to a Realtor before the next month's rent was due. With the carpentry skills his father had taught him, and the hours of spare time he seemed to have, he was a fool not to buy a little fixer-upper in town to turn a profit on. But then he'd see the saggy porch where he'd carried Amy over the threshold, he'd look out at the chicken coop where she'd kept her beloved hens. He'd walk up the creaky stairs to the room where Trev had been conceived, and smile up at the sparkles on the ceiling that Amy had pretended were stars while they snuggled under the quilts on cold winter nights, and he'd know he couldn't leave. Not yet.

If there was an ounce of comfort in losing them both on the same day, it was that they'd gone together. Sometimes a picture would come into his head—playing like a movie—his wife and son holding hands, laughing and skipping through a misty meadow. It comforted him. Amy had always lamented the Bible's description of heaven as a city. She hated anything "city." He'd barely been able to get her to Wichita for a day of shopping twice a year. The day he'd pointed out the green pastures and still waters of the psalms and told her he thought they would surely be a part of heaven for her, she cried and rewarded him with a kiss.

Halfway up the long lane, the farmhouse came into full view. The sky blue paint was fading on the west side of the house, but the honey-suckle vines hid the evidence well. He rounded the curve of the drive and tapped the brakes when he saw the SUV sitting in front of the house.

Shoot. Amy's parents. Their Explorer sat empty, the windows rolled down a crack against the heat. He expelled a breath that puffed out his cheeks. He was in no mood for this. He wondered how long they'd been waiting for him. Long enough for Verna to tidy up the living room and clean out the refrigerator the way she had last time they'd come. Not that he minded. It was the lecture he'd get about eating right and not working so hard and letting a little air in the house, for heaven's sake, that he wasn't looking forward to.

That, and the heavy coat of memories he could never shake off after a visit with Hank and Verna. He loved them both like his own parents, but he was grateful they lived in Kansas City and only dropped by a couple of times a year. He suspected the visits were as painful for Hank and Verna as they were for him.

Steeling himself, he climbed out of the pickup and went in through the back door, depositing Wren's cheesecake in the deep freeze in the mudroom before stepping into the kitchen.

Hank was reading the *Courier,* Clayburn's weekly newspaper that was printed at Trevor's shop. Verna had her head in the refrigerator.

"Hey there."

"Trevor!" Verna whirled and came at him like a cyclone.

He took a step backward and held out his hands. "I'm covered with dust. Let me take a quick shower and change clothes, and you can hug me all you want."

She laughed as if he'd told a sidesplitting joke. He prayed her laughter wouldn't dissolve into tears as it too often did.

Hank slid his chair back from the table and rose to shake Trevor's hand. "How's it going, Son?"

"Busy. Busier all the time." It was a safe answer. But a true one too. He made sure of that. "How are you folks doing?"

"Getting along . . . getting along. We had a funeral over in Coyote, and Verna wanted to stop by on the way back home. I told her you'd probably be working, but you know how she is."

Trevor smiled. He knew. Like mother, like daughter. Hank let Verna walk all over him just like he'd let Amy. And they were happy men for it.

"Can I get you something to drink?"

He opened the refrigerator. He was right. Verna had done a job on it. No more moldy leftovers, no more takeout boxes. She'd congregated an assortment of bottled fruit juice at the back of the top shelf, as if she thought he wouldn't notice her contribution.

"Some juice, maybe?" He winked at Verna and returned her sheepish smile with one of his own.

"I'm fine, thanks," Hank said. "We grabbed something before we left Coyote."

"Verna?"

"No, but let me get you something."

"I got it." Trevor pulled out a bottle of some cranberry concoction and poured himself a tall glass. He downed it all at once, then wiped his mouth with the back of his hand. "That's pretty good stuff."

"Amy drank it by the gallon . . . always said it kept her from getting bladder infections." Verna's voice faltered. "The girl should have been a doctor, as much as she knew about medical stuff."

Trevor took his cue and backed down the hall toward the bathroom. "I'm going to change. I'll be back in five minutes."

"Don't rush on our account," Verna shouted after him, her voice composed again.

In the shower, he let the stinging water pelt his skin while he tried to think of something he could talk to Hank and Verna about that wasn't ripe with Amy's memory. That was the trouble. Everything was ripe with Amy's memory. Everything.

He dried off and put on a pair of clean blue jeans and a T-shirt. Hair still wet, he padded barefoot back out to the kitchen.

"Oh, much better," Verna said when she saw him. She crossed the room with her arms outstretched.

Trevor let her hold him and pat his back for a long minute, knowing that when she pulled away, her eyes would be wet and her face contorted. Sometimes he wondered why she and Hank tortured themselves by coming to see him. It would be easier for all of them if they just forgot about him. Went on with their lives. They had no connection to him now. Not really.

But they'd played this polite game since the day of the funerals. Almost two years now. It seemed like an eternity ago.

And it seemed like only yesterday.

A stab of jealousy
cut through her, but
she quickly reminded
herself of what she was
escaping.

Chapter Seven

Maggie stood to the side while the clerk in the store waited on a man wearing cowboy boots and a wide, tooled leather belt with RICK burned into the back.

When his transaction was finished, she stepped up to the counter. The young man behind the cash register eyed her. "Can I help you?"

She tossed her head in the direction of the interstate. "I was supposed to be on that bus that just left."

The clerk rolled his eyes. "Sorry, miss, but those buses don't wait for nobody. There should be another one through here in a couple of hours. Where you headed?"

"Ohio. But I—"

"Excuse me." Behind her, the middle-aged cowboy who'd been in front of her in line cleared his throat loudly. "I couldn't help but overhear. You're goin' to Ohio?"

She nodded, wary.

"Whereabouts in Ohio?"

"I was supposed to be on that bus to Columbus."

The man's shoulders sagged. "Oh. Well, my wife and I are headin' to Cleveland, but that's a sight north of Columbus."

A pretty brunette came to stand beside the man, putting a manicured hand possessively on his arm. But she gave Maggie a winsome smile. "You'd be more than welcome to ride along with us. Long as you don't mind country music." She extended her hand. "I'm Sandy."

Maggie shook hands and sized up the situation. The couple seemed harmless enough. That assessment almost made her giggle. After all she'd been through today, *harmless* was a relative term.

"You're sure you wouldn't mind?"

The man pushed back his white Stetson and hooked his thumbs in the front pockets of his jeans. "Don't take no more gas to carry three people than it does two. But like I said, we're not goin' that far south."

"That doesn't matter. I can catch another bus or something once I get there."

"If that suits, come along. Oh, by the way, I'm Rick. Rick Henry."

Maggie shook his hand and flashed Sandy a smile of thanks. The couple stood there looking at her expectantly. "Oh. Sorry. I'm Mag—" She clamped her mouth shut, slicing off the last syllable of her name. For all she knew, Kevin might already have alerts out on local radio stations. In case they were broadcasting her name, she'd do well not to use it.

She feigned a cough and prayed her fiery cheeks wouldn't give her away. "Excuse me . . . sorry. My name is Meg. Meg Anders." The amalgam of her real names rolled off her tongue before she had a chance to think it through. She'd always wanted to be called Meg, but she'd never convinced anyone to make the change. She only hoped Meg Anders sounded different enough from Maggie Anderson to conceal her secret.

"You ready to leave now?" Sandy asked. "Don't you have any luggage?"

"It was"—she gestured toward the street—"on the bus."

"Oh, man. That's a bummer. Well, come on. We'll get you on down the road a ways. Over here." Rick led the way through the parking lot to an ancient Volkswagen bus.

"It's kind of a pigsty in here. I apologize." Sandy unlatched the door and started slinging clothing and wrinkled wildlife magazines over the middle seat into the back. "Didn't exactly count on having company ridin' along."

"I sure appreciate this." Maggie climbed up and slid across the narrow bench, easing the rusted door shut behind her. She latched it, instantly feeling safer than she'd felt on the Greyhound bus. Never in a thousand eons would Kevin think to look for her in an old VW bus headed to Ohio.

On the interstate again, the gentle rocking of the van and the drone of tires on the asphalt lulled her. She curled up on the bench seat and closed her eyes.

She didn't think she'd fallen asleep, but when she opened her eyes next and peered out the window, the half circle of the moon was perched above the highway.

Sandy Henry, sandal-clad feet propped on the dashboard, dozed in the front seat beside her husband. Tim McGraw crooned a ballad over the crackle of the radio. Maggie sat up and ran her hands through the tangled mass of her hair.

In the rearview mirror, Rick caught her eye. His fatherly smile warmed her. "You hungry? We could stop . . . get something to eat."

Sandy stirred but settled back against the seat again, her jaw slack.

"I'm okay," Maggie said. "Unless you want to stop."

"Could you make it another forty-five minutes? We're almost to Aurora."

"Is that close to Cleveland?"

"It's another hour or so past Aurora."

"Wow. That was quick."

Rick chuckled. "You've been asleep for almost three hours."

That meant three hours farther away from Kevin. She couldn't decide whether that thought excited or terrified her. She was in a frightening no man's land—not far enough away to be out of his reach yet, but so far that he'd be mad enough to kill her when he found her.

She wondered what he was doing right now. Was he searching for her, growing more angry and irrational by the hour? Or had he just gone to sleep? It probably wouldn't take him long to replace her. He'd had other girlfriends before her and had never hidden that fact. Kevin's good looks and ability to turn on the charm had captivated her too, for a while. It was the very thing that had reeled her in. A stab of jealousy cut through her, but she quickly reminded herself of what she was escaping. She felt sorry for the next woman he caught in his snare—and a little guilty that her freedom might put someone else in danger.

Now that she'd broken loose, she had a hard time seeing why she hadn't done it sooner. Of course, she *had* run away, more than once, after one of Kevin's particularly brutal tongue-lashings. But even when she'd made it to a women's shelter once, she'd always known deep inside that she'd end up back with Kevin. The only reason she'd taken refuge at the shelter was because she'd hoped it would finally make him realize what he was doing to her, make him appreciate what he had. In the end, it had accomplished none of that. If anything, it had made things worse. Made *him* worse.

She wondered now if men like Kevin ever appreciated another person—*any* other person. No. The mental self-lecture began. Men like him lived only for themselves. Kevin was no different than her father. Though she barely remembered the man, she somehow knew her father was to blame for what had happened to Mom. Maggie herself should have learned that hard lesson long ago. Now she'd wasted two years of her life. This time she wouldn't make the mistake of thinking Kevin had changed. This time she wouldn't go back.

She thought of her sister again, and her heart sank to her feet. She couldn't call Jenn. At least not until she was sure Kevin had quit looking for her. She shot up a muddled prayer that Jenn would somehow know she was all right. With Mark seemingly out of a job every other week, Jenn had enough to worry about without wasting time fretting over a runaway sister.

When she mouthed a silent *amen*, a shiver rippled through her. She leaned to gaze out at the heathery night sky. She'd tried to pray before, and it had seemed a superstitious exercise at best. But now she dared to hope her prayer for Jenn had reached the heavens.

Their simple
touches seemed deeply
intimate—something
she had no right to
witness, but something
she longed to know.

Chapter Eight

Maggie yawned and stretched on the seat of the VW bus as Rick Henry pulled into the parking lot of a small diner and cut the engine. The clock on the dashboard flipped from 3:59 to four o'clock. Was it only yesterday—twenty-four hours ago—that she'd left the apartment in New York? It seemed like an eternity.

Rick reached across the seat and brushed the hair from Sandy's forehead. "Hey, Sleepin' Beauty. How about some breakfast?" He pointed with his fingers laced over the steering wheel. "Place up ahead open twenty-four hours."

Sandy's eyes flew open and a drowsy smile grew. "Mmm . . . sounds good." She patted her husband's cheek. "What time is it anyway?"

"It's only four, but I gotta have some coffee if I'm gonna stay on the road."

"You want me to drive, babe?"

The couple's affectionate exchange warmed Maggie even as it made her squirm. Their simple touches seemed deeply intimate—something she had no right to witness, but something she longed to know.

As if Sandy had just remembered they had a passenger, she turned in her seat and gave a little wave. "Mornin'. Did you get some sleep?"

Maggie nodded, feeling very much a fifth wheel. Sandy climbed out and opened Maggie's door. She eased her achy legs to the curb, stretched, and followed the couple into the diner.

The clock over the bar counter reminded her that it was now Wednesday morning. She could barely believe she'd lived for one day without Kevin. And he without her. Did he feel as liberated from her as she did from him right now?

Rick ordered the short stack with bacon and eggs for the three of them, waiting while Maggie told the waitress how she wanted her eggs.

Rick shook out his napkin and tucked it in the neck of his shirt. "So, Meg, what takes you to Ohio?"

She took a long drink from her water glass, stalling. "I'm just visiting."

"Oh?" Sandy smiled. "You have family there?"

"No . . . friends." She gave a quick smile, then glanced away.

"That's nice." Sandy ran her fingers over the Formica tabletop. "What part of Columbus do they live in?"

Maggie cast about for an answer that wouldn't give her away. "I'm not sure. I-I don't really know the town that well."

"You have an address though," Rick said, more a statement than a question.

Sandy's voice took on a motherly timbre. "Did you find out where to meet the bus for your luggage?"

"My luggage?" For a minute, she'd forgotten the story she'd told them about her bags being on the bus. "Oh, yeah. I have a number to call."

Sandy rummaged in a huge leather purse. She came up with a cell phone and handed it across the table to Maggie. "Here, you can use my phone."

"No . . . I mean, I already called." Lies were rolling off her tongue like buses out of Port Authority.

"Oh, that's good."

Maggie nodded and looked past Sandy to see the waitress approaching with a loaded tray. She prayed it was their order. Again she had that odd sensation that heaven was suddenly hearing her prayers, for the waitress stopped at their table and slid overflowing plates in front of each of them.

At the fragrant steam of pancakes and maple syrup Rick and Sandy seemed to forget their interrogation.

They ate their food in silence, Rick and Sandy engrossed in the morning newspaper they'd picked up in the lobby, and Maggie concentrating on each morsel she lifted to her mouth. She didn't know when a meal had tasted so good. They hadn't even looked at menus, but a cardboard tent propped between the salt and pepper listed the short stack at $3.99. She calculated what the meal would be with a tip. After their waitress refilled their coffee cups, Maggie excused herself and followed the woman to the register.

"Can I get the check for our table?"

"Sure." The woman scrounged in the pocket of her uniform until she came up with the right ticket. She rang it up while Maggie peeled a ten and a five from the wad of bills in her pocket. It would deplete her cash seriously, but it was the least she could do for the couple who'd helped her get almost five hours farther down the road—away from Kevin.

With the receipt in her pocket, she followed the signs to the rest room at the back of the diner. She brushed her teeth and combed her hair, glad she'd thought to buy those things at the first bus stop. She worked her hair into a wispy French braid, cringing to discover that her hair was greasy enough to stay braided without a rubber band. When she got back to the table, the Henrys were standing by their table, in animated conversation with another couple about their age.

She nodded and started to slip back into the booth. Rick interrupted himself, stopping her with an upraised hand. "Meg, this is Ted and Corinne Blakely. They're old friends of ours. Can you believe we just happened to stop at the same diner for breakfast? Especially this time of morning?"

"Hi." Maggie gave a weak smile, wishing she'd stayed in the rest room a few minutes longer. She slid behind Sandy into the booth.

While the husbands and wives carried on simultaneous and noisy conversations, she felt as if she were eavesdropping. She pleated accordion folds into her napkin and rearranged her silverware on the empty plate, as if these were tasks of great importance.

"Did you hear that, Meg?"

She lifted her head at Rick's effusive question. "Sorry . . . no."

"Ted and Corinne are going through Columbus. They said you'd be welcome to ride on with them." A satisfied grin split his face, as though he'd just handed her an expensive gift.

And in truth, he had. "Really?" She sought Mrs. Blakely's eyes, trying to read the sincerity there. What she saw was the kindest, most welcoming expression she could have hoped for.

"Of course. We'd love to have the company. Wouldn't we, Ted?"

Her husband nodded but looked pointedly at his watch. "We're kind of needing to get on the road. We're headed on to Kansas City, and our daughter's expecting us for a late supper. We'll pick up I-70, but whereabouts in Columbus do you need to go?"

"Oh, you can drop me off anywhere. I . . . my friends can come and get me wherever you drop me off."

"Well, we'll see how the time goes," Ted Blakely said, checking his watch again. "Maybe your friends can meet us somewhere. Don't want to leave you stranded."

"Oh, that's okay. I'm grateful for the ride."

Mr. Blakely turned to the Henrys and offered his hand. "Sure good to run into you guys."

They exchanged warm good-byes, then Mr. Blakely turned to Maggie. "We'll drive over to where Rick is parked and get your bags."

Rick stepped in to explain, saving her from repeating the lie.

"Well, all right then. This way." He took his wife's arm and ushered her toward the exit. Maggie followed.

"Good luck to you, Meg." Rick tipped his Stetson.

"Thank you for everything."

"Glad to help," Rick and Sandy said as one.

Mr. Blakely held the door for her, and from the corner of her vision, she saw the Henrys walk toward the cashier.

She was torn between wanting to hurry out to the Blakelys' car before Rick and Sandy discovered she'd paid for their meals, and wanting to go back and say good-bye and a proper thank-you. An odd lump rose in her throat as the door swung closed and the Henrys disappeared from sight. Was she so needy that she'd formed an attachment to complete strangers in the space of a few hours?

The Blakelys drove a small Toyota. Half of the backseat was packed with cardboard boxes, but Ted Blakely transferred them to the trunk before motioning for her to climb inside.

"Are you sure you got everything, Ted?" Mrs. Blakely turned to Maggie. "All my garage-sale goodies are back there . . . stuff I picked up for our grandkids." Mrs. Blakely's voice was apologetic, but her eyes bright with pride.

"Oh? How many grandchildren do you have?" Maybe if she could get them talking about themselves, they wouldn't ask her too many questions.

"We have six and one on the way. Only two of them are in Kansas City though. The others live in Buffalo . . . just an hour from us."

Her ploy worked. The woman turned and propped an elbow over the back of the seat. For the next fifty miles, she prattled on about her family. Maggie tried to follow the detailed descriptions of the grandchildren, tried to smile in the appropriate places, but she soon felt herself grow drowsy. She eased into the corner of the backseat and rested her head against the window, her eyelids weighing heavy and Mrs. Blakely's chatter mingling with the noises of the highway.

Maggie dialed
~~the bogus number and~~
crossed her fingers ~~that~~
~~it was invalid.~~

Chapter Nine

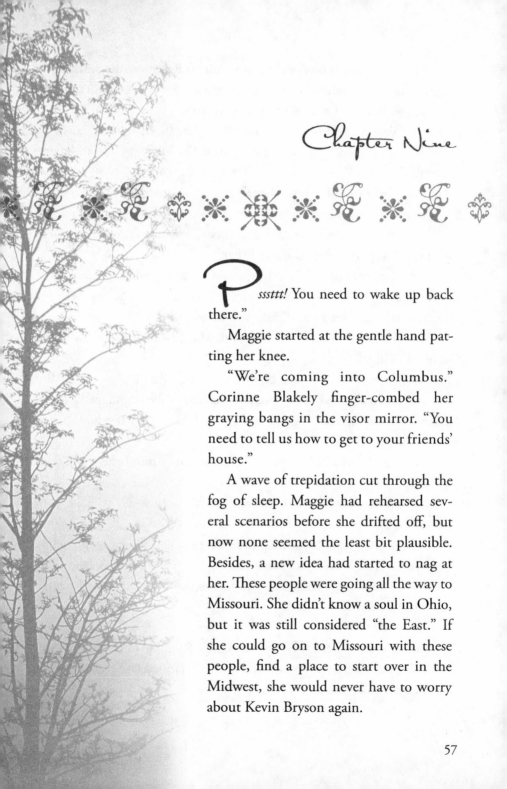

P*ssssttt!* You need to wake up back there."

Maggie started at the gentle hand patting her knee.

"We're coming into Columbus." Corinne Blakely finger-combed her graying bangs in the visor mirror. "You need to tell us how to get to your friends' house."

A wave of trepidation cut through the fog of sleep. Maggie had rehearsed several scenarios before she drifted off, but now none seemed the least bit plausible. Besides, a new idea had started to nag at her. These people were going all the way to Missouri. She didn't know a soul in Ohio, but it was still considered "the East." If she could go on to Missouri with these people, find a place to start over in the Midwest, she would never have to worry about Kevin Bryson again.

She cleared her throat and sat up a bit straighter in the seat. It was beginning to get light outside the car windows. "I was wondering . . . would you mind if I rode on farther with you?"

Mrs. Blakely's eyebrows shot up. "But what about your friends?"

"They didn't know I was coming. And I'm kind of . . . I'm having second thoughts."

"But where would you go then?"

"I have some other friends . . . in Missouri," she said.

A shadow of suspicion flitted across the woman's face. "But *they* wouldn't know you were coming either."

"Oh, they wouldn't care," Maggie said, injecting what she hoped was credible energy into her voice. "They've been trying to get me to come out and see them for ages. Would you mind too much?"

Mrs. Blakely glanced at her husband. Maggie caught the slight shrug of his shoulders.

"Well, I guess that would be fine with us," Mrs. Blakely said. "But . . . maybe you'd like to call your friends first?" She unplugged the cell phone from the cigarette lighter and handed it back to Maggie. "Do you know the number?"

"No, but I can call information. If you don't mind me using your minutes."

The woman waved off the idea. "Don't worry about it. Take your time."

"Thanks." Maggie took the phone. She studied the faceplate before she dialed 411. What if the Blakelys could hear the voices on the other end? She faded as far back into the seat as possible and waited for the operator to answer.

"What city?"

She smiled at Mrs. Blakely, who was hanging over the backseat watching her with an expectant smile on her tanned face.

"Kansas City, please."

"Go ahead."

"I'd like the number for Jennifer Anderson." Her sister's maiden name had rolled convincingly from her lips, but she immediately regretted using it. What if the Blakelys got suspicious, checked out her guise, and it somehow led them to Jenn in Baltimore?

"There are several listings," the operator said. "Do you have an address?"

"No—" She sneaked a quick look at Mrs. Blakely. "This would be . . . Fred. Fred and Jennifer."

Good grief. Where had that come from? She didn't even know anyone named Fred.

Mrs. Blakely was digging in her bag. She unearthed a pen and a scrap of paper and handed them to Maggie just as the operator said, "I'm sorry. Nothing listed for Fred Anderson in Kansas City."

"Thank you." Maggie took the paper and pen Mrs. Blakely thrust at her.

The line went dead, but Maggie nodded and pretended to be listening intently. Avoiding the older woman's gaze, she jotted "Jenny and Fred" at the top of the page. She wrote down Jennifer's area code but made up the rest of the phone number.

"Got it," she said, punching the phone off.

"Hopefully they can give us instructions on how to get there," Mr. Blakely said, his eyes meeting hers in the rearview mirror.

Maggie dialed the bogus number and crossed her fingers that it was invalid. No such luck, but the next best thing—an answering machine picked up on the third ring. A peppy voice informed her that "Brett and Cindy" weren't home now but requested that she please leave a message.

She waited for the tone. "Hi." She floundered, then found her cue on the scrap of paper. "This is . . . Meg. Hey, I'm headed out to see you guys." She pretended it was her sister she was talking to and tried to urge some genuine enthusiasm into her voice. "I'm in Ohio right now, but I'll probably get to your place sometime this afternoon."

"It'll be around five," Mrs. Blakely mouthed.

"Probably around five," Maggie parroted. "I'll call later when we get into town."

She hung up and handed the phone back to Mrs. Blakely. "I left a message," she said, as if the woman hadn't been eavesdropping on every word.

"Oh, well, at least they know to expect you. We can try to reach them again when we get a little closer to Kansas City."

Maggie nodded. Poor Brett and Cindy—whoever they were. They'd be frantically cleaning house and wracking their brains to think who they knew named Meg. Maggie felt the way she had in seventh grade at Alisha Pierpont's slumber party when they'd made prank calls late into the night. If it hadn't been so mean, it would almost be funny.

Mrs. Blakely twisted in her seat as if she were going to settle in for a heart-to-heart. Maggie's pulse quickened. She did not want to talk. She was having enough trouble keeping her stories straight. Feigning a yawn, she settled back into the seat and closed her eyes.

It wasn't long before she fell asleep for real.

Maggie awoke to the splatter of rain on the windshield. The sky was gray, and the cars on the interstate all had their lights on. Maggie peeked through half-lidded eyes, trying to determine if Mrs. Blakely was dozing in the front seat or simply waiting for Maggie to wake up so she could pounce on her with a barrage of questions.

The woman was curled up in the seat, her head lolling with the motion of the car. She seemed to be asleep. Her husband had tuned the radio to some sports talk show and seemed intent on the on-air banter.

Maggie adjusted her position, being careful to place herself where her eyes didn't meet the driver's in the rearview mirror. She rode that way until they exited the interstate a few hours later for fast food—a

McDonald's drive-thru. They were back on the road in minutes. Maggie took her time eating the cheeseburger Mr. Blakely insisted on paying for. When it was gone, she leaned her head against the window, playing possum.

After an hour, her muscles ached with the need to stretch. It was going to be a long trip. She consoled herself with the knowledge that every mile she suffered put her that much farther from Kevin.

The radio blared louder as a commercial started. A minute later an announcer read the latest news in a monotone. But when national news gave way to a local update, Maggie froze. She didn't know how far this particular station's signal reached, nor did she have a good sense of how far away they were from New York by now, but what if they reported her missing or kidnapped in yesterday's carjacking? Or worse, what if Kevin had them broadcasting her description?

She slunk back into the corner of the seat.

She ran blindly,
instinctively in the
direction that would
take her farthest from
the life she'd known
before yesterday.

Chapter Ten

T he newscaster on the radio rambled on . . . something about the Illinois Department of Education. Maggie shot up in her seat and gave a little gasp. "Are we in Illinois?"

"Just crossed the state line." Mr. Blakely reached to turn the radio down.

Good. Way out here they surely couldn't care less about yet another New York City carjacking. She kneaded the knotted muscles in her neck and shifted to the other side of the car. Before long, the white noise of the rain and the road lulled her back to sleep.

"Meg . . . wake up, Meg. We're in Kansas City."

Maggie struggled to the surface of a dream so real it took her a few seconds to separate it from reality, even after she was sure she was fully awake. Yawning deeply, she stretched and peered out the car window. Relief flowed through her to see wide, rolling plains in every direction. In her dream she'd been slogging through a jungle thick with bamboo. The stalks grew so dense she could only move a few inches before she'd have to clear another step of the path. The reeds snapped apart at the joints as easily as if they were toothpicks, but in spite of that, she felt as if she was getting nowhere—going backward even. And when she glanced behind her, she saw Kevin's scowling face hovering over an endless highway.

She shivered and looked outside again, trying to supplant the disturbing image with the reality of the lush landscape outside her window. The sun hovered above the ribbon of highway spooling over the plains before them, but it shone warmly and bore no sinister visage.

"What time is it?"

"Almost five. I'm going to stop for gas at this next exit," Mr. Blakely said. "You might want to try calling your friends again. See if we can get some directions."

As they pulled into the QuikTrip, Mrs. Blakely awoke. At her husband's nudging, she located the cell phone and handed it to Maggie.

While Mr. Blakely got out and gassed up the car, Maggie dialed the number again, willing Cindy and Brett—whoever they were—to not be home yet.

The same exuberant voice from the recording answered—Cindy, obviously—only unmistakably in person this time. Maggie waited past three "hellos," hoping the woman would hang up so she could carry on the pretend conversation she'd hastily written a script for in her mind.

"Hello? Is anyone there?"

The voice was so loud in her ear, Maggie was afraid Mrs. Blakely could hear. She took a breath and plunged in. "Hi! It's Meg."

"Meg? I'm sorry. *Who* is this?"

"I'm in Kansas City."

"I'm sorry. Who did you say this was?"

"Yeah, I missed my bus and . . . well, it's a long story. I'll tell you all about it later, but anyway I'm here in town and thought I'd stop in and see you guys. But I need directions to your house."

A long silence.

"Um . . . I think you have a wrong number."

"Yes. Sure." She waited a few beats. "Main Street? Okay. Turn left. Then what?"

"Listen," Cindy said on the other end, "I don't know what's going on, but I'm hanging up."

"Okay." Maggie stalled, waiting for the telltale cellular silence. "—Fifteen eighty-seven you say?"

Mrs. Blakely scrounged on the console for the pen and paper, handing them back to Maggie. She could almost see the woman's ears prick as she listened to every word of Maggie's side of the convoluted conversation.

Maggie mouthed her thanks and took the pen and paper. She wrote down 1587 and a capital R followed by a scribble she hoped looked like it could be a street name. "Great," she said, smiling into the phone, almost convincing herself she was talking to a long-lost friend. "We'll see you in a little while then."

"Who *is* this?"

Maggie nearly dropped the phone. Apparently Cindy hadn't hung up as threatened, and whatever perkiness she'd had at the start of the conversation was exhausted.

"Can you hear me?" shouted Cindy. "Who is this?"

Maggie stole a glance at Corinne Blakely, who wore a confused frown. Had she overheard Cindy's end of the conversation in the quiet of the idling car?

From the corner of her eye, she watched Mr. Blakely cross the parking lot and go into the convenience store. She launched into her final performance. "I can't wait to see you either, Jenny," she said, speaking loud enough, she hoped, to drown out the stranger's frustrated shouts.

She clicked the phone off and handed it back to Mrs. Blakely.

"Is everything all right? You got directions?" The woman craned her neck and turned a skeptical eye to the information on the notepad.

Maggie whisked the paper into her palm. "Yes, I got it." She was in deep now and had no idea how she was going to get out of this.

"What street do your friends live on?"

Maggie opened her palm and stared at the scribbled R on the page. "Remington," she plucked out of thin air. "Fifteen eighty-seven Remington."

"Did your friend say how to get there from here? I didn't hear you tell her where we were."

"She said it's just off of Main Street." Did Kansas City even have a Main Street? She didn't know, but she was on trial now. Mrs. Blakely's pinched face made that clear. Somehow she had to extricate herself from her lies before Mr. Blakely got back to the car.

She reached for the door handle. "I'm going to go use the rest room. I'll be right back." She climbed out of the car before the woman could protest.

When Maggie reached the door, Mr. Blakely was coming out with three steaming coffees in a cardboard drink tray. He smiled, oblivious to her charade. But Maggie knew he'd get an earful as soon as he got back to the car.

"I'll pull up in front of the door for you," he said. "I got us a little something to tide us over." He pointed to several granola bars clustered in the fourth compartment of the drink holder.

"Oh . . . great." She forced a lightness to her tone. "Thanks. That was very kind of you."

Which made what she was about to do even worse.

She located the rest room in the back corner, thankful it was a single stall. She locked the door behind her. Her hands were trembling as she stared into the soap-splattered mirror. What had she done? These people had been kind enough to help her, and she was treating them like dirt. Worse, she'd probably made them late getting to their daughter's house.

But she'd dug her own grave. She couldn't go back out there. For all she knew, the Blakelys were calling the police right now to report the psycho girl they'd hauled cross-country in their backseat.

She inspected her reflection in the dingy, pitted mirror. Her hair had worked itself out of the braid and hung in limp strings around her face. Desperation sharpened her bloodshot eyes and turned the blue of her irises to a dim gray. She glanced back at the door, her heart thudding in dull rhythm, her thoughts scrambled like so many eggs.

If she didn't hurry, they'd come looking for her. They'd be knocking on the door, wondering if she had fainted or something. And how would she get out of her predicament then?

She had to leave now. There had to be a back entrance to the store—the one the delivery trucks used. It wouldn't be locked from the inside. She went through the motions of flushing the toilet and washing her hands, in case anyone was listening outside the door. Then she turned the handle, opened the door a crack, and looked outside.

Two teenage girls waited in line, but she didn't see either of the Blakelys. She couldn't see through the plate-glass windows in front to tell if their car was there, but she couldn't risk going out to check.

She made a dash, sidestepping the two girls and turning the opposite way she'd come in. She walked through a break room where a petite, older woman was mopping the floor. Behind the woman was the back door, an emergency bar crossing the front to discourage use. It appeared to be the kind that set off an alarm if it was pushed. She'd have to risk it.

She strode toward it as if she knew what she was doing.

"Hey! You can't use that d—" The woman lofted her mop, but in vain.

Maggie pushed through the heavy door and broke into a run. She raced across the side parking lot and made a beeline for the auto body shop next door. There were no alarms going off behind her, but the janitor probably thought she'd stolen something, so the police would no doubt be summoned.

She wondered if the Blakelys had figured out yet that she wasn't coming back. Behind the shop, clumps of scrap metal and concrete seemed to sprout up wherever she set her feet. She ran blindly, instinctively in the direction that would take her farthest from Kevin, and the Blakelys, and everything about the life she'd known before yesterday.

She whipped around, searching for the source of the voice.

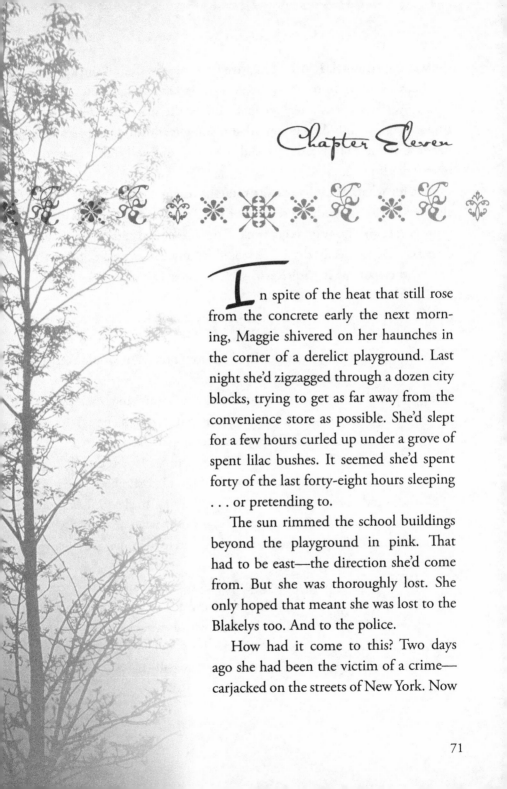

Chapter Eleven

In spite of the heat that still rose from the concrete early the next morning, Maggie shivered on her haunches in the corner of a derelict playground. Last night she'd zigzagged through a dozen city blocks, trying to get as far away from the convenience store as possible. She'd slept for a few hours curled up under a grove of spent lilac bushes. It seemed she'd spent forty of the last forty-eight hours sleeping . . . or pretending to.

The sun rimmed the school buildings beyond the playground in pink. That had to be east—the direction she'd come from. But she was thoroughly lost. She only hoped that meant she was lost to the Blakelys too. And to the police.

How had it come to this? Two days ago she had been the victim of a crime—carjacked on the streets of New York. Now she was the criminal. A virtual fugitive from the law, for all she knew.

She reached up to touch her hair. Ugh. It was a tangled mess, laced with leaves and sticks after her night under the lilacs. She felt in her pocket for the comb she'd bought that first night at the bus stop. Careful not to lose the roll of cash, she slid the comb out and did her best to make herself presentable.

But for what? Why hadn't she thought things through before she'd climbed in the car with those people? Now she was hundreds of miles from home with no way to get back. Sure, Kevin had treated her like a dog. But did she really think life would be any better on her own? At least at the apartment with Kevin she'd had a soft bed to sleep in and food on the table.

Her stomach yowled at the thought. She hadn't had anything to eat since the cheeseburger at McDonald's. She'd have to part with a couple of dollars this morning. If she keeled over from hunger, it wouldn't matter that she had money in her pocket.

She glanced around, making sure no one was watching, then pulled the roll of cash out of her pocket and counted it. She had enough to get a room. She could get cleaned up, get something to eat.

But then what? The answer was disheartening. If she did that, it might not leave her enough cash for the bus. Had she been crazy to think she could survive on her own? Was starving to death, being on the streets homeless, really an improvement over what she'd had with Kevin in New York? If she called him, he'd surely help her get back to the apartment.

Her mind raced, formulating a plan. She'd call from a pay phone, feel him out first. Find out what he knew about the car. If it had turned up in the possession of that jerk who'd carjacked her, maybe Kevin would take pity on her. Maybe he'd believe her story. She could tell him the guy had forced her to drive all the way to Kansas City.

She blew out a puff of air. Yeah, right. Like he'd believe that. Besides, he always knew exactly how many miles were on the Honda. Unless the carjacker had taken it on one whale of a joyride, Kevin would know she was lying the minute he checked the odometer.

She fingered a twenty-dollar bill. If she hung out here in this empty playground, found a grocery store and bought a few snacks, she probably had enough money to last a few days.

But what then? She had no ID with her, she didn't own a credit card. She had no way to get into Kevin's bank account. Even if she had, using an ATM card would clue him in to her whereabouts in a flash. Besides, if he figured out what she'd done, he would close the bank accounts she knew about as soon as the bank opened this morning—if he hadn't done it already.

She scrambled to her feet and shook the kinks from her legs. The oxygen she breathed in cleared her head and brought her to her senses.

I am not going back. Ever. She didn't care if she died homeless and alone. She'd been handed the gift of freedom on a silver—well, a *tarnished*—platter, but valuable all the same. She was going to grab on to it and never let go.

But for now, she needed a place to hide out.

No.

She whipped around, searching for the source of the voice, then realized it hadn't been an audible whisper. Her mind must be playing tricks on her.

But she had heard that word. She was certain. And the thought that followed was as clear as if someone had breathed it in her ear: *Keep moving. Get out of this city. Keep heading west.*

An eerie urgency overtook her, and she started walking. She followed the sidewalk, keeping the sun at her back. Half an hour later she came to a small convenience store. She hesitated at the door, leery after what had happened yesterday, but this place had a mom-and-pop feel to it. It drew her inside the same way the inaudible voice had drawn her westward.

She wandered down the aisles, searching for something to eat that would fill her up and stick with her for a minimum of cash. She chose an oversized PayDay bar and a bottle of chocolate milk. Waiting in line at the checkout, she snagged a large bag of popcorn. The sign said the expiration date had passed, but it was on sale for ninety-nine cents and would provide a couple of days' worth of filler. The price on a bag of beef jerky was almost three dollars, but it made her mouth water and she added it to her stash.

She'd probably gain three pounds eating all this junk. *Kevin will have a fit.* She nodded to herself and corrected her tense. He *would have.* If he'd known. But he would never find out. Not now. Just one more reason she needed to get away.

Her turn came in the queue, and she placed her items on the counter. But before she counted out the money, a note tacked to the bulletin board behind the clerk's head caught her eye.

Greyhound—Fare to Salina $45.

She tipped her head. "Where is Salina?"

The clerk followed Maggie's line of vision. "Oh . . . that? It's three, maybe four hours up the interstate. You just missed the early route. Next bus doesn't leave until twelve-thirty."

"It's in Missouri?"

"Salina? No, Salina's in Kansas." He pronounced it with a long *i*. *Suh-line-uh.*

She liked the sound of it. And it was in Kansas. Kevin would be more likely to search for her in Siberia than in Salina, Kansas.

"I'd like a ticket for that bus, please."

"Oh, we don't sell tickets here. You'll have to go to the bus station."

"Where is that?"

He looked past her and pointed through the windows at the front of

the store. "That's Eleventh Street. Runs east and west. You want to go west
. . . maybe five or six blocks. It's on Troost Street. You can't miss it."

"You want to go west," he'd said.

It had to be a sign. She thanked him, paid for her items, and walked
to the street. Excitement welled up inside her. Something was going to
happen. She felt it in her bones.

Alarm rose in her
throat when the
vehicle slowed,
lurched, then started
backing toward her.

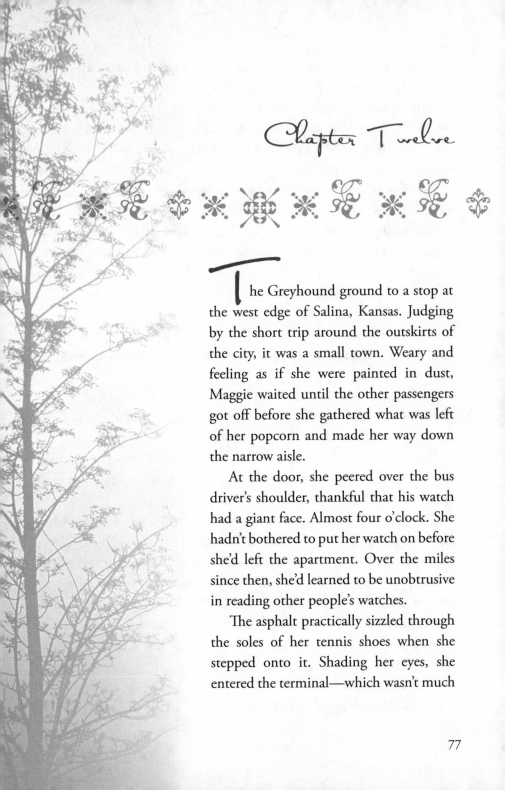

Chapter Twelve

The Greyhound ground to a stop at the west edge of Salina, Kansas. Judging by the short trip around the outskirts of the city, it was a small town. Weary and feeling as if she were painted in dust, Maggie waited until the other passengers got off before she gathered what was left of her popcorn and made her way down the narrow aisle.

At the door, she peered over the bus driver's shoulder, thankful that his watch had a giant face. Almost four o'clock. She hadn't bothered to put her watch on before she'd left the apartment. Over the miles since then, she'd learned to be unobtrusive in reading other people's watches.

The asphalt practically sizzled through the soles of her tennis shoes when she stepped onto it. Shading her eyes, she entered the terminal—which wasn't much more than a convenience store—and bought a can of Diet Coke from a vending machine.

A man wearing cowboy boots and a leathery complexion tipped his Stetson to her as she exited the building, but no one paid much attention when she headed for the highway. Traffic zipped past as she walked along the graveled shoulder.

She walked half a mile or so to an overpass. From there she looked west, her eyes taking in the sun-scorched landscape. The corner of her mouth quirked in a sardonic smile. She'd landed smack-dab in the middle of a *Little House on the Prairie* movie set. The terrain wasn't pancake flat the way she'd always heard Kansas described, but the sparseness of trees on the gently rolling hills extended the vista for what seemed like a hundred miles.

She moved to the left side of the road and crossed the overpass, hugging the dented guardrail and praying no one tried to add another dent while she was there.

Every driver who passed waved or honked until she checked to see if she had toilet paper trailing her shoe or something. Was it that unusual to see a girl walking along the road in Kansas?

The last of the Coke was warm and syrupy by the time she drained the can. Sweat trickled down the bridge of her nose, stinging her eyes, and her blouse was plastered to her back.

But soon the sun dipped to the horizon, and a breeze fanned her face. Behind her the town had disappeared save for a row of grain elevators peeking over the sphere of the earth. On one side of her was a field of golden plumes she guessed to be wheat. Wasn't that what Kansas was famous for? And on the other stretched miles of rocky pastureland. The grassland was fenced in with barbed wire strung through tilted posts of gnarled wood, or in some places, thick posts carved from porous yellow stone.

A pickup barreled over the hill behind her, spraying sandy dust as it passed. Alarm rose in her throat when the vehicle slowed, lurched, then started backing toward her. She kept walking, and the truck shifted gears again and crawled along beside her.

A man who looked remarkably like the man with the Stetson back at the bus terminal rolled down his window and leaned out, resting a tanned elbow on the window frame. "You need a ride?"

"No," she said. "I'm fine."

"You have car trouble?"

"I'm just . . . walking. Thanks." She quickened her pace.

He shook his head as if he thought she were crazy but put the truck in gear and drove on.

A few vehicles whizzed past, not seeming to notice her. But she hadn't gone half a mile when another truck stopped, and another tanned farmer in a cowboy hat offered her a ride. Maggie was starting to feel as though she was a player in some sort of bizarre *Stepford Wives*–type movie.

Again she declined. Did these people really think she was such a fool that she'd accept a ride with a man—a complete stranger—on a deserted country road?

But as twilight pulled a cloak over the landscape she started to wonder if she *was* a fool. Whirling in the road, she looked back toward Salina. A haze of light rode the horizon where the town was sprawled. She'd probably walked thirty or forty city blocks, and there wasn't a building or a light in sight, save for a couple of white grain elevators that occasionally peeked over the rolling terrain. Maybe she would be better off going back into town for the night.

Go west.

That voice again—or whatever it was. She couldn't go back.

She traversed a narrow bridge, and when she came to the next crossroad, she decided to turn off the main highway and walk south. Maybe there wouldn't be so much traffic on a side road. She stopped short, seeing two small wooden crosses jutting up from the prairie grasses in the ditch. She scrambled down the gully and stooped to inspect them closer. The crosses, one slightly larger than the other, were carefully constructed, and Maggie could tell they'd once been varnished to a sheen, though now they showed signs of being left to the elements. There was evidence on the ground around the monuments—dried flower petals and a bit of tattered sun-faded ribbon—that someone had tended them at some point. Like a grave. Someone's pets, perhaps? Or did they denote the scene of a fatal accident? She shivered and climbed back up to the road.

At the next intersection, she turned west again. The road was asphalt-paved for half a mile or so, then turned to gravel and sand. As she stopped to shake a pebble out of her shoe, it struck her that, for the first time all summer, she had put her tennis shoes on before she left the apartment in New York that fated morning. Tennis shoes *and* socks. A little chill snaked up her spine at the fluke. What if she had been wearing her flip-flops the way she usually did when she went out on a quick errand? As it was, she could almost feel the blisters raising on her heels. If she'd been in sandals, her feet would have been torn to shreds. She'd never have made it this far on foot.

She trudged on, her muscles aching with the effort of the miles. The utter silence was broken by a murmuring *whoosh whoosh* as she came upon wheat fields on either side of the road. The bushy stalks danced with the breeze, an ocean of golden waves rolling around her as far as she could see. She had never experienced such space! It made her feel small. Yet an odd sense of freedom had started to well up in her chest.

The sunlight ebbed further and shadows of memory clouded her thoughts . . .

Kevin, telling her she couldn't have coffee with the sweet woman who lived in the apartment next door.

Kevin, ordering her what to make for supper, how he wanted it cooked, and what time he wanted it served.

Kevin, forbidding her from taking a job.

Kevin, making her step on the bathroom scales every morning, and putting her on a diet if she gained half a pound. She'd always tried to count her blessings that she had a personal trainer of sorts.

Now, out here in this wide-open territory that seemed like a foreign country, her brain seemed to clear, and the truth of her situation unfolded like a clearly marked map. How had she ever allowed herself to come under his control? What was it about him . . . ?

She stopped dead in the road, stirring up little whirls of dust around her feet. No. That was the wrong question. What was it about *her*? That's what she *should* be asking.

She plodded on another mile, weariness almost overpowering her. She came to a little turnoff in the road that led to a fenced pasture. Slumping against a pale stone post, she rested for a while before hauling herself up again. The road ahead of her was covered by a canopy of trees, leafy branches entwined overhead. They rustled as the wind picked up. The tunnel they formed was almost pitch-black inside, reminding her that night would fall in a few minutes. She quickened her pace. It wouldn't be good to be caught out here after dark.

As if to confirm that thought, an eerie howl split the quiet evening. It was probably some farmer's dog, but a sign a few miles back, before she'd turned off the main road, had said it was twenty miles to Coyote. She didn't want to think about how that town got its name.

The last crescent sliver of sun slipped below the prairie and, as if the sunset had triggered some switch, a chorus of insects started in. Cicadas? Crickets? She didn't know, but within seconds, their *chirrup chirrup* rose to an earsplitting crescendo.

Maggie walked on. She didn't know what else to do.

After exiting the canopied mile, she looked up. The sky overhead was inky black, but that only showed off the pinpoints of light to better advantage. She traced the Big Dipper, amazed at how clearly it was outlined in the Milky Way. She had seen starry displays like this in the movies, but she'd always assumed they were achieved through some genius of special effects. The spectacle of lights took her breath away.

She'd lost her sense of direction, but at a rise in the road, she spotted another cluster of lights twinkling in the distance. These were close to the horizon and obviously man-made. Out here it was hard to tell how far away they were, but as the night grew ever blacker, she took courage in their presence. They gave her something to go toward, a goal.

If she could just make it to those lights, everything might turn out okay.

She glanced furtively
over her shoulder and
was blinded by
headlights cresting
the hill behind her.

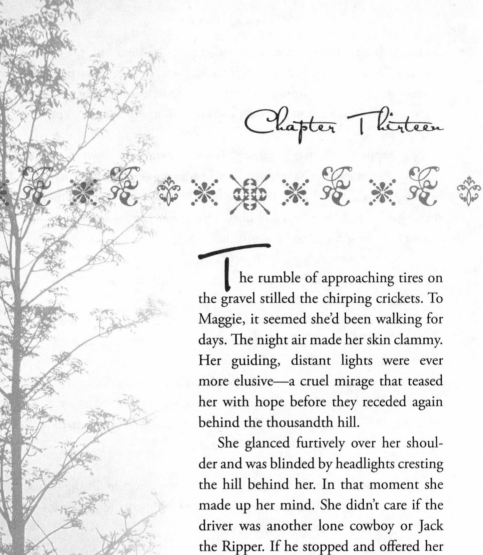

Chapter Thirteen

The rumble of approaching tires on the gravel stilled the chirping crickets. To Maggie, it seemed she'd been walking for days. The night air made her skin clammy. Her guiding, distant lights were ever more elusive—a cruel mirage that teased her with hope before they receded again behind the thousandth hill.

She glanced furtively over her shoulder and was blinded by headlights cresting the hill behind her. In that moment she made up her mind. She didn't care if the driver was another lone cowboy or Jack the Ripper. If he stopped and offered her a ride, she would take it. She moved closer to the ditch on the left side of the road and slowed her pace, walking between the edge of the ditch and the ruts that had been worn deep into the road's surface by decades of eastbound vehicles—or perhaps even by covered wagons.

In the hours she'd been trudging along this Kansas road, the centuries had seemed to fold back on themselves. Now, strangely, she wouldn't have been any more surprised to see a stagecoach pull up behind her than she was to see the old wood-paneled station wagon that crept to a stop at her side.

She stopped in the road, waiting. The window rolled down in a series of jerky movements. The interior lights came on and a young woman's head appeared. At the same time the back window also slid down. Two matching curly blond heads bobbed into sight, then a third, a spike-haired boy she guessed to be about six.

"Hey!" the woman yelled. "Everything okay?"

The children echoed her question and she turned to shush them.

Maggie approached the car.

The front window jerked halfway up again. Maggie backed off a couple of steps. She, of all people, understood the woman's caution.

"I could use a ride."

"Your car break down?" Again three towheads popped out the back window. The woman rolled her eyes at Maggie and stretched over the backseat. "Landon Michael DeVore! Sit. Now. You girls buckle back in."

"No. It's a long story. I'm kind of stranded."

"Well, where you headed?"

"That town up there." Maggie pointed in the direction of the lights, which had withered into the night again. She hoped she hadn't imagined them. She was beginning to wonder.

"Clayburn?"

She nodded, relieved there *was* a town.

"I can give you a ride. You live in Clayburn?"

"No, I'm just visiting."

"Well, come on. Hop in."

Maggie jogged around to the passenger side, all at once weak with relief. The woman pushed the door open and scraped a collection of coloring books and McDonald's Happy Meal bags off the passenger seat onto the floor. Maggie got in and gingerly found a place for her feet on the cluttered floorboard.

"Where'd you come from? Oh. Sorry. I'm Kaye." She nodded toward the backseat. "These are my kids. Well, three of them anyway."

Maggie turned to smile and wave at the children. "I'm . . . Meg," she said, remembering in the nick of time.

The children sat in a row on the backseat—statues watching her with unguarded eyes.

Their mother laughed. "I ought to hire you to ride with us all the time. I haven't seen them that quiet since the last time I got a speeding ticket."

"The cop made Mama cry," the little boy offered.

"Hush, Landon," his mother said. She gave Maggie a conspiratorial wink. "It worked like a charm. I got away with nothing but a warning . . . well, that and a good workout for my heart."

Landon piped up again. "You shoulda seen how fast that cop had to go to catch Mama."

"Landon! I said hush." Kaye turned to Maggie. "So where are you from?"

Apprehension stole her voice for an instant. "From Salina."

"Well, I hope you didn't hitchhike."

"No . . . I walked."

Kaye tapped the brakes and stared at Maggie agape. "You walked? Not from Salina?"

Maggie nodded.

"No way. That's like, fifteen miles."

"It is?" Maggie was a little stunned herself, until she looked at the clock on the station wagon's dashboard. It was after nine. She'd been on the road for almost five hours. No wonder she was tired to the bone.

"Where are you staying?"

"Um . . . one of the hotels. I don't remember the name."

"*One* of the hotels?" Kaye threw her head back and laughed. "You must mean Wren's?"

"Wren's?"

"Wren's Nest is the closest thing Clayburn has to a hotel. It's more like an oversized bed-and-breakfast."

"Oh, yeah . . . that's it. Do you think they'll have a vacancy?"

"Honey, you could probably have two rooms there if you wanted."

"Oh, good." She wanted to cry with relief. She was so weary she didn't know if she could walk another ten steps. "I hope it's not too expensive."

Kay scratched her head. "I honestly don't know how much it is to stay there. But knowing Bart and Wren, it won't be unreasonable. And if you're a little short, Wren'd probably let you wash pots and pans to make up the difference."

Maggie tucked that tidbit away.

They rode the next few miles in silence. The station wagon rumbled over an old wooden bridge wide enough for only one vehicle. A green sign declared they were crossing the Smoky Hill River. Maggie saw the lights twinkle again, closer. This time they appeared very real and welcoming. She relaxed a little.

Five minutes later the town materialized in front of them. It was tiny. Not much more than a stop in the road. But if there was someplace for her to lay her head, she didn't care how big it was.

Kaye drove down the main street, which appeared to be almost the only street. Though neat white lines sectioned the curbs into parking spaces, every space was empty and not one vehicle cruised the road. If not for the glow of the streetlamps overhead, Maggie would have thought she'd landed in a ghost town.

"The inn's right up there." Kaye pointed through the windshield to an old building that took up an entire corner of the block. Lamplight shot through a filigree of lace curtains at the window. A spotlight shown on a weathered sign that declared, Wren's Nest: Country living inside the city limits.

It was so quaint, her nose could almost detect the spice of homemade apple pie and strong coffee. Her mouth watered in response to the mere thought. She hadn't had anything to eat since she finished off the bag of stale popcorn along the road outside Salina.

"You can let me out here."

"Nonsense. As far as you walked today, the least I can do is take you to the door. You didn't have any bags?"

"They're coming later. They got lost . . . on the bus."

"That's a bummer."

"Yeah." For a minute, she had an image of that mammoth Greyhound bus pulling up in front of this inn tomorrow morning to deliver a pair of suitcases filled with her clothes, her drawings, and her precious pens and colored pencils carefully wrapped amongst the folds of cotton and khaki . . .

Brother. She was starting to believe her own lies.

She climbed out of the car and leaned to peer into the backseat. "Bye kids."

Landon waved, and the twins giggled, suddenly shy.

"Thanks so much for the ride. I don't know what I would have done if you hadn't come along."

Kaye waved her off. "Don't think a thing of it. It wasn't much out of my way at all."

Maggie shut the door and took a step back. She watched the station wagon make a U-turn and head back the way they'd come. Taking a labored breath, she turned to look up at Wren's Nest. Might as well get it over with.

She didn't know
if her mother was even
alive. She wasn't sure
she wanted to know.

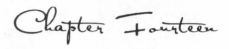

Chapter Fourteen

✳ ❀ ✳ ❀ ❀ ✳ ❀ ❀ ✳ ❀ ✳ ❀ ❀

Maggie opened the screen door facing Main Street and pushed the brass kick plate of the front door. A bell tinkled when she closed the door behind her.

"I'll be right with you," a gravelly male voice called out from somewhere to her right.

She waited, scanning the large lobby, which had as its centerpiece an ornately carved L-shaped counter that served as a check-in desk. A massive fireplace to her left was cold, yet its wide mantel, decorated with antiques and whimsical figurines, offered a different kind of warmth to the room. Beyond, to the right of the hearth, a long hallway stretched, punctuated by perhaps eight or ten doorways, each with a lighted sconce illuminating the recessed entry.

In a dining room beyond an arched doorway to her right, a jumble of tables and chairs had been pushed against the walls under the windows. In the middle of the room, an assortment of lumber spanned two sawhorses. Instead of the apple pie and coffee she'd dreamed of, the tang of sawdust hung in the air.

A clatter of dishes came from somewhere beyond the room. A man who would have been a dead ringer for Santa Claus, had he been wearing a red fur-trimmed suit, ducked under the arched doorway. The woman who bustled out behind him wasn't far off from the way Maggie imagined Mrs. Claus to look with her white topknot and gingham apron.

"Good evening. Welcome to Wren's. How can we help you?" Mrs. Claus said.

"I'd like a room for the night. I don't have reservations but—"

"No problem. Let me get you set up here." She waddled around the check-in desk and lifted a key off the wall behind it. "Bart," she ordered, handing the key to Santa Claus, "Go out and get this young woman's luggage and take it to 208, please."

Maggie stepped forward, managing a weary smile. "Oh, that's all right. My luggage . . . got put on the wrong bus. I don't have anything to carry."

Mrs. Claus inspected Maggie over her reading glasses. "Nothing? Not even a purse?"

She shook her head. "But I have cash to pay," she added quickly.

The woman waved her off. "Goodness, we're not worried about that. Don't you fret. We'll get you taken care of." She leaned out over the counter and studied Maggie again. "You look flat exhausted, honey. Bart, you get her checked in and I'll go round up the things she'll need for the night."

The man moseyed behind the counter and took out an invoice pad. With stubby fingers, he struggled to get the carbon in place. "Well, let's see now. First I need your name and address."

"It's Meg. Meg Anders."

"Anderson, you say?"

She froze. Had she given her real name? She was so exhausted she wasn't thinking straight.

"Sorry." Bart cupped a hand to one ear. "I'm a little hard of hearing."

"It's Anders."

"A-N-D-E-R-S?"

She nodded and watched him print the letters in painstaking strokes. He finished and peeked up at her through bushy white eyebrows. "That dear wife of mine is a stickler about the paperwork. Wren lives in fear of an IRS audit."

"Oh, so that's Wren?" She pointed in the direction of the hall Mrs. Claus had disappeared down.

"The one and only. I'm Bart, but you can just call me Mr. Wren." He gave a low, jolly chuckle, searing the Santa Claus image into her mind. "Okay, let's see . . . I guess I need your address next."

Maggie had decided during her fifteen-mile walk that she would "be" from California. She'd had a pen pal from that state. After copying Trudy March's address every week from third grade until she outgrew the novelty during middle school, Maggie had never forgotten it. Trudy's address also happened to be the date Columbus "sailed the ocean blue," an easily remembered line from an elementary school song. "1492 Rainwater, Fall River, California." She gave Bart the zip code, trying to make it sound as if she'd been giving out her address for years. She had to repeat it twice before he heard. There wasn't a computer or even a cash register on the counter, so maybe they wouldn't try to verify her information. Besides, she was paying cash.

"California, huh?" Bart said. "Whereabouts is Fall River?"

"Oh . . . in northern California. Nowhere near LA or Hollywood." She quoted Trudy's introductory letter and racked her brain for some other tidbits from her pen pal's old correspondence.

"How many nights will you be staying?"

"Just one. Just for tonight."

He mumbled to himself as he finished filling out the invoice, then looked up at her and gave an obviously memorized speech. "We're in the middle of remodeling our kitchen and dining room, so breakfast will be served here in the lobby from six until nine. Checkout time is noon, unless you need a later time. Wren's not too picky about that as long as we're not full up. If you want to give me your credit card information now, you can just leave your key in the room in the morning and you'll be all set."

She dug in her pocket. "I'm paying cash, but I'll go ahead and take care of it now. How much is it for one night?"

"Sixty-five dollars plus tax." His pudgy fingers punched the keys of an old manual adding machine. The *plunk* of the keys and the *whirr* of paper tape feeding through the machine jerked her back to a childhood memory . . .

Her mother at the kitchen table late at night doing bookwork for the apartment manager after she'd already put in a long day on her feet in the factory . . .

Maggie hadn't thought of that in at least a decade. *But that was before.* She stuffed the next thoughts back inside. She didn't know if her mother was even alive. She wasn't sure she wanted to know.

Bart rang up the sale, ripped off the white and yellow tapes, and laid her copy on the counter in front of her. He pointed to the total. "Sorry, but we have to charge room tax and sales tax. Jacks it up pretty steep."

Maggie peeled off four twenty-dollar bills. He made change, and she tucked the bills back in her pocket.

"Right this way," he said, leading her down the hallway where Wren had disappeared.

He stopped at the first room on the left. The door was open, and Wren was beside the bed. She was bent over picking at something on the carpet, her round, gingham-clad backside facing them like one of those tacky lawn ornaments Maggie had seen in suburban yards.

Bart cleared his throat, and Wren popped up and whirled to face them. "Good gravy, Bart. You pert near scared me to death. Okay, miss, you should have everything you need until your luggage arrives. Are they sending it here?"

"My luggage?" Maggie groped for an answer. "No. I had them send it on . . . ahead."

"Oh?" Wren planted plump hands on her hips. "And where are you headed from here?"

If she were in a New York hotel, she would have told the concierge it was taken care of, not to mention it was none of his business. But somehow she didn't mind the question coming from this grandmotherly woman. Unfortunately, she didn't have an answer.

"I'm not sure." It was the first honest reply she'd given since Opal Sanchez had picked her up on that off-ramp Tuesday morning.

Wren cocked her head, waiting.

"I'm still considering some options."

"I see. Well . . ." She grabbed a dust rag off the corner of the dresser and gave Bart a shove. "We'll get out of your hair so you can get cleaned up and get some rest." She motioned toward the door in the corner of the room where a dim light shone on a spotless tile floor. "I put a tooth-brush and some other things you might be needing in the bathroom. And there's a nightgown I never wear hanging in the closet. You holler if you need anything else, and we'll try to rustle it up."

"Is there anyplace around here to get something to eat this time of night?"

"Read?" Bart put a beefy hand on his wife's shoulder. "Wren here has all kind of reading material. You just—"

Wren tugged on her husband's sleeve. "She said *eat*, Bart. *Eat*." She pantomimed shoveling food into her mouth.

"Oh . . . *eat*. Sorry. I thought you said *read*. I'm a little hard of hear-ing," he said again. "You mean like a snack?"

"Well, I haven't had dinner yet."

"Good land!" Wren clutched a hand to her breast. "Why didn't you say something, honey? Listen, you get out of those clothes and put them out in the hallway. I'll get them washed up for you."

"Oh, you don't have to—"

"Now you just go draw yourself a nice bath and get comfortable, and I'll put a tray by your door. You probably noticed my kitchen is slightly out of commission, but I can whip up a sandwich. You like corned beef?"

"You don't need to go to the trouble. Is there maybe a vending machine somewh—?"

"Nonsense! It's no trouble at all." The woman clicked out a *tsk-tsk* and gave Maggie a little push toward the bathroom. "You go hop in that tub. We'll take care of the rest."

Maggie was touched—and too tired to argue. She closed the door behind them and went into the tiny bathroom. An antique claw-foot tub sat in one corner, a pile of plush green towels stacked beside it. She popped the plug into the drain and turned on the hot water. It felt wonderful to slip out of her dust-crusted clothes. Wrapped in a towel, she went to slip them outside the door. She hoped the woman would pick them up before some prankster came down the hall and swiped them. She'd look pretty funny walking along the highway tomorrow in an old woman's nightgown.

Back in the bathroom, she examined the assortment of products the woman—Wren—had left beside the sink. There were sample sizes of luxury shampoo and soap and lotions. She smiled when she noticed they were labeled for various well-known hotel chains. The lavender scent of a little bottle of bubble bath enticed her and she squirted some under the steaming stream of water. A mountain of suds billowed up, and Maggie climbed into their warmth.

Fifteen minutes later she drained the lukewarm water and rinsed the sludge out of the tub. Then she refilled it and soaked for another twenty minutes. She didn't know when a bath had ever felt so heavenly.

The water was starting to cool when a sharp rap at the door startled her. She sat up and smoothed her wet hair back from her face with fingertips that had turned to prunes. "Yes?"

"I'm putting a tray by the door, dear." Wren's voice drifted from the hallway.

"Thank you," Maggie called back. She waited for a response, but hearing nothing, slipped back into the water. Finally the grumbling of her stomach urged her from the tub. She made a turban of one of the towels and slipped into the crisp cotton nightgown before opening the door.

She gave a little gasp at the feast she found sitting there on a little metal TV tray. She didn't even wait until she'd brought it inside before tasting of its offerings. There was a thick corned beef sandwich with cheese and lettuce, a bowl of potato salad that would have fed three people, two giant oatmeal cookies wrapped in waxed paper, and a carton of chocolate milk.

Maggie ate every crumb and cleaned the last of the potato salad out of the bowl with her fingers. She felt like a slob, but right now she didn't care. They would probably charge an arm and a leg for the room service, but right now she would have turned over every last dime in her pocket for the feast.

She was too exhausted to worry about a plan of action for tomorrow. Right now the clean sheets and plump feather pillows were chanting a siren song, and she left the empty tray by the door to heed their bidding.

Maggie sat bolt upright in bed, her heart hammering.

Chapter Fifteen

"Uh . . . I think I jammed the printer again." Mason Brunner stood in front of Trevor's desk with a hangdog frown on his pimply face, kicking absently at a loose tile.

Trevor bit back a harsh word and marked his place in the galleys he'd been proofreading. Dana was home sick, but he'd promised Bob Swanson at Clayburn State Bank that their employee handbook would be printed in time to distribute at the company picnic.

He pushed out of his chair. He'd been hoping to take off early today and help Bart finish hanging drywall in the kitchen at the inn. He didn't have time for some wet-behind-the-ears college kid mucking things up in the pressroom. "Let's go take a look."

Ducking his head, Mason stepped

back and waited for Trevor to come around from behind his desk.

The two of them worked together to free a jammed sheet of paper. Ten minutes later the press was *kachunking* out posters again. Trevor wadded up the mangled sheet that had caused all the trouble and sent it arcing across the room. The wad of paper landed crisply in the center of the waste barrel—nothin' but net. He gave a self-satisfied smile. Still had the touch.

Brushing off his hands, he returned to the handbook proofs, and half an hour later he left the finished pages on the front desk for Bob.

Trevor stopped back in the pressroom to check on Mason before heading across the street to Wren's.

At the inn, he pushed open the front door and let it close with a slam and a jingling of bells. The lobby was empty and the place eerily silent. "Anybody home?" he hollered.

In answer, Wren came flying out of the laundry room, arms flapping like wings. "Quiet! We've got guests." She pointed down the hall.

"Sorry." He tried to look appropriately apologetic but caught a glimpse of the clock over the check-in desk and wondered why she was walking on tiptoe at two o'clock in the afternoon. "I didn't see any cars out front. Glad you've got guests though." He glanced over his shoulder to the empty street outside the front window.

Again Wren shushed him. She lowered her voice to a whisper. "Well, it's just one. A young girl. Came into Salina on the bus. Stupid Greyhound lost the poor thing's luggage. She looked like something the dogs dragged in when she got here last night. Hadn't had supper, so I fixed her a tray. She said she was checking out this morning, but we haven't heard a peep out of her since."

"Are you sure she didn't climb out a window and skip town without paying her bill?"

Wren apparently didn't see his wink. She scowled at him. "She's a nice girl," she said defensively. "She wouldn't do a thing like that. Besides, if she did, she's headed down the highway in my nightgown."

He raised a brow in surprise, making Wren giggle.

"The girl didn't have so much as a pocketbook on her. Only the clothes on her back. I did up her laundry last night and loaned her something to sleep in."

"That was nice, Wren. But you'd better be careful. You'll have every beggar from five counties away knocking on your door if word gets out that the inn offers free laundry service. Wait—don't tell me—this girl didn't have a credit card on her, did she?"

Wren had a heart as big as the prairie. Bart too. It was no wonder they could barely keep their heads above water when it came to the inn.

"Oh, stop." Wren cuffed him playfully. "And that's where you're wrong. This one paid when she checked in. Cash. That's why I didn't mind her staying past checkout time."

"Oh, like you would've kicked her out otherwise," he teased.

"Shush." She leaned over the desk and looked into the dining room. "You're not going to be making a racket in there, are you? Hammering?"

He sighed. "A man can't win for losing with you, Wren. Seems to me just yesterday you were griping because I wasn't hammering fast enough. Now which will it be? Keep the noise down or get the kitchen done?"

She folded her arms across her chest and bobbed her head. "Both."

Shaking his head, he tiptoed across to the dining room with exaggerated steps.

Wren harrumphed. "By the way, Mister Smarty-Pants, I need to run to the IGA. Do you think you could hold down the fort here for a few minutes?"

"Sure." He tipped an invisible hat and gave her a grin.

"If our girl wakes up, I saved some cinnamon rolls from breakfast. You can have one, too, but be sure and save a couple for our guest."

"Got it. Thanks, Wren." He grabbed a tape measure and pencil and headed for the kitchen. He could get some nice quiet measuring done while he waited for Sleeping Beauty to wake up.

Maggie sat bolt upright in bed, her heart hammering. For a minute she'd thought she heard someone beating the door down.

Kevin.

She blinked and looked around the sunny room.

It took a minute for her to remember where she was. A little Podunk hotel somewhere in Kansas. Safe, and far from Kevin's reach.

She slid back under the quilt, but her pulse accelerated again when she heard pounding again . . . somewhere down the hall. She threw off the covers and eased her legs over the side of the bed, bending to inspect the roman numerals on the windup alarm clock perched on the nightstand. It was ticking like a time bomb, but it couldn't be right. Surely it wasn't two thirty in the afternoon.

She stretched her hands over her head but gave a little gasp of pain when she went up on tiptoes. Every muscle in her body was in knots from her marathon walk yesterday. She massaged her calves in vain, then padded barefoot to the window and pushed back the frothy white curtains.

The little town had come to life since last night. Cars and trucks lined the curb, and traffic puttered up and down the street.

She turned and saw the TV tray by the door. If it was really two thirty, she'd missed breakfast. Her stomach growled at the thought, but at least maybe they wouldn't charge her for last night's spread. She glanced at the clock again. She'd be paying an extra night if she didn't hurry up and get dressed and out of here.

But where were her clothes? This old-lady nightgown with its puffy sleeves and perky-daisies-and-watering-cans pattern made her look like a clown. She opened the door a crack and checked the hallway outside.

Nothing.

There was a brief list of local numbers posted beside the phone on her nightstand, but nothing about how to call the front desk.

She went into the bathroom and did the best she could with her hair. At least it was clean. That was a huge improvement. She would ask for a bag to put the toiletries in before she left. The items would help get her through another night or two on the road. Sooner or later she was going to have to break down and buy a few things—socks and underwear for sure.

And a new pair of shoes if she was going to put fifteen miles a day on them. She wouldn't mind a bit of makeup too, though the Kansas sun had painted a natural blush on her cheeks yesterday.

She peeked out the door again and down both ends of the hallway. The hall was empty, and she couldn't see the front desk. Propping the door open against the safety latch, she crept to the lobby.

Empty. No one behind the desk either.

She heard a commotion coming from the dining room across from the hallway. "Mrs.—?" She searched her brain for the woman's last name. "Wren?" she called, finally, hoping the woman wouldn't think her rude.

There was no answer, but louder rumblings came from the dining area—what sounded like furniture being moved. "Is anyone here?"

A man in jeans and T-shirt, wearing a carpenter's apron and a backward baseball cap, appeared in the arched doorway. "I'm the only one here." He ducked through the doorway, a smile on his face. One look at her in Wren's nightgown, and he quickly averted his eyes, his smile following suit.

The gown covered more than most of her shorts outfits did, but she suddenly felt exposed. She wrapped her arms around herself. "Do you know where Wren is? Or her husband?"

He doffed his cap, revealing neatly clipped hair the color of sand. Thick-lashed blue eyes met hers briefly before he focused on the door-jamb, running his hand along the painted wood. "Wren went for a few groceries. Should be back any time now. I don't know where Bart is."

"Oh. Okay. Wren did my laundry last night. I was wondering where my clothes were."

He cleared his throat, still inspecting the intricacies of the arched doorway. "Yeah. She told me."

"She did?" What kind of place left the carpenters in charge and filled the guy in on all the details of a guest's situation?

He nodded and chanced a look back, his gaze not straying below her face. "I don't know where your clothes are, but the laundry room would be a pretty good first guess." He gave her a crooked smile and headed back into the dining room.

Maggie followed him, hugging her arms tighter around her midsection. The fragrance of coffee and cinnamon mingled with the scents of pine and sawdust. Silvery motes danced on the rays of sunlight that spilled through the windows. "Excuse me, but . . . the laundry room? Where would that be?"

He tugged his cap back on, picked up a ladder, and moved it a few feet. When he set it down, a pathetic yowl split the air, and a huge cat shot across the room and out into the lobby. Maggie's heart swelled. The striped tabby was an oversized version of her Buttons back in New York.

"Fool cat," the carpenter muttered under his breath.

Maggie started after the animal. "What's her name?"

"It's a he, and his name is Jasper."

She found the cat in the lobby, huddled beneath a low bench by the front door. "Come here, Jasper. Here, kitty."

The cat sniffed her outstretched hand, and after a minute, crept out, keeping low to the ground. Maggie scooped him into her arms. He outweighed Buttons by a good five pounds, but holding him made her ache for Buttons something fierce. She rubbed her face against his soft fur.

The carpenter shouted something over an eruption of hammering. She walked over to the doorway. "Were you talking to me?"

He looked up, hammer midswing. "I said the laundry room is behind the check-in desk." He indicated with a nod. "First door on the right."

"Oh, thanks." She'd almost forgotten why she came out here.

She let the cat down with one last, longing stroke and went to the door he'd indicated. Feeling like an intruder, she knocked softly, then pushed the door open. Sure enough, neatly folded on the edge of one of two washing machines were her khaki slacks and the rest of her things. The woman had even managed to get the grass stains out of her white blouse.

She grabbed the stack of clothes and headed for her room. It would be almost three by the time she got dressed and out of here. At least if Wren wasn't here, she might be able to leave before they charged her for an extra night. A ghost of guilt hung over that last thought, but she pushed it away, knowing she needed to stretch her cash.

She sat on the bed and let her eyes wander over the furnishings. She'd been too tired to notice last night, but it was a pretty room. The sun streamed through pale wooden venetian blinds and lay in thick slices across the blue and white quilt. The dresser and a little table and chairs in the corner by the windows were painted white, and the walls were covered with a cheery blue and white toile print.

She gazed with longing toward the bathroom. The thought of another long soak in that tub was enticing. Shaking off the thought, she slipped into her clean clothes, then scooped up the money from the dresser, counting it twice.

She started for the door but halted halfway there. She wasn't anxious to hit the road again. She plopped back onto the plump bed pillows. She didn't have enough cash to pay for another night. She remembered what the woman who'd picked her up outside Clayburn had said about Wren letting her work it off washing pots and pans. It was tempting. But she needed to get on the road. With a sigh, she stuffed the cash deep in the pocket of her clean khakis.

In the bathroom she gathered up all the little soaps and shampoos and put them in a plastic bag marked *Laundry* that she'd found hanging in the small closet. She tied the sack in a knot and slung it over her shoulder. She was officially a hobo now.

Through her sun—
induced stupor, an
odd feeling came over
her again—the feeling
that something was
about to happen...

Chapter Sixteen

Maggie closed the door to her room behind her and crept down the hallway. She peered around the corner to the lobby. Still empty. No sign of Wren or her husband.

The carpenter was whistling in the dining room. She poked her head through the doorway. "I'm leaving now. I'm already checked out. I checked out last night," she explained.

He studied her over a sheet of drywall. "I see you found your clothes."

She looked down at her clean outfit. "Oh. Yes. Would you tell the owners thanks for me? I'm Meg, by the way. I really appreciate everything they did."

"Meg." He bobbed his head. "Sure. I'll tell them." He carried the unwieldy drywall toward a torn-up kitchen, apparently dismissing her.

After a moment, she turned to leave.

"Oh, hey! Meg!"

His shout brought her back around.

"I almost forgot. Wren wanted me to be sure you got some of the cinnamon rolls she fixed for breakfast. I'll be in a whale of trouble with her if you don't eat something before you leave." That lopsided smile again. "You'd be doing me a personal favor."

Maggie chuckled at the thought of him being in trouble with the elderly proprietor. "Well, I guess I did miss breakfast."

He glanced at his watch. "Only by four or five hours." The crinkles around his eyes deepened. "But Wren saved some rolls back especially for you."

"That sounds really good right now," she admitted.

"They're in the oven, wrapped in foil. I tested them. Wren didn't make them from scratch like she usually does, but they're edible." He grinned.

He had a nice grin.

"I'll be the judge of that," she said.

"Here." He propped the slab of Sheetrock against the bare studs and squeezed through the labyrinth formed by the refrigerator, stove, and dishwasher. He opened the oven door as far as the maze would allow and pulled out a packet of foil. "There are plates and forks on that little table out in the lobby. There might even be a cup of coffee you could nuke. Or you could make a new pot. Everything you need is out there."

"Thanks." She took the rolls from him and went back to the lobby.

An overstuffed chair facing the window invited her to sit. She rested her head against the upholstered back, relishing the sun on her face. Outside, the village street was picturesque, with geraniums and petunias blooming in flower boxes in the middle of the street and every store decked out in a colorful awning.

The passersby appeared to be in no hurry to get anywhere. She watched as people stopped on the street to greet one another like old friends. Everyone seemed to know everyone else, and their smiles were contagious. Did people really live like this? She felt as if she'd fallen into an old rerun of *Mayberry RFD* . . . or *The Twilight Zone.* Come to think of it, Wren *did* favor Aunt Bee.

She unwrapped the foil and tore off a bite of cinnamon-crusted roll. She'd taste one bite and save the rest for later, when she was on the road. After the feast Wren had fixed for her last night, she shouldn't have been hungry, but the cinnamon was sweet on her tongue. Before she knew it, she'd polished off both rolls and licked the last bits of icing from the wrapper.

She curled up in the chair, growing drowsy with the sun and the rhythmic pounding going on in the dining room. What would it be like to live in a town like this? To have friends like Bart and Wren?

She gazed out the window and imagined what it would be like to live in this sleepy little town. She could almost feel a muddy riverbank beneath her bare feet, cool water lapping at her toes. Overhead, the full moon. And silhouetted in its golden light, ancient trees seemed to whisper her name. She had crossed that river last night, seen that full moon overhead. Through her sun-induced stupor, an odd feeling came over her again—the feeling that something was about to happen . . .

The jangle of bells on the front door brought her upright in the chair. Wren flounced in, wearing the handles of half a dozen plastic grocery bags like bracelets up and down her arms.

Maggie jumped up. "Oh, here, let me help." She cleared the bags from one of Wren's plump arms.

"Whew." Wren wiped her brow with her free hand and tucked a wayward snowy tress behind her ear. "Thank you, honey. I thought I was only going to the store for milk and bread." She studied Maggie. "Did you decide to spend another night with us?"

"Oh, no," Maggie said quickly. "I just overslept. I guess I should have set the alarm."

"Are you going to make your connection?"

Maggie consulted the oversized clock above the mantel, as if she had a schedule to keep. "I should be fine."

With her free hand, Wren motioned to the grocery bags Maggie still carried. "Follow me. If Trevor will let us through, I'll show you where to put those. Have you met Trevor?"

"The carpenter?"

Wren laughed. "Trevor is a man of many talents, a true jack of all trades. He owns the print shop in town. But yes, he's *our* carpenter." Wrinkles creased her forehead. "He saved you some of those cinnamon rolls, I hope."

"Oh, yes. Thank you. And thanks so much for dinner last night. It was delicious."

Wren waved her away. "Goodness, sweetie, it was a sandwich . . . the least I could do after your ordeal." Wren led the way through the arched doorway into the small dining room where the carpenter—Trevor—was still hammering away. "Hey, keep it down, would you?"

He turned, a far-off look in his eyes, as if he hadn't noticed their presence. But then a light came to his eyes and that grin from before spread across his face, and he was fully with them.

"Hey, Wren. She's awake now." He winked at Maggie, then nodded in Wren's direction. "Please inform this woman that I was nice and quiet while you were sleeping."

Maggie looked from him to Wren and back. They'd obviously had words about this. "Well," she said, trying to decide which one of them to side with, happy to be in on their playful dispute, "I couldn't say for sure it was hammering, but *something* woke me up at the crack of . . . well, two thirty."

Wren laughed. "At least you're honest."

Maggie winced. If the woman only knew.

"Here, honey"—Wren reached for the grocery bags Maggie still held—"I'll get these put in the cupboards. You're probably wanting to be on your way. I didn't see a car out front. Where did you park?"

"Oh, I got a ride . . . from Salina." She didn't mention that she'd walked fifteen miles first.

Wren and the carpenter exchanged glances. "Where are you headed?" Wren asked.

"California." Her well-rehearsed answer came a hair too swiftly.

"Back home, huh?"

Maggie had to think for a minute why the woman would assume that was home. *Oh. The hotel bill her husband filled out last night.* "Yes, home. Eventually."

"You weren't expecting the bus to come through Clayburn, were you? Closest place to get on again is back in Salina."

Maggie calculated the miles. If she'd walked fifteen miles and hitched a ride for a dozen more, cab fare to Salina would probably eat up the rest of her cash. Then what would she do? But what choice did she have? She could walk back to town or she could take her chances and accept a ride with one of the farmers who was sure to stop. "I guess I'd better call a cab," she said, thinking aloud.

Again Wren and Trevor exchanged looks, then burst out laughing.

"Honey, the day Clayburn has cab service is the day I retire. And it'd cost a small fortune to have a cab come from Salina."

When Trevor stopped laughing, he turned to her with a kind expression. "When does your bus leave?"

"I don't know," she hedged. "I mean, I don't exactly have a ticket yet. This stop was sort of a detour . . . after I lost my luggage."

"Where are they sending your bags?" Trevor asked.

"Back home." She was starting to believe her own lies.

Wren opened her mouth to say something, then clamped it shut. But Maggie saw doubt flit in her eyes. Or was it suspicion?

Trevor scraped the toe of his work boot in the sawdust on the tile floor. "I guess I could run you to Salina. You find out about the bus and let me know what time you need to be there."

She wasn't sure what this guy had up his sleeve, but in that moment,

Maggie made up her mind. "I think . . . maybe I will stay here another night if that's okay. Until I decide what to do."

Trevor shrugged and went back to work, bowing out of the conversation. Wren still wore a skeptical expression.

"Do you have a vacancy tonight? I can pay ahead like I did before. At least part of it." Remembering the comment of the young mother who'd given her a ride, she added, "If I run a little short, I'd be glad to work it off . . . wash dishes or cook or something. I'm a pretty good cook."

Wren reached out and put a warm hand on Maggie's arm. "I know you're good for it. You just hang on to your money. I'll address an envelope for you, and when you get home you can mail me a check. In the meantime, I best get your room ready for tonight."

Guilt seized Maggie. "Oh, no, please. It's fine the way it was. I have everything I need."

"Well, I won't change the sheets, but made beds are part of the package, sweetie. Hey!" Wren's eyes lit up. She snapped her fingers. "I bet I know where we can get you an extra set of clothes." She doffed her bibbed apron and beckoned Maggie. "Follow me."

Maggie tagged after her up a narrow stairway across from the laundry room. The door at the top of the stairs opened onto a cozy upstairs suite that apparently served as Bart and Wren's apartment. "This is nice," she said, panning the sunny rooms that opened onto each other accordion-style—a kitchenette, a small dining area, and a sitting room beyond that.

Wren gave a grunt. "Well, we don't get to spend much time up here, but we like it when we do. Here . . . come on back."

In a small bedroom off the sitting area, Wren lugged a grocery bag from the closet. "Our church is collecting clothes for the fall rummage sale, and I bet there's something your size in this bag of stuff Clara Berger sent over. Her granddaughters are about your size." She dumped the contents on the bed and started weeding through the jumble of clothing. "What size do you wear?"

"Usually a six or an eight."

Wren inspected a tag in a pair of capris. "Do you see anything here that looks like it would fit?"

Maggie started to pick up a lime green blouse, then hesitated. "Are you sure it's okay?"

Wren waved off her question as if swatting at a pesky gnat. "If it'll make you feel better, you can pay a quarter for each piece. That's about what we'd get for it at the sale. But I'm sure Clara would be delighted to have someone get some wear out of these."

Maggie held up the lime-colored blouse.

Wren clapped her hands. "Oh, Meg! That's such a nice color on you with your blond hair. You take that. And what about these pants? I don't know much about fashion, but wouldn't those go cute together?"

They came back downstairs with two different outfits. "I'll get these washed up tonight," Wren said. "Then at least you'll have something to change into on your trip home. I'll send some toiletries with you too. Wouldn't mind cleaning some of those out of our cupboards."

For some silly reason, Maggie felt a lump lodge in her throat and tears burn behind her eyelids. "Thank you. I-I really appreciate that." Embarrassed, she mumbled an excuse and bolted to her room.

In her rush to
be free of Kevin,
had she abandoned
Jenn in the same
way her mother had
abandoned them both?

Chapter Seventeen

Huddled on the unmade bed, Maggie let the tears fall. She couldn't have told anyone what her tears were about, much less explain them to herself.

The sobs came almost violently now. *Why* couldn't she stop crying? Was she losing her mind? Was this how it had been for her mother—before she'd been committed?

Terror struck at Maggie, and she fought to rein in her emotions. She had always wondered what it had been like for her mother. Whether Mom had even been aware of what was happening when they moved her from the hospital to the institution. The *asylum*, as Maggie's fifth-grade teacher had called it.

Would she end up like Mom? How many times had Kevin accused her of being there already? How quickly he'd used it against her . . . not two days after she'd first confided in him about what had happened to her mother. "You're crazy! A regular loony tune, just like your mother," he'd shouted. And he used it against her again and again. Anytime she tried to persuade him that she had a right to a different opinion than his, he declared her nuts.

She tossed her head, forcing the memories away. She wouldn't be like her mother. Giving up on life, abandoning her daughters, causing them to be separated from each other until they were almost teenagers.

Jennifer. The thought of her sister brought the tears raging back. In her rush to be free of Kevin, had she abandoned Jenn in the same way her mother had abandoned them both? The possibility made her sick to her stomach. Surely Kevin had phoned Jennifer in Baltimore by now. Had he told her that she'd called from that convenience store in Jersey . . . or Pennsylvania . . . or wherever they'd been? Had he told the police about her call?

The questions were sobering. Steeling herself, she slid off the bed and went into the bathroom. The mirror over the sink reflected back her puffy, red-rimmed eyes. She reached up to touch her straggly dishwater-blond hair. Kevin would have had a fit if he'd seen her like this. She could hear him barking now: "Go do something with your hair. You look like—"

Stop! She pressed the fluffy towel against her face and held it there, as if that would silence Kevin's voice in her head.

She ran her comb through her hair and straightened her clothes. She needed to find out if Jenn was okay. Maybe she could get online at the library—if Clayburn, Kansas, even had a library.

She tiptoed to the door and peered out into the hallway. On the carpet beside the door was a small plastic grocery bag containing the clothes Wren had helped her pick out. She grabbed the bag and tossed it on the dresser, then checked the hallway again. Not seeing anyone, she tiptoed out to the lobby. The hammering had stopped, but dishes clanked in the dining room. She let their noise cover the clanging of the bells as she slipped out the front door, relieved not to have to face Wren or Trevor.

Clayburn's Main Street was abuzz with activity, in vast contrast to the ghost town of the night before. She paced in front of the inn, then strolled to the corner where a candy-striped barber's pole advertised seven-dollar haircuts. Down the side street, on Elm, she spotted a flag flying over the post office. A library would probably have a flag flying too. At the north end of Main, about four blocks ahead, she could make out another flagpole rising above the trees in front of an old, square brick building. She headed that direction, taking in the layout of the downtown area as she walked.

In the next block, a little art gallery stopped her in her tracks. The elegant, eclectic décor said anything but small-town Kansas and drew Maggie inside. A man with a ponytail sat behind a counter in the back of the gallery reading a newspaper. He glanced up and acknowledged her with a smile and a nod before burying his head in his newspaper again.

The artwork displayed throughout represented a variety of artists. Mediocre described most of it, but several of the watercolors were beautifully done. Not that she was an expert, but she knew what she liked.

She thought with longing of her secret stash of paints and brushes back at the apartment in New York and wondered if Kevin had discovered it yet. When she got wherever she was going, got settled and found a job, she would go without food if she had to, so her first paycheck could be spent replacing her art supplies. She looked down at her hand and realized her fingers were posed as if they cradled a paintbrush.

She shook her head and gave a little snort. She had no business thinking about job applications. What did she have to put on a résumé? It had been two years since she'd quit the job she loved—working as a designer in a graphic-arts firm.

Kevin had persuaded her to quit her job a week after he'd talked her into moving in with him. "Taking care of me is a full-time job, babe," he told her. "I'll take care of you if you'll take care of me." She cringed to think how romantic she found that at the time.

In spite of his love of the bottle, Kevin had managed to hold down his engineering job. He made a decent living. She couldn't say he hadn't held up his end of the bargain. They lived in a nice apartment, he bought her nice clothes, let her get her hair done whenever she wanted, and even sometimes treated her to spa days. Of course, he threw all those things back in her face if she ever dared to question why he dictated her activities, why he alone chose their friends—what few friends they had.

"See anything you like?"

A voice behind her startled her from the disturbing thoughts. "Oh. I was just . . . admiring these watercolors."

The man beamed. "Thank you. Those happen to be mine."

"You're the artist?"

"Jackson Linder."

He put out a hand, and she shook it.

"They're beautiful."

"You paint." It wasn't a question.

She eyed him. How would he have known that?

His telling nod said he must have seen the question in her eyes. "I can usually recognize another artist. Something about the way you look at a piece—the tilt of your head and the way you examine every brush stroke."

"Well, I dabble a little. I don't really know what I'm doing. I'm better with pen and ink . . . design work. But I like to paint." She pointed to a luminous, pale landscape. "How did you keep the colors so soft without losing the depth?"

The artist launched into a long explanation, and Maggie listened with rapt attention, wishing she could experiment with his advice.

"Listen," he said finally. "I teach watercolor classes every spring and fall. We'll probably start up early in September. We meet on Tuesday nights here at the gallery. Had a good group this past spring. Almost a dozen of us. You saw some of the better work that came from that class hanging over there." He indicated a wall of paintings adjacent to the counter.

"Oh, I don't live here. I'm just staying at the inn. On my way through . . ." She was having trouble concentrating for the fantasy that danced in her head. She imagined herself sitting at an easel in this gallery, painting a fanciful watercolor as sunlight slanted across the wooden floor.

She massaged her temples, trying to get her head out of the clouds. She barely had a dime to her name, and no way of even applying for a job since all her identification was lost. And if she applied for new documents, Kevin would be in town before she knew what hit her.

She gave a cynical laugh at the phrase. *Before she knew what hit her.* It threatened to be true in the most literal sense of the words.

She certainly had no business daydreaming about putting down roots and living the bohemian life of an artist in a Podunk Kansas town.

"At the inn, huh? It's a nice place."

"Oh, it is. It's a little torn up right now, but they've taken good care of me. Wren has. She's such a sweet woman."

He opened his mouth, then closed it as if he'd thought better of whatever he started to say. "Yep. She's a good woman. Salt of the earth."

They made small talk for a few minutes before Maggie eased toward the door. "Well, thank you. I enjoyed your gallery."

"Thanks for stopping in." He followed her to the door. "Come back whenever you're in town."

"Thank you. Oh, hey, is there a library here in Clayburn?"

"Not a very big one, but it's just a couple of blocks up the street." He pointed north up Main Street.

She thanked him and headed that way.

The library was dark and quiet. Except for the librarian and a middle-aged woman browsing through a rack of free paperbacks, Maggie appeared to be the only person in the building.

The librarian showed her to one side of the stacks where a study carrel held four computers. She hadn't worked on a computer much since Kevin made her quit her job, but the mouse felt instantly familiar in her hand. The librarian helped her open a browser, and Maggie logged on to the *New York Times* and skimmed the news. Carjackings were a dime a dozen in the city, and a search of the past two days' issues of the *Times* didn't turn up anything.

She was about to log off the site when she scrolled past an ad for a free online e-mail account. Jennifer had an e-mail address, though Maggie couldn't remember what it was. If she could find out, maybe she could contact her sister without giving away where she was.

She clicked on the link to sign up for the account. She started to type in her name as Meg Anders, then decided against it in case it might show up in a search. She played with the letters of her new name, rearranging them until she came up with "gemsander." Gem Sander. She smiled to herself at the image it evoked. A diamond in the rough, just in need of a little sanding, a little polishing. Kevin would never figure that one out.

Now if she could only remember Jenn's address . . .

On a whim, she did a search for the Realtor her sister worked for. There was a contact link. The e-mail addresses of several principals in the company were listed, and they all followed the same pattern. First initial, last name, and the company's Web address. Using that, she composed a message to her sister, choosing her words carefully.

> Dear Jenn,
>
> I don't know if he has tried to contact you yet or if you even know what's happened, but I wanted to tell you that I'm fine. Things were scary for a while, but I'm okay. I'm someplace safe for

now, and I'll never have to go back.

Please don't say anything to anybody about this (except Mark, of course). No matter what certain people might have told you, I promise you I haven't done anything wrong. I just had to get out. An opportunity came, and I took it. I'll tell you all about it as soon as I can, but I'm sure you understand why I can't say anything yet.

I love you and will try to post again when I can. You can write back to this e-mail address. I'm not sure when I can check it again, but I'll be anxious to know you got this and that he hasn't bothered you.

Love,

M

She read her note again, looking for anything that might give her away if Kevin somehow got hold of it. She hesitated, her hand poised over the keyboard. Finally satisfied that it was safe, she clicked Send.

He felt as though
he were hiding some
deep, black secret.

Chapter Eighteen

Trevor sucked in a breath, steeling himself before he opened the door to the day-care center.

He stepped inside, books in hand, and was immediately swarmed by half a dozen four-year-olds. Gleeful whispers of "Story time! Story time!" rippled through the room.

At her desk, Mickey Valdez spotted him and rolled her eyes. "You're a tough act to compete with, mister, you know that?"

He laughed. "Sorry . . . do I need to come back later?"

"No, no, it's too late now. I've lost 'em completely." Her tone was cynical, but her wide smile told him she was teasing.

He returned it with a grateful one of his own. Mickey knew how hard it was for him to be here. But it was supposed to be good therapy. Face your fears. Don't crawl in a hole and lick your wounds. The voices of many concerned counselors—from Amy's parents to his best buddies to Wren—echoed in his head. And, in truth, it did get a little easier each time.

At least while he was with the kids.

It was leaving that tore him up. Walking out those doors alone, with no tiny hand tucked in his. Going to a car that was glaringly empty of a car seat or a mommy waiting in the passenger seat.

Well, he was here now. No use worrying about leaving until it was time to leave.

One day at a time. One day at a time.

He gently extricated himself from the octopus of preschoolers and led the way to the story pit.

He held up one of the picture books he'd brought. "So what do you think our story is about today?"

"Dinosaurs!" eighteen preschoolers shouted in unison.

"That's right." He opened the book, holding it so the children could see the colorful illustrations. From the moment he read the first line, he was caught up in the fantastical world the author had created. For a few minutes he was able to escape his sorrow and soak up the delight on the faces of the eager children in front of him.

The counselors had been right. It had been good for him to get involved with children, to find a place he could give of himself and think of others' happiness, rather than wallow in his grief. He knew that tonight at home he would once again wrestle with the specter of all he'd lost. But for now, he felt uplifted and almost whole again.

He turned the page and winked at Seth on the front row. The boy's eyes were wide and his mouth open in anticipation of the next silly rhyme of the book. Trev's eyes had been that same rich shade of brown. Eyes like his mother's. Trevor thrust the comparisons out of his thoughts and read the next page in a singsong voice.

Later, with the children out for recess, Trevor perused the bookshelves trying to come up with something for the following week's story time. He'd donated most of Trev's books to the day-care center, and they were lined up on a special shelf with a memorial plaque that read, In Loving Memory of Trev Ashlock. Trevor usually avoided them when he selected books to read. There were too many memories wrapped up in some of those titles.

"Finding what you need?"

He looked over his shoulder to find Mickey Valdez leaning against her desk, watching him.

"I've about exhausted the selection here. Maybe I'll go over to the public library and see what I can find there. Or better yet, next time I'm in Salina I'll pick up some new ones. You have a list of books you've been wanting?"

"I'd be more than happy to go with you sometime," Mickey offered. He recognized the too-eager gleam in her eyes. She'd been hinting for him to ask her out ever since he'd started spending his Friday afternoons at the day care. Mickey was a sweet girl. Pretty, too, with her olive skin and curly black hair. But he couldn't lead her on. He wasn't interested. Not now. Maybe not ever.

"Thanks, Mick. I appreciate the offer, but . . ." He shook his head. "Maybe I'll order some off the Internet. Didn't you tell me there was a place online that you order from?"

"Yeah," she said.

He could almost see her spirits deflate.

"I'll send the link to your e-mail at the print shop."

"Okay. I'll watch for it." He felt bad, but there wasn't a thing he could do about it. He started toward the door. "I'd better run."

"Yes . . . sure. I need to go round up kids." She held up a hand and gave him a close-mouthed smile.

It was almost time for Main Street to roll up its welcome mats, but he decided to make a quick stop at the library before he headed to the inn. He could choose a few books from the children's department for next week's story time. If he left the task until next week, he was bound to forget.

He mounted the stairs of Clayburn's public library and opened the massive doors. As he walked into the cool sanctuary of the main room, musty remnants of dust and old ink met him. He breathed them in with satisfaction. This library always took him back to his own childhood. His mom had taught the weekly story hour here for as long as he could remember—until his dad retired and they became snowbirds. Now his parents lived in Florida year-round. He missed having them close by, but it was also nice to have a warm destination for a week every year when the bitter cold of February in Kansas rolled around.

If he didn't hurry up with Bart and Wren's project, he'd find himself stuck in Clayburn all winter with no relief. He turned to go downstairs to the children's wing but stopped short near the checkout desk. The girl from the inn—Meg—was sitting at one of the clunky computers at the back of the room. Engrossed in whatever was on the screen, she apparently hadn't noticed him. He wondered what had brought a California girl across the country by bus. She hadn't said where she'd been, but if she'd been farther east than Salina, she was a brave woman. That was a lot of miles on a Greyhound and she had a few to go before she was home.

He felt a twinge of guilt about his halfhearted offer earlier. He should have been grateful to take her to the bus station, grateful for another assignment that would keep his mind occupied. But he wasn't looking forward to half an hour in the car with a stranger.

Amy had always called him an extrovert. She'd been shy and on the quiet side. And he *was* outgoing with friends and family, but he wasn't crazy about meeting new people—especially since what had happened to Amy and Trev. The subject was bound to come up within ten minutes of meeting someone new, and if it didn't, then he felt as though he were hiding some deep, black secret.

But even without the haze of his tragedy hovering over everything, he didn't exactly relish spending time with a stranger from California. He shook his head and took the stairs two at a time down to the children's library.

But when he came back upstairs twenty minutes later, a stack of picture books in one arm, she was still at the computer.

His conscience wouldn't leave him alone. He glanced up at the big clock above the doorway and sighed. It was closing time. Approaching the study carrels, he cleared his throat to announce his presence.

She looked up from the computer screen, her eyes glazed. It took a minute for recognition to light her face. "Oh . . . hi."

"Hi. I'm Trevor."

"I remember. From Wren's."

"Yeah. Actually, I run the print shop in town—that's my real job. Wren's is just on the side."

He waited for her to respond. When she only stared up at him, an odd sensation filtered through him. If he didn't know better, he would've pegged it as nervousness.

"Listen," he went on. "I meant it this morning when I offered to take you to the bus station. We're not real busy at the print shop this time of year, and I can get away pretty much anytime I need to, so I'd be glad to take you . . . whenever you decide to go." His mouth was running, and he couldn't seem to shut it off.

She blinked twice, her cornflower blue eyes narrowing ever so slightly. He read in them the same wariness he detected the first time they met. For whatever reason, this girl didn't trust easily. His insides suddenly knotted tight, and his belly churned the way it had the first time he asked Amy for a date. The comparison sobered him.

He cleared his throat a second time. "When you find out your bus schedule, just get in touch with me."

Meg tipped her head to one side, studying him. "Thanks. I'll let you know."

Her eyes drew him in, and he couldn't seem to break his gaze. "The library's closed, you know. Do you want a ride back to the inn?"

She looked past him toward the checkout desk. "What do you mean, closed?"

He pointed over his shoulder at the schoolhouse clock on the wall behind him. "They close at five."

"Then how come we're still in here?" Those blue eyes held skepticism.

He grinned, hoping to win her trust. "They're not going to kick us out. You watch. If we don't leave in a couple of minutes, Mrs. Harms will start flipping off lights."

She wasn't warming to him, and he was starting to feel a little foolish. "Do you want a ride or not?"

She shook her head. "I can walk. It's only a couple of blocks."

"It's still pretty hot out there. I could deliver you to the front door in the comfort of air conditioning." He shot up a prayer that his air conditioner would work today. "It's the closest you'll find to a taxi cab in Clayburn." He almost turned around to see who'd said that. It was as if he had no control over the words that came out of his mouth.

The girl does not want a ride, Ashlock. Leave it alone.

She glanced at the clock. "You're going back to the inn anyway?"

He nodded. "Wren'll kill me if I don't get her kitchen put back together in the next couple of days."

She looked dubious. "You really think you can finish it in two days?"

He laughed. "Well, by 'put back together,' I don't necessarily mean finished. She just wants to be able to plug in the oven each evening. It'll take me a couple of months to finish the whole project." He started for the door.

At the squeak of her tennis shoes on the tiled floor behind him, he curbed a smile.

"That your pickup?" She pointed to the truck parked in front.

"That's it. Here, let me get that." He switched the stack of books to his other arm and opened the door for her.

She stood by the open door and eyed the books. "*The Cat in the Hat?* You have kids?"

He winced to himself but managed to smile and shake his head. "I read for the day-care kids."

"Really? You doing community service or something?"

Where had *that* come from? He laughed and started to open his mouth, but how did a guy answer a question like that?

"No, I mean, that's cool," she said, obviously back-pedaling. "You don't find a lot of macho guys checking out kids' books—at least not in broad daylight."

"Toto, I don't think you're in California anymore," he said, trying to deflect her "macho" comment.

Now it was her turn to laugh. "Sorry. I'm still trying to figure this place out."

He opened the door wider, hinting for her to get in.

She climbed up and settled into the seat, then reached out for the books. "Here, I can hold those."

"Thanks." He handed them to her and walked around the truck to the driver's side.

"Your name was Meg?" he asked as he got behind the wheel.

She grinned. "Still is."

He acknowledged her correction with a self-deprecating roll of his eyes. "You have a last name?"

"Anders."

"Oh? Any relation to the Anders families around here?"

"No," she said a bit too quickly. "My family is all in California."

"So how long have you lived out there?"

"California?" She stared out the windshield. "A couple of years."

"I wondered. Your accent *sounds* more like New York."

Her head jerked up, and he caught a spark of surprise in her eyes. But then she smiled. "Yours is more like Texas."

"Really? Texas? Never been farther south than Oklahoma City."

She eyed the keys in his hand pointedly. "Were you headed back to the inn?"

He followed her gaze. After fumbling to put the keys in the ignition, he backed out of the parking space, trying to avoid her eyes as he checked the oncoming traffic.

They drove the few blocks to the inn in silence. As soon as he parked, she jumped out of the truck. "Thanks for the ride." Her words were cut off by the slam of the door.

Trevor rested his forearms on the steering wheel and watched her hurry in the front door. "Yeah, sure . . . you're welcome. Anytime," he told the empty air.

Why hadn't
she just told the
truth? Nobody here
was going to give
away her secret.

Chapter Nineteen

The inn's lobby was empty. Maggie hurried down the hall to her room, not wanting to face Trevor again, yet sorry at the same time that she'd ruined the pleasant conversation they'd begun.

She closed her door and leaned against it, regret swelling her throat. She'd been terse and rude when all he'd done was show an interest in her life. But he was getting too chummy, and it made her nervous. It took too much energy to keep up her charade.

Her stomach rumbled, reminding her that she hadn't had anything to eat since the cinnamon rolls when she first woke up. She emptied the pockets of her khakis onto the dresser top. She had less than sixty dollars left. And that was without paying for tonight's stay at the inn, thanks to Wren's offer to let her send a check later. Where she'd get a check, she hadn't a clue.

And where was she going tomorrow? If she let Trevor take her to the bus station, what line would she ask for? Having known him for only a few hours, she suspected he would insist on going into the station with her. On making sure she got on the right bus. Funny thing was, she didn't suspect his motives for an instant. Once upon a time—before Kevin Bryson—she'd known men like Trevor. Donald Tarkan at the first foster home she and Jenn had been sent to. And Pastor Fred at the Tarkans' church. The memories were coming back now, of good men who treated women as though they had worth, and whose motives were pure.

She thought of Rick Henry and Ted Blakely. In her desperation for a way of escape, she'd trusted these men. And they'd proven to be kind men who only wanted to help her. She watched the way they treated their wives and caught a glimpse of what a loving relationship should be.

Shoving the cash back in her pocket, Maggie went into the bathroom to comb her hair. In the mirror, she looked over her shoulder with longing at the reflection of the deep tub. It would be nice to have one more soak before she left tomorrow. But first she had to find something cheap for dinner. She turned out the bathroom light and went to the hall.

Wren's voice warbled from the lobby. "That you, Meg?"

Maggie locked the door to her room behind her and tucked the key into her pocket.

"Yes. I was just going to find someplace to eat."

"I wonder if this is yours?" Wren held out a small folded slip of paper.

Maggie reached for it and unfolded it.

"I found it in the washing machine with your clothes. It must have been in your pocket."

Maggie turned over the paper. There was a brief note, but it was smudged and faded, and Maggie could only decipher a few words. It looked like "All things work . . ." and something about a call. But there was no number to call.

Aware of Wren's eyes on her, Maggie refolded the paper and put it in her left pocket. "Thanks."

"Now if that's important, don't you be sending it back with your laundry tonight," Wren teased.

"Oh, you don't have to do my laundry again."

"Might as well. I've got a load to run anyway. Did those clothes fit you?"

"I haven't tried them on yet. But thanks so much for leaving them for me. I'll try them on after dinner."

"You're welcome to eat with me and Bart," Wren said. "Nothing fancy—just my tuna noodle casserole. And we'll have to eat in amongst that mess." She raised her voice and called over Maggie's shoulder into the dining room, "I haven't cooked an honest-to-goodness meal since Trevor Ashlock tore up my kitchen."

"Don't think I didn't hear that, Wren Johannsen." His deep voice came from beyond the arched doorway. The words were gruff, but Maggie heard the smile behind them.

She hadn't heard him working in there. Why did it unsettle her to know Trevor was just on the other side of that wall?

"You're welcome to stay for tuna casserole, too, Mr. Ashlock," Wren hollered.

No answer.

"It's one of Bart's favorites," Wren told Maggie. "At least that's what he's been telling me ever since we were newlyweds."

"Thank you, but I couldn't impose."

"Nonsense. It doesn't make good leftovers—noodles get too sticky, you know. Help us eat it up. I insist. We'll sit down around six."

Maggie looked into the dining room, wishing Trevor would decline the invitation so she could accept. But either he hadn't heard, or he was waiting to see if she would decline.

In the end her stomach—and the thinness of the wad of bills in her pocket—won out. "Thank you, Wren. I'd love to have dinner with you and Bart."

※ ❀ ※

The entire inn seemed to carry the savory aroma of onions and garlic. Maggie's mouth watered as she walked through the lobby to the dining room.

Wren was flitting around the room like a bee in full pollination mode. The ladders and a toolbox stood in the corner on a tarp, but Wren had pulled one of the tables away from the Sheetrock walls and spread it with a cheerful red-and-white-checked tablecloth. Tapers in candlesticks waited to be lit, and a tiny milk pitcher held a fuchsia geranium blossom and a sprig of asparagus fern.

Maggie noticed with dismay that there were four places set at the table. Trevor must have accepted the invitation after all.

"Everything looks beautiful, Wren. What can I do to help?"

Wren spun around, her face alight. "Meg! Good. I was hoping you'd come in time to help." She went to the cabinets in the torn-up kitchenette, rummaged in a drawer, and came up with a book of matches. "Here. You can light the candles. And fill the glasses with ice. I made lemonade."

Jasper lay curled up on a chair in the canted evening sunlight. Maggie picked up the cat and snuggled him for a minute before carrying him to the lobby and depositing him there.

When she returned to the kitchen, she lit the candles on the table, filled the glasses with ice, and came back to Wren for her next assignment. They worked together, turning do-si-dos around each other in the cramped space, Wren grumbling good-naturedly about the mess her kitchen was in. Maggie was happy to keep the talk off the subject of Meg Anders.

"Do you have many guests?" she asked, when a long minute of silence made her fear Wren would start prying.

A hint of a shadow passed over Wren's face but disappeared with her smile. "Not as many as we did when we first opened—back in the eighties. It's a little better on the weekends, but we're hoping with some updating and a little advertising, we can get things back up to snuff again. I'll send some of our cards with you, and you can tell all your California friends about us. We find big-city people appreciate us more than anyone." She gave a soft chuckle. "If I had a nickel for every time I've heard some city-slicker guest comment on how many stars there are in Kansas, I'd retire a rich woman."

"I noticed that, too . . . the stars. That night when I walk—" She caught herself and back-pedaled. "When I first got here."

Wren studied her, then put her hands on her hips. "Honey, God put the same sky over your California as He put over our Kansas. We just haven't seen fit to block out the stars with skyscrapers and neon lights."

Maggie cringed at Wren's reference to "your California." Why hadn't she just told the truth? Nobody here was going to give away her secret. It hurt to admit it, but she wondered if Kevin Bryson was even looking for her anymore. He'd probably have one of the women he worked with—one of the many she'd suspected him of cheating on her with—ensconced in his apartment before the summer was over.

The thought caused a twinge of pain, until she remembered how free—how utterly unfettered—she'd felt since she first stepped onto that bus headed west.

Bart came into the dining room, whistling a song Maggie was pretty sure he was making up as he went. The meandering melody made her feel happy and at ease.

Bart kissed Wren on the cheek, slid out a chair, and sat. "Where's Trevor?"

"Oh, I expect he'll be here any minute." Wren placed a steaming casserole dish in the middle of the table and paused to straighten the napkin under a fork. She gave Maggie a sidewise glance. "Why don't you go ahead and have a seat, Meg? We won't wait too long on him."

Bart jumped up and pulled Maggie's chair out for her. Just then the bells jingled on the front door. A few seconds later, Trevor

Ashlock appeared in the doorway. He'd changed out of his work clothes into clean jeans and a cotton shirt. His hair was still wet from the shower, appearing darker than it had before. As Trevor approached the table, Maggie thought he smelled even better than the dinner on the table.

"You need any help, Wren?" he asked, his hand poised on the back of the chair adjacent to Maggie's.

"You just sit. Everything's ready." Wren brought a basket of fragrant brown bread to the table and plopped into the chair Trevor held for her.

As he sat, he nodded a greeting to Maggie.

Without a word to each other, the three of them bowed their heads. Maggie bowed quickly, hoping they hadn't caught her hesitation. But she couldn't resist peeking around the table, fascinated with their easy expression of faith.

Bart's voice boomed, as if he needed to crank up the volume to reach God. "Thank you, Lord, for these, Thy gifts, which we receive with a grateful heart, a humble spirit . . . and a hungry belly."

"Bart!" Wren pretended to be shocked, but Maggie caught the twinkle in her eyes.

Trevor hid a grin from the woman but winked at Maggie as he picked up the wicker basket in which Wren had placed the casserole dish. He held it while she spooned out the biggest serving she dared.

The food was as luscious on her tongue as it had been to her nose, and she had to restrain herself not to wolf it down like a starved dog.

"Well, Meg, did you get a ride worked out for tomorrow?" Wren asked when all the serving bowls and the breadbasket had gone around the table. "What time does your bus leave?"

"The bread is delicious," she said over a mouthful, to no one in particular, hoping to divert the subject. "You must have a good deli in town?"

"Wren made that herself." Bart puffed out the bib of his overalls, as though he'd had a hand in the bread making.

"It's wonderful. As good as any we get in the kosher delis in New York."

"New York?" Wren laid her fork down, all ears. "Is that where you've been visiting?"

Maggie fought to catch her breath without letting on. She'd blown it big time. Trevor had accused her earlier today of having a New York accent. She scrambled to remember how she'd explained that to him.

"Um . . . yeah. I was in New York for a few days."

"Never had much desire to visit that city," Bart offered.

"Were you there on business?" Wren asked.

"No. Just to see some friends." She felt as if she was being chased on a treadmill.

Trevor caught her eye. He seemed to sense her discomfort with the topic at hand. "The offer still stands," he said matter-of-factly. "I'll be glad to take you to the bus station."

"Thanks. I don't know the schedule, but if you could just get me to the station, I'll take care of the ticket when I get there."

"Oh, you don't want to do that, honey." Wren frowned. "You might get there and find out there's not a bus leaving until the middle of the night. I'd feel a lot better if you had a ticket lined up before you go. We can call after dinner."

"Wren's right," Bart said. "You don't want to be hanging around the bus depot any longer than you have to." He turned to Trevor. "You'll make sure she's safely on that bus before you head back."

It wasn't a question.

Trevor gave a single decisive nod, and Maggie did a mental scramble for something to change the subject. She wanted to get out of this town before she showed herself to be the liar she was to these people who had shown her nothing but kindness. Somehow she would pay the Johannsens what she still owed them for her stay. She didn't need that guilt on her conscience.

But how was she going to avoid going back to Salina with Trevor tomorrow? Maybe she could just leave—start walking and pray one of those Kansas cowboys picked her up on the highway.

The crazy thing was, she'd barely been in Clayburn twenty-four hours, yet she'd started to feel at home here.

"What if I decided to stay one more day?"

The surprise on the faces of her dining partners couldn't have been more pronounced than her own. Until her words registered in her own ears, she hadn't realized she'd blurted out her thoughts. Her temples pounded, and she would have sworn the walls of the room were closing in around her.

Wren put down her fork. "Well, of course you're more than welcome to stay as long as you please, Meg. But don't you have people at home wondering where you are?"

"I-I'll let them know." She pushed back her chair. It scraped the tiled floor, echoing in the curtainless room. "If you don't mind, I think I'm going to go to my room now. Thank you for the wonderful dinner, Wren."

Bart threw up his hands. "You can't go without a slice of Wren's strawberry pie."

But Maggie was already halfway across the room. In the mirror that hung at a tilt beside the door, she caught Wren's reflection as she flew past. The woman was motioning frantically for Trevor to go after her.

Fearing just that, Maggie quickened her pace through the lobby and into the hallway. She fumbled in her pocket for the key to her room.

"Wait!" Trevor's voice behind her sounded uncertain. "Meg, wait a minute."

She slowed. She couldn't run out on him again. With one hand on the doorknob to her room, she turned to face him.

"Is everything all right?"

Her shoulders slumped against the door. Tears threatened. "No," she whispered. All the fight had left her. "Everything is not all right."

"You . . . you want to talk about it?" His voice cracked like an adolescent boy's.

The poor man had been roped into coming after her. Wren meant well, but Trevor shouldn't have to play psychologist to her. "You don't even know me."

He didn't miss a beat. "Oh, but I do, Meg Anders from California who wears a size six-maybe-eight and loves tabby cats and Wren's home-made rye bread." He was close enough for her to catch the citrus tang of his aftershave. Maggie took a deep breath and exhaled heavily. She couldn't help but smile, even though she suspected he was flirting with her. And though he had a few of the details wrong—thanks to her lies— he'd memorized more about her than Kevin Bryson had managed to learn in two years of living with her.

It would be easy to love a man like this.

She recoiled at the thought. What was her problem? The whole rea-son she was standing here while Bart and Wren enjoyed strawberry pie was because she didn't want to get involved. Besides, Trevor had only come after her at Wren's bidding.

Still, his nearness unnerved her. She tried to back up, but she was already pressed against the door like a sock with static cling. She reached behind her for the doorknob. "Listen . . . you think you know me, but you don't."

"Maybe I'd like to."

She barked out a sarcastic laugh. "Maybe you're crazy."

He drew back slightly. "Why would you say that?"

"Are you serious? I'm only passing through. You'll never see me again after tomorrow. Why would you want to . . . invest the time?"

He took two steps backward into the dim light of the hallway. "You let me know what time your bus leaves tomorrow, Meg, and I'll see that you get there. Wren can give you my number at the print shop." He turned and strode into the lobby.

She unlocked the door to her room and opened it. But before going in, she stood under the lintel for a long minute, waiting to hear his voice mingle with the Johannsens'.

Instead she heard the distinct clatter of bells on the front door.

Maggie studied
Wren's expression.
Was there more that
the older woman
wasn't telling?

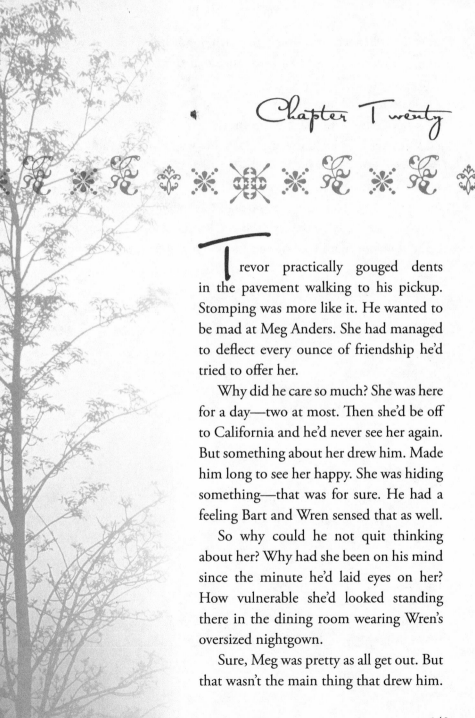

Chapter Twenty

Trevor practically gouged dents in the pavement walking to his pickup. Stomping was more like it. He wanted to be mad at Meg Anders. She had managed to deflect every ounce of friendship he'd tried to offer her.

Why did he care so much? She was here for a day—two at most. Then she'd be off to California and he'd never see her again. But something about her drew him. Made him long to see her happy. She was hiding something—that was for sure. He had a feeling Bart and Wren sensed that as well.

So why could he not quit thinking about her? Why had she been on his mind since the minute he'd laid eyes on her? How vulnerable she'd looked standing there in the dining room wearing Wren's oversized nightgown.

Sure, Meg was pretty as all get out. But that wasn't the main thing that drew him.

In spite of her reticence to share much about her life, there was something about her fresh-faced innocence that captivated him. Then it hit him.

She reminded him of Amy.

The thought brought him up short.

With her fair hair and complexion, her willowy figure, and those blue eyes, Meg was Amy's polar opposite physically. But she had that same wide-eyed amazement with the world that Amy had possessed. He saw how Meg took everything in—delighting in Bart and Wren's repartee, loving on Jasper. Even the way she inhaled the yeasty scent of Wren's rye bread somehow reminded him of the way his Amy had seen the world.

His Amy.

That all-too-familiar ache lodged in his chest.

He climbed into the pickup and revved the engine. Why was he letting himself get tangled up in this woman's life? Dusk was setting in. He flipped on his headlights and closed his eyes. But he couldn't shake the feeling that there was something special—precious, even—about Meg Anders. Some connection they shared.

But how could that be? Meg would be gone tomorrow.

A cloud of dust followed Trevor's pickup westward. Maggie stopped running and stood in the street, watching the dust settle. Against her better judgment she'd tried to catch him before he drove away from the inn. But either Trevor hadn't seen her in his rearview mirror, or he'd decided he wanted nothing more to do with her. A heavy melancholy settled over her. Something even deeper than the sadness and hurt she'd felt when Kevin gashed her with critical, bitter words or that too-familiar look of disdain. Why did she care so much what this stranger thought of her? Why was there such an emptiness in her chest watching him drive away?

"Meg?"

She turned to see Wren standing in the doorway.

"Is everything all right? Where did Trevor go?"

She shrugged. "I don't know."

"Did something happen between you two?"

Did something? Maggie didn't know. It was crazy. She barely knew him, yet she felt the rift between them as if they'd once belonged to each other and something had torn them apart.

"I was kind of rude to him. I think he was just trying to be friendly and—" She shook her head, not able to understand it herself, let alone explain it to Wren.

Wren came out on the sidewalk and put a hand on Maggie's back, rubbing feather-light circles in the space between her shoulder blades. The simple act offered a comfort and warmth Maggie hadn't felt since she was a little girl being coaxed to sleep by her mother's tender hand.

"Why don't you come inside? Eat some pie. We'll talk."

Maggie smiled. Pie seemed to be Wren's solution to everything. Well, it couldn't hurt, could it?

Bart had disappeared, but the dirty dishes were stacked on the panel of plywood that served as a temporary countertop during the remodeling. Wren poured coffee and dished up generous slices of strawberry pie. They carried their plates to the table and sat across from each other, eating and sipping in silence for a few minutes.

"I don't know what happened between you and Trevor at dinner, honey, but whatever it was, don't let your feelings be hurt. Trevor . . . well, he's hurting and sometimes doesn't quite know what to do with his pain. Once in a while it spills out on other people. He doesn't mean it to be that way. It just is."

Wren's words took Maggie by surprise. "I didn't realize—"

"Of course not. He doesn't talk about it. Keeps it locked up inside. It'd be better if he'd let someone share his pain."

"What happened . . . if it's all right for me to ask?"

"He lost his wife and little boy a couple of years ago—in a car accident."

A little gasp escaped Maggie's throat at the horror of it. She rested her fork on the edge of her plate, her appetite gone.

"I know." Wren's head bobbed in sympathy. "It's been tough. Real tough."

"He was checking out kids' books at the library earlier today. Said he reads to the day-care kids. Does he have other children?"

"No. He lost his only child—his son. He lost everything that day." Wren stared past Maggie, her eyes glazed with old sorrow.

Maggie tried to remember what she'd said to him at the library. Some stupid joke about doing community service. She winced.

"I think reading to the day-care kids is Trevor's way of working out his grief. I sometimes wonder if it's the wisest thing." Wren set her cup in the saucer, and the tinkling filled the quiet room. "It can't be easy being around kids who are just the age his little boy would have been. But maybe it helps."

Wren didn't really seem to be fishing, but it was hard to miss the woman's motherly affection for Trevor. Perhaps an explanation would set Wren's mind at ease.

"He offered to take me to the bus station tomorrow. I-I didn't know about—you know." She hung her head. "I thought he was flirting with me or something. I was pretty rude to him."

"Trevor was flirting with you?"

Maggie shook her head. "I probably imagined it. I'm so stupid—"

"Oh, honey, I hope he *was* flirting with you. That would make me one happy woman."

Maggie took another sip of her now lukewarm coffee, not knowing how to respond.

Wren didn't seem to notice. She went on, her words gathering steam. "It's about time he came out of mourning. Maybe it just took a pretty girl like you to bring him around. Nothing would make me happier than for Trevor Ashlock to find a sweet girl like you and fall head over heels." That faraway look came to her eyes again.

Maggie studied Wren's expression. Was there more that the older woman wasn't telling?

Feeling suddenly uneasy with the conversation, Maggie pushed away from the table. Leaving her coffee and the last bite of pie, she murmured an excuse and practically sprinted down the hall to her room.

She closed the door behind her, her breath coming in uneven gasps. She had to get out of this place. Everything was getting too confusing.

As awkward as it would be, she would take Trevor up on his offer and leave tomorrow. First thing. Before she was in so deep there was no getting out.

A small voice
seemed to whisper
inside her that he was
different. Did she
dare hope it were so?

Chapter Twenty-One

'll wait to make sure you get your ticket okay." Trevor shifted the pickup into park in front of the convenience store that served as a bus terminal. He cut the engine and jumped out of the truck before Maggie could stop him.

She jogged after him as he strode toward the building. "You don't need to stay."

He shrugged. "I don't mind. Just till we make sure you can get a ticket."

"Please, I'm a grown woman. I'm perfectly capable of purchasing my own bus ticket."

"Yes, but are you capable of keeping track of your luggage?" He eyed the canvas bag slung over her shoulder, and a slow grin lit his face.

Wren had given Maggie the bag this morning—packed with sandwiches, fruit, and enough food for at least two days—

149

along with two freshly laundered outfits. But she knew Trevor's comment didn't refer to this new "luggage." He was talking about the bags she'd supposedly lost when the bus left without her. She looked down at the rummage-sale castoffs she was wearing. Everything she now owned had been given to her in sympathy—mostly for stories that weren't even true. A phrase spooled through her mind: *ill-gotten gain.*

"It wasn't my fault my luggage got lost." Guilt made her bite out the words more harshly than she intended.

"I never said it was."

"You implied it."

"No, you inferred that I implied it."

She rolled her eyes. "A woman needs a dictionary to have a conversation with you."

He grinned like he'd won some prize.

"What?" she barked.

"I didn't say anything."

She put her hands on her hips. "Listen. I appreciate all your help—I really do—but please go now. I feel bad enough that you had to take off work to get me here."

"There's nothing at work that won't still be there when I get back. Besides, it's Saturday. I usually work a short day anyway."

"Please, Trevor. I'll be fine." Frustration colored her words. She walked toward the station, hoping he'd give it up.

But he dogged her steps. "Sorry. I wasn't raised that way."

She kept walking. "What are you talking about?"

"My dad raised me to be a gentleman, and I intend to make sure you get safely on that bus. Besides"—he flashed a goofy grin—"Bart will give me what for if I don't."

"Fine." She ignored him and headed for the ticket counter, praying he would stay back far enough that he wouldn't hear the transaction.

She got in line behind a burly man in a Hells Angels jacket. When he turned to leave, he looked her up and down and wolf-whistled just loud enough for her to hear. She glanced back to see if Trevor had noticed the exchange. He watched intently from the edge of a booth bench and visibly relaxed when the bearded man left the building.

"May I help you?" The impatience in the clerk's voice told Maggie she'd asked the question more than once.

She lowered her voice to a near whisper. "I'd like to buy a bus ticket."

The woman stared at her for an overlong second. "Your destination?"

She stole a glance over her shoulder. Trevor had settled in the booth with his elbows propped on the table, raking his hands through his hair.

"What's the next stop west?"

"That would be Hays."

"Hays?"

"Hays, Kansas."

"Oh . . . still in Kansas? How far is that?"

"The bus leaves at 4:25 this afternoon and arrives at approximately 6:00 p.m."

"How much is that?"

"A ticket to Hays is twenty-seven dollars."

She studied a route map behind the counter. Hays was only a couple of inches from Salina. At this rate, she'd never make it past the state line. "What's the next stop after that? Does that bus go on to Colorado?"

"Yes, Greyhound has service to Colorado." The clerk's voice rose a few decibels.

Maggie hiked Wren's canvas bag up on her shoulder and reached into her pocket to finger the ever-thinning roll of bills. "What's the farthest I could get on fifty dollars?"

The woman typed something on the keyboard and waited for the screen to change. "You could get to Denver for seventy-seven dollars."

"I don't have that much. Is there anyplace else a little cheaper?"

"Meg?"

She winced at Trevor's deep voice directly behind her.

"Is everything okay? Do you need some money?"

She gave the clerk a long-suffering look. "Excuse me. Sorry." She wheeled to face Trevor. "I'm fine. I said you didn't have to wait."

"Are you sure everything's okay? I heard you ask—"

She turned back to the clerk. "I'm sorry. Hang on . . ." She stepped out of line to let two elderly women go ahead of her.

"I thought you were going back to California." His tone was even, but his eyes challenged her.

"I am."

"Then why are you trying to buy a ticket to Denver?"

"Denver is on the way home." Why was she explaining herself to this man? She didn't owe him any explanations.

"Come here, Meg." He motioned toward the door of the convenience store.

"What?" She kept her feet planted.

"Would you please come here for a minute? I want to talk to you."

Huffing out her frustration in a ragged breath, she trudged after him. He held the door for her, and she stepped outside. The sun was already hot and wavering off the asphalt parking lot. Exhaustion came over her like a gust of hot wind. She wanted nothing more than to crawl back into the soft bed at Wren's Nest and burrow there until she figured out the rest of her life.

She followed Trevor across the lot where a row of cars had lined up next to his pickup. Just then the sun caught a familiar flash of white, and Maggie recognized a Honda Civic parked at the end of the row. It took a minute for the significance of the vehicle to register.

Kevin.

Her heart lurched. Her hands turned into clammy appendages. She forced herself to step closer and examine the back of the vehicle.

The car had Kansas plates—and pinstripe detailing that didn't match Kevin's Honda. Relief flooded her.

She was being ridiculous, and she knew it. But even the thought of him tracking her down had left her lightheaded and trembling.

She felt Trevor's hand on her elbow and turned to face him. He seemed oblivious to the terror that had just coursed through her.

He squinted against the sunlight, the silvery blue of his irises flashing through the narrow slits. She squirmed under the intensity of his gaze. His touch was exquisitely tender, yet his fingers seemed to burn into her flesh. "What? What do you want?"

"Something is wrong here." He dropped his head briefly, scuffing the toe of his tennis shoe on the asphalt before meeting her eyes again. "It's none of my business, Meg, but I . . . I get the sense that you're in trouble. I don't want to see you get hurt."

She glared at him, silent, intent on keeping the rise of emotion within her at bay.

"Well? Am I totally wrong about that?"

She wriggled out from under his hand. Yet, even when she'd removed herself from the heat of his touch, something about his expression made her want to pour her heart out to him. She braced herself against the thought. All that would accomplish would be to make him feel guilty.

"Meg, please. Would you tell me what's going on? Maybe I can help."

Her brain told her to turn back toward the building. But she stood rooted in place, unable to make herself move. Emotional walls, once so tightly erected—and higher than she could have imagined—were beginning to crumble. She was a little girl again, and they were taking her mother away, then separating her and Jenn. Then Kevin was destroying the few good things left inside her—her self-worth, her talent as an artist, her dignity, her good judgment.

She looked into Trevor's kind eyes, and the dam finally broke inside her. She couldn't stop the outpouring of her fears. Barely able to stay on her feet, she dropped her face to her hands and felt tears slip through her fingers. "I don't know what I'm going to do. I . . . don't even have enough money to get to Denver."

"Meg." Trevor lifted her chin and forced her to look at him. "Why didn't you say something?"

She wanted to run away as fast as her legs would carry her, and at the same time, she wanted to fall into the shelter of his arms and stay there forever.

Then, immediately, she hated herself for the thought. For being so weak. She'd fallen for Kevin just as quickly, and look at the abyss *that* had plunged her into. But there was something about this man. A small voice seemed to whisper inside her that he was different. Did she dare hope it were so?

"How much do you need?" Trevor dug in his back pocket and brought out his wallet. "Where is home?"

She drew back and stared at him.

"What city in California are you trying to get to?"

She wagged her head. "I-I can't pay you back. I don't know when I'd be able to—"

"No. This isn't a loan. I want to help, Meg. Tell me where you're going." He started walking toward the convenience store, steering her along beside him with a light touch to her elbow. "Let's go see how much a ticket would be."

She stiffened and stopped walking. "Trevor . . . I'm not going to California."

He dropped his hand from her shoulder and took a step back. "You're not?" He hesitated, studying her, as though waiting for her to tell him something he already knew.

She felt his eyes on her and wanted to offer him the truth. But she didn't know where to start. Or if she could fully trust him.

For a long while he said nothing. Just stood there, waiting. Finally he spoke. "So where *are* you going . . . *Meg?*"

The way he said her name made her wonder if he knew even that was a lie. She rubbed her brows with the tips of her fingers. "I don't know. I need to get away."

"Away from what? What is going on, Meg? I can't help you if I don't know the truth."

"I need to get away from someone who . . . isn't good for me."

"Your husband?"

She lifted her head, surprised, and watched a shadow play across his face. Why had he guessed *that*? She shook her head, then dropped her chin to her chest, her face burning with shame. "No . . . we're not married. But I can't go back to him. I can't go back."

"Back to where?"

She shook her head. She wanted desperately to trust Trevor. But if Kevin tracked her down, or if he—or any of the people she'd lied to along the way—had the police searching for her, she didn't want them to be tempted to rat her out.

"Then where will you go?"

"I don't know. West, I guess."

"West isn't a destination. You can't just buy a ticket 'west.'" His lips curved in a quick half smile before his expression turned serious again. "Why don't you come back to Wren's? Stay there, at least until you know what you want to do. Where you want to end up . . ."

Oh, how wonderful that sounded. How safe. Absently she touched the roll of bills through the fabric of her pocket. "I don't have enough to pay for last night, let alone stay another night."

"We'll worry about that later. You don't have enough to stay anywhere else either. At least this way you'll be with people you know. You'll be safe."

She tried not to let him see the relief that flooded over her. "Do you know someplace I could get a job, even for a little while? Until I earn enough to . . ." She didn't know how to finish the sentence. Didn't know what was next for her. "Maybe I could help Wren out at the inn?"

His expression turned skeptical. "Business hasn't been too good lately. I don't think they have funds to spare."

"But all that remodeling. I thought—"

"I think that's wishful thinking on their part," he said. "But hey, Bart and Wren would probably let you stay at the inn for a while. They have plenty of extra rooms."

"I'd help out any way I could." She tried not to sound too eager, but hope swelled her throat. She swallowed hard. *Oh, please, God . . . if you're really there . . . ?* She started inwardly at her own words. Did she really think God might hear her? She had to admit there was a strange comfort in the mere utterance of the words, the . . . Was it a prayer?

Trevor reached out a hand. "Come on. Let's get out of here."

The smile she gave him through the pickup window did strange things to his insides.

Chapter Twenty-Two

ouncing along the country roads back to Wren's Nest, Trevor kept both hands on the pickup's steering wheel and sneaked a peek at Meg in the seat beside him. Conversation was apparently the last thing on Meg's mind. She sat staring out her window, her shoulders hunched and angled away from him.

He turned on the radio to drown out the silence that hung between them. A Mozart violin concerto filled the cab, and Trevor willed the beauty of the chords to work their soothing magic on the woman beside him.

They were halfway back to Clayburn before she finally spoke. "I'm sorry you had to make this trip for nothing."

He turned down the radio. "It was no big deal. I didn't have anything more important to do."

She gave a cynical little laugh. "I know better than that."

"No, I mean it, Meg. I'm glad you didn't get on that bus. And it wasn't for nothing." If her situation was as he was beginning to suspect, he meant every word. The stooped shoulders and the pale blue eyes that were so often downcast made sense now. Anger rose in his throat. What had some nameless man done to Meg to cause her such pain?

"I'm sorry."

He didn't quite realize he'd spoken the words aloud until she looked up, her brow knit in a question.

"For whatever he did to you, I'm sorry."

"Why should you be sorry?"

He harrumphed. "Because men can be real jerks sometimes."

She shrugged in seeming agreement with his statement.

He waited an awkward moment for her to say something, but she turned back to stare out the window instead.

Watching her surreptitiously, he couldn't help but compare Meg to Amy—and be glad he'd never seen the dull glaze of sadness in Amy's dark eyes. No, his Amy had always worn a knowing smile, as though she carried all the secrets of the universe in her heart. Even at the funeral home, people had commented how Amy's expression in death was beatific, as though she'd seen her eternal destination a split second before she became absent from her body.

Amy. Sometimes he was utterly overwhelmed with the longing—the ache—to hold her just one more time. He shook off the thought. Amy was okay now. This woman was not. Maybe he could help her find a place to belong.

He turned off the road, taking a shortcut into town. A blanket of shadows fell over them as they passed under the canopy of Dutch elms that grew on either side of Bill Wyler's pastureland.

"Oh." Maggie strained against the seat belt and peered intently through the windshield at the trees overhead. "This is the road I came in on the other day—well, *night*, actually. A woman picked me up here. Kaye somebody. She had a bunch of kids."

"Probably Kaye DeVore. Her mother lives east of town. Had surgery last week, I think. Kaye's probably been taking care of her."

"What a coincidence."

A coincidence? He gave her a questioning look.

"That you just happen to know her."

He shrugged. "I don't really know her that well. I went to school with her husband. She and Danny have half a dozen kids and one on the way, I hear."

"You know an awful lot about her for not knowing her very well."

He laughed. "You're definitely not from around here, are you? Clayburn is a tiny town. And this is Kansas. Everybody knows everybody."

She shook her head as if she didn't quite get it. "Seven kids? Really? Can you imagine?"

"Well, I might be exaggerating a little. But I know they have at least four or five. A set of twins, I think."

"Yes, I remember the twins. A handful." She smiled. "Did you grow up in a big family?"

"No, I'm an only. You?"

The sadness crept back to her eyes. "I have a sister."

"I always wished for a brother. Are you and your sister close?"

She seemed to think about the question for a minute. "We are now. We . . . we didn't grow up together."

"Oh?"

"We were raised in foster homes—after our mom—" She fanned a hand in front of her face, as if swatting away a gnat. "It doesn't matter."

"Sure it does. It's your history. Your story."

Again that self-deprecating shrug. "I guess."

He fumbled to think of something pleasant to say. It was obvious she didn't want to talk about herself. "Once you get settled at Wren's, do you want to have lunch with me? My treat," he added quickly, remembering her financial status. "I can show you around Clayburn."

She eyed him, as if deciding what his intentions were. "Okay . . . thanks. I'd like that."

Apparently he looked safe—either that or she decided to risk him for the free lunch. Either way suited him fine.

He glanced at the clock. "I have a couple things to take care of at the print shop, but I'll come by the inn around eleven-thirty. We can beat the lunch crowd that way."

She giggled.

"What's so funny?"

She covered her mouth, stifling more laughter. "I'm sorry, but is there really such a thing as a lunch crowd in this 'tiny town?'" She drew quotations marks in the air.

"You're not making fun of our fair city, are you?"

A playful spark came to her eyes, and she wagged her head. "Not me. Wouldn't do to bite the hand that feeds me."

"Good point. And hey, you'd be surprised how Clayburn packs out our three restaurants. What else is there for excitement?"

"Another good point." She was as close to beaming now as he'd seen her.

They drove out of the alley of trees into the sunshine, and Meg squinted against its brightness. She was quiet again after that.

They drove to the center of town in silence. She thanked him when he dropped her off at the inn. He considered going in with her to explain things to Wren but sensed she would rather do that herself.

"See you at eleven-thirty," he reminded her.

"I'll be waiting."

She shut the door to the pickup, but the smile she gave him through the pickup window did strange things to his insides. Maybe it was just the natural reward of being a Good Samaritan. But it seemed like more. Much more.

※ ✾ ※

hen Maggie entered the lobby, Wren looked up from the desk with the same formal smile she'd first greeted Maggie with. Then her expression changed to one of concern. "Meg? What happened? Did you miss your bus?"

"No. I—" She teared up. What was wrong with her? She was usually a master at shoving down her emotions. But she had shed more tears in five days than she had in five years.

Trying again, she opened her mouth, her mind manufacturing another lie to explain her return. But she caught herself. Coming clean—well, mostly—with Trevor Ashlock had felt good.

She decided to adopt the same policy with Wren, who had been so kind to her. "I don't have any place to go, Wren. I asked Trevor to bring me back here."

"No place to go? I don't understand."

"I needed to get away from . . . a situation. I'm . . . out of money, but if I can find work, I'd like to stay—until I figure out what to do."

Wren put a hand to her bosom. "Oh, honey. Is everything all right?"

Maggie wondered if the woman was fishing for details, but the concern on the older woman's face convinced her that wasn't the case. "No. It really isn't. I don't know what I'm going to do."

Wren jumped up and hurried around the desk. "Oh, Meg. What's going on?"

The canvas bag that held all of Maggie's worldly possessions dropped to the floor as the warmth of Wren's motherly arms enveloped her. As Maggie let herself be held, a sweet, long-forgotten fragrance brought memories flooding back. The perfume conjured the scent of her mother. Mom had held her tight like this that day in the solarium. Someone— she couldn't remember who—had taken her and Jennifer to the hospital where Mom lived. It was the last time they ever saw her.

The social worker had driven her and Jenn to another new foster home that afternoon. They'd barely gotten to say good-bye to their first foster parents, the Tarkans. To this day, she didn't know why they'd had to leave. She and Jenn had huddled together in a cold double bed that night, keeping each other warm.

But the next morning the social worker came again. And this time she took Jenn away in her car. "To a nice new home," the lady told Maggie. "With a mommy and daddy to love her forever." But that family didn't have room for Maggie. They wanted a *little* girl, and Maggie was four years older than Jennifer, and more "self-sufficient." At the time Maggie didn't even know what that big word meant. She'd quickly learned it wasn't a good thing.

Her foster mother told her she could visit Jennifer soon. But a week went by, then two, and no one ever said anything about Jenn again.

When Maggie started sixth grade, she and Betsy Tavenger became best friends. That eased the pain of losing Jenn a little. That, and knowing her sister was in a nice home with a nice family.

And Mr. and Mrs. Manning were nice enough, even if they seemed to spend all their time with the babies and never paid much attention to her.

"Come." Wren loosed her arms from around Maggie and went behind the counter for a set of keys. She took Maggie by the hand, leading her down the hall to the same room she'd stayed in before. "You get settled here and rest awhile. We'll figure out the rest later—on a full stomach."

"Oh!" Maggie scooped up the canvas bag. "I almost forgot. I still have the lunch you made me. I didn't eat any of it." She thrust the bag at Wren.

"Why don't you take that to your room? I'll have Bart move one of our little dorm fridges in there, and you can keep a few things on hand."

Trevor had lunch covered, and the food Wren had fixed would keep her going for another day or two. Maybe she could help Wren with some housecleaning to pay for her room for a few nights. She wouldn't have to leave quite yet.

He barely knew the
woman. Why had he
become so obsessed with
thoughts of her?

Chapter Twenty-Three

he back door to the print shop was unlocked, and Trevor opened it to a blast of cool air from the pressroom. Maybe a few minutes out of the heat would bring him back to his senses. It almost seemed like a dream that he'd already made a trip to Salina this morning. With a beautiful woman. And he'd brought her back with him.

The things he found himself doing since Meg Anders showed up at Wren's were so out of character for him it made his head spin. He hit the Play button on the CD changer in his office, closed the blinds on the window that overlooked the front office, and plopped down at his desk. The same Mozart concerto that had been playing in the pickup came on. It reminded him of Meg.

Why did he feel so drawn to her? She wasn't even his type. Even before he'd met

Amy, he'd always gone for the petite, dark-haired beauties.

Meg was beautiful all right but in a very different way. He frowned. Maybe that was the point. Maybe he'd subconsciously chosen to befriend a woman who wouldn't remind him of Amy every time he looked at her.

He huffed out a sigh. If that were the case, it wasn't working. Meg did make him think of Amy. Or at least made him remember what it was like to be in love. To feel the way Amy had made him feel—strong and competent. And needed.

Since he'd lost Amy and Trev, he sometimes felt that nobody would even notice if he fell off the edge of the earth. Oh, sure, Bart and Wren appreciated his helping around the inn, and the kids at the day-care center obviously enjoyed his stories, but anyone else could have stepped into those shoes and done a fine job. None of them truly needed him.

But Meg seemed like a lost kitten yearning for a place to belong, and he liked the idea of maybe becoming that place for her.

"Trevor?" Jamie Marlowe, the high-school girl who worked as his Saturday receptionist, stood in the doorway of his office. "Do you have a minute?"

"Sure. What's up?"

"Can you come and talk to someone about an order?"

He followed her to the front counter and greeted the owner of the local lumberyard who served as president of the chamber of commerce. The man was waiting to talk about a printing project for the chamber. For the next twenty minutes Trevor's thoughts were absorbed in business matters. But the moment Trevor entered the pressroom, Meg Anders jumped to the forefront of his mind again.

His feelings troubled him. He barely knew the woman. Why had he become so obsessed with thoughts of her? Why had he gone out of his way to help her? He was as nice as the next guy, and sure, if he saw someone lying injured in the street, he would be the first to help. But he didn't go around looking for good deeds to perform.

Yet that's what he'd done for Meg. And in spite of the fact that she was a troubled woman, and obviously running from some relationship, he was drawn to her. Why? He'd had women practically throw themselves at him ever since Amy's death. He'd never even been interested until now.

He wished he could talk out his conflicted feelings with someone. But he didn't really have a confidant. A stab of guilt pierced him at the thought. Of course he did. God was always waiting to hear him whine. But right now he wouldn't have minded someone made of flesh and bone.

In the first weeks after Amy and Trev's accident, his friends had gathered around him and let him talk endlessly about his loss. It had helped too. But most of their friends had been couples, and it seemed to be the wives who were most willing to let him talk. And that got awkward. When weeks and then months went by and he lost interest in anything but nursing the crushing grief, one by one, his friends drifted away. He couldn't blame them. Sometimes he got tired of his own company.

And then there was Jack. The one friend he'd known from the time they were boys covering each other's backs on the playground at Clayburn Elementary. He'd always known Jack would stick with him through anything. But the accident had changed all that.

Oddly, when he wished for a confidant now, Wren was the first person who came to mind. But amazing as it was under the circumstances, that she had chosen to take him under her wing, he'd never been able to confide in her about anything to do with Amy's accident. Wren had too much at stake in the whole mess.

It surprised him to realize that he hadn't thought of the accident itself—the ugly, difficult details—for a long time. The revelation encouraged him. There'd been a time when he thought about it every single minute of every single day. Ironically he had Wren to thank for much of his healing. He thanked God every day that he had a reason to stay away from home. He sometimes worried that Wren had manufactured her little remodeling project purely out of sympathy for him—or worse, out of her own misplaced guilt.

He shook off the thoughts. Maybe he'd give his father a call tonight. It had been awhile since they talked. Unfortunately, since his folks moved to Florida, out of sight had soon become out of mind. But Dad was a good listener, and whether he simply let Trevor talk or offered a word of advice, it helped to spend some time with him—even if it had to be over the telephone wires.

He went back to the pressroom, where Mason was stuffing fliers and coupons in an advertising tab slated to go out with next week's *Courier*.

"You want me to do all these before I leave, Trevor? I could finish up first thing Monday morning." Mason's hopeful expression left no doubt what his preference was.

"What's the deal? You have a hot date tonight or something?"

When Mason flushed ten shades of red, Trevor almost regretted teasing the kid. "I don't care when you do them. As long as they're done by eight or so Monday morning. I'm going to need you for that chamber job first thing."

"No problem."

A grin split the young man's face, and Trevor couldn't resist. He punched him in the bicep. "You mean to tell me you'd rather take some cute girl out than work late on a Saturday night? Think of all that over-time you're giving up."

Mason laughed. "Ha! If you saw her, you'd do the same thing. Hey, I think she has an older sister."

Trevor tried to shrug off the suggestion. For the past few months it seemed the entire population of Clayburn had conspired to get him married off—or at least dating again. He wasn't in the mood for this conversation, but Mason didn't take the hint.

"Seriously, I could probably set you up. Audrey goes to some college back East, but she's home for the summer."

He clamped a hand on Mason's shoulder. "She's probably a tad young for me, Mason. I think I'll pass, but thanks for thinking of me."

"No, wait. Audrey's a lot older than Mandy. I think she's divorced or something and going back to college again. She's not as hot as Mandy, but you could do a whole lot worse."

Trevor shook his head. "You've got it bad for that girl, don't you?"

Mason turned the backward bill on his cap around and hid beneath its shadow. They both laughed.

But Trevor's smile faded as soon as he closed the door to his office. He turned on his computer and pulled up the documents for a printing project that was due Monday. The four-color job required some photo retouching before he could put it on the press, and he hadn't quite mastered the Photoshop program. He was grateful for the concentration the task required. He wasn't in the mood to think too hard.

He glanced at the clock before settling in with the job. Why he'd offered to take that woman from the inn—Meg—to lunch, he didn't know. It seemed like a good idea at the time. She was in a bad spot. But now that it was almost time to pick her up at the inn, he wondered what he was going to tell people about her. Trevor Ashlock couldn't just show up at the Clayburn Café with a pretty girl in tow and not explain her to people.

Maybe he'd pick up sandwiches at the grocery store and they could do a quiet picnic in the park. He'd make it short and sweet. Feed the girl and take her back to the inn. He needed to knock off work early anyway so he could get in a few hours on Wren's kitchen tonight.

Meg would understand that even though it was Saturday, he had work to do. He was a business owner. And he'd already taken off half the morning on a wild-goose chase to Salina on her account.

He kneaded the bridge of his nose. What had he gotten himself into? Meg Anders seemed like a nice enough woman, but she was hiding something. Something besides the fact that she was running from some jerk who had treated her badly. He was certain of it.

※ ✳ ※

aggie surveyed her reflection in the full-length mirror. She'd paired the maroon print blouse from Wren's rummage-sale bag with her khaki pants. It wasn't exactly what she would have chosen for a job interview, but it would have to do. By the looks of things, she didn't think Clayburn was too concerned with formality.

She ran the comb through her hair one last time, took a deep breath, and stepped into the hallway.

"Well, don't you look nice," Wren said when Maggie walked through the lobby.

"Wish me luck. I'm going to see if I can find a job."

"Already?"

Maggie nodded. She didn't want to tell Wren how little money she had left.

The wrinkles in Wren's forehead grew pronounced. "You might have better luck if you wait until Monday, honey. A lot of the shops close early on Saturday."

"Oh." Maggie hadn't thought about that. In some ways, it seemed as though it had been one long day since her adventure began in the early hours of Tuesday morning.

"Well, you never know." Wren brightened. "It sure can't hurt to try. But you come back in time to eat lunch with us, okay?"

"Oh . . . thank you, Wren, but Trevor invited me to have lunch with him."

A slow smile tipped Wren's mouth. "He did, did he? Well, I'd invite you to have supper with us, but Bart's taking me out to dinner and a movie. The sweet man thinks I need a break."

"That *is* sweet."

Wren chuckled. "Well, Bart's idea of dinner out is Taco Bell, but it's the thought that counts, right?" She turned back to the papers she was sorting. "But listen, Meg, you feel free to raid the refrigerator. If you can get it open in that crazy wreck of a kitchen."

"Don't worry about me. I'll be fine. I'm not used to eating that much anyway. Besides, I still have the sandwiches you made for me."

"Well, good luck with your job search. You just smile that pretty smile and you'll get hired in a flash. I'd hire you myself if we had the money."

Well, that answered that question. Trevor had said as much, but she'd held out hope. But there was no sense getting discouraged before she'd even made one inquiry. Her heart fluttered a little, but it was more with excitement than with nerves. She hadn't figured out what to do yet about her lack of identification, let alone the fact that she hadn't held a job in two years.

Breathing in deeply, she shook off the thought. She had to think positive. If she did find a job, it meant the opportunity to stay here in Clayburn. And start a new life.

She was beginning to like that idea very much.

Maggie faced the moment she'd hoped for—and dreaded.

Chapter Twenty-Four

With one hand on the door, Maggie checked her reflection in the window of the children's clothing shop. She sighed, pasted on a smile, and tried to straighten her sagging shoulders. How much rejection could one woman handle in the space of a morning? She'd gotten a firm "sorry, we're not hiring" at every other shop on this side of Main Street's business district—such as it was in Clayburn.

She took in a deep breath, opened the door, and went to give her now well-rehearsed spiel to the woman behind the counter.

Before she even finished, the woman frowned. "I'm sorry, but I barely have enough work to keep myself busy."

"Do you know *anyone* in town who's looking for help?" She hoped the proprietor didn't detect the desperation in her voice.

"Have you tried the Dairy Barn out on the highway?"

Maggie shook her head. "I don't really have any experience with animals."

The woman looked askance at her, then a spark of realization came to her eyes and she started laughing. "It's not that kind of dairy barn, hon. It's an ice-cream place—like a Dairy Queen."

"Oh." Heat crept up Maggie's neck, but she smiled past her embarrassment. "I'm new in town."

The woman grinned back at her. "I guessed that. Unfortunately they probably don't need anyone now. They hire on a lot of high-school kids in the summer. But they're usually looking for people as soon as school starts."

Maggie's hopes flagged. She couldn't wait a week, let alone two months. Besides, even if they would hire her today, how would she get to work?

The next two shops on Main Street gave her the same story—and the same suggestion to try the Dairy Barn.

She started across the street. Lunch customers were already lined up at the café, so she decided it would be best to wait until later to inquire there. She knew beggars couldn't be choosers, but she'd worked as a waitress for a few months while she was in college, and waitressing held no appeal whatsoever. But if they were hiring, she'd be game.

At a tiny flower and gift shop beside the café, Maggie faced the moment she'd hoped for—and dreaded. The florist handed her a two-page job application. She slid it to the end of the counter and started to fill it out. She printed Meg Anders and her Social Security number, but as she'd feared, the application asked for information she didn't have access to, nor did she feel safe including the address of her former employer at the graphics firm in New York. Not yet.

She completed every part of the form she could, then paused. She would have to admit to the florist that she didn't have the birth certificate they required for tax purposes, then pray he wouldn't ask her to get more specific about her job history.

She cleared her throat, trying to get the man's attention. "I'm staying across the street at Wren's Nest for a few days. Would it be okay if I use that address and phone number until I find a permanent place?"

The man scratched his head and seemed to consider her request. Then his smile turned to an apologetic grimace. "It might be better for you to come back when you have a more . . . permanent address. To tell you the truth, we're not really looking for anybody right now."

Deflated, she left the shop and crossed the street to the art gallery down the street from Wren's. She'd saved the best for last, but now she was afraid to have her hopes dashed once again. She steeled herself and opened the door. *Here goes.*

Entering the shop, she paused to breathe in the pungent oil and turpentine. Standing on the oak floor, surrounded by walls of canvases and prints, she felt a sense of excitement. What a dream come true it would be to work in an art gallery—even a small one like this. Maybe the owner would have a space where she could work in her spare time. Approaching the front counter, she forced herself to shake off the fantasy. She dared not allow herself to dream that big.

Jackson Linder wasn't behind the counter today, but she heard someone whistling in the back room.

She gave the old-fashioned bell on the countertop a tentative tap. She rang a second and third time before a middle-aged woman walked from the back room. The woman swept back a hank of salt-and-pepper hair and considered Maggie over reading glasses looped to a chain around her neck. "May I help you?"

"I was in here the other day, talking to Mr. Linder. I wondered if you might have any openings?"

"Oh, I'll let you talk to Jack." The woman disappeared through the narrow doorway behind the counter.

Seconds later, the artist himself emerged from the same door, drying his hands on a paint-splotched rag. As he came around the counter, he tripped over something Maggie couldn't see but quickly steadied himself and came toward her.

"Can I help—Oh! It's you! Still in town, huh?"

For an instant Maggie thought she detected whiskey on his breath. For one terrifying heartbeat, the man's face morphed into Kevin's. It took every ounce of will power she had not to turn around and run for the door.

But then Jackson Linder's kind, suntanned face came back in focus. She offered her hand. "Yes. I'm . . . well, I'm *back* in town, actually. I've decided to stay in the area. I'm Meg Anders." It still felt strange to introduce herself that way. "I wondered if you had any openings here in the gallery?"

He scratched the short stubble on his chin. "I'd be happy to take a look at your work, but I'll be honest. Business is slow. Even if I could hang your stuff tomorrow, I couldn't guarantee—"

"I'm sorry. I didn't mean . . . I'm looking for a job—as a receptionist or framing paintings, cleaning up, whatever. I'm not picky. I just need a job."

"Ah, I misunderstood. Unfortunately, I'm not sure I can help you there either. I—"

He looked past her out the windows at the front of the shop, and she turned to follow his gaze. But he seemed to be staring at nothing. His eyes glazed over almost as if he'd forgotten she was even in the room.

"Well, thank you. I appreciate your help."

His eyes came back into focus, and he shook his head almost imperceptibly, as if coming out of a trance. He reached out and braced a hand on the counter. "Yes," he said. "Well . . . good luck. You have a good day now."

Maggie had the impression that he was merely going through the motions. She wondered if he was even aware of the conversation they'd just had. She shuddered. Kevin had done that sometimes. Spaced out. Not losing consciousness or giving any physical sign that his brain was malfunctioning, but suddenly he wouldn't be there mentally.

She couldn't get out of the gallery fast enough. On the sidewalk out-side, she forced herself to take slow, deep breaths. She wasn't sure what had happened in there, but she hated the thoughts of Kevin Bryson that were so close to the surface.

Still, she was disappointed. Her hopes of landing a job at the gallery—perhaps having access to a studio, and maybe even a mentor—had been dashed. And she was fast running out of options.

He seemed
perfectly sober now.
Had Maggie only
imagined the hint of
liquor on his breath?

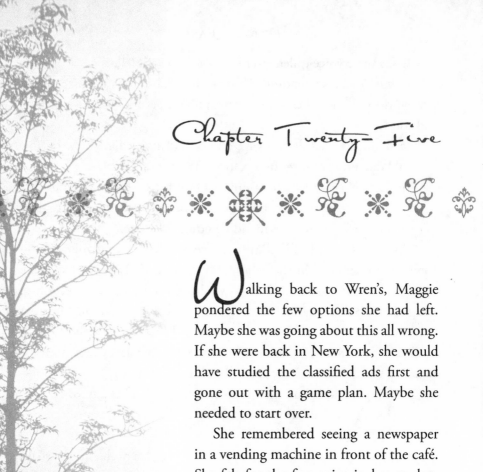

Chapter Twenty-Five

alking back to Wren's, Maggie pondered the few options she had left. Maybe she was going about this all wrong. If she were back in New York, she would have studied the classified ads first and gone out with a game plan. Maybe she needed to start over.

She remembered seeing a newspaper in a vending machine in front of the café. She felt for the few coins in her pocket. She'd buy a paper and take it back to the inn to study. There had to be *something* available in this town.

She turned to go back to the café but realized she would have to pass the gallery again unless she crossed the street to the other side. That seemed petty, but she quickened her steps and hurried past the gallery storefront with affected purpose in her demeanor.

Just when she breathed an inward sigh

of relief, a male voice called after her. "Miss! *Miss!* Hello?"

She considered pretending she hadn't heard, but then footsteps thudded on the pavement behind her. She spun on her heel to face a smiling Jackson Linder.

He skidded to a halt and gave a nervous laugh. "I'm sorry. I know you told me, but I've forgotten your name already."

His ready charm made her think again of Kevin. She wanted to take a step back, move away from his closeness. But she forced herself to hold her ground, refusing to cave to old demons. "It's Meg."

"Yes, of course. Meg. Well, listen, I've been rethinking your offer— someone to help out in the gallery. My mom comes in when she can. You met her." He jerked a thumb over his shoulder in the direction of the gallery. "But she has her own business, so you can imagine how that works. Or doesn't work. It struck me that if I had regular help, I might be able to get some new paintings out to a few other galleries and maybe make up the difference." He seemed suddenly hesitant. "I'm still thinking it through, and if I did decide to hire you, I couldn't pay you much, but I thought I should at least talk to you—before someone else snags you."

She gave a wry laugh. "That's not seeming to be a problem. I'm striking out so far. Everyone I've talked to says they're not hiring. But I'm only getting started," she added quickly. If she didn't quit stuffing her foot in her big fat mouth, she was going to convince him that she was completely unemployable.

He seemed perfectly sober now. Had Maggie only imagined the hint of liquor on his breath? At least here on the sidewalk the only aromas she detected were strong coffee and homemade bread from the café across the street.

She extended her hand to him. "Thank you, Mr. Linder. I—"

He held up a hand. "Jackson, please."

"Jackson," she corrected. It was an effort to keep her smile toned down to polite instead of giddy. "Thank you again. I'd really appreciate if you'd let me know what you decide. I have some experience with framing, and I've worked in graphic design, so I think I could really help out. And I'd be willing to do secretarial work or janitorial . . . whatever."

He smiled. "I'll keep that in mind. Nice to see you again, Meg. I hope you like living in Clayburn. I'll give you a call in the next couple of days and see what we can work out." He hesitated. "You're still staying at the inn?"

She nodded.

He looked as though he might say something, then shook his head slightly. He slipped a ballpoint pen and a business card from his breast pocket. "Why don't you give me your cell-phone number?" He waited, pen poised.

She winced an apology. "I don't have a cell phone. But I'm sure it would be okay for you to call me at the inn." Guilt chided her. She'd already taken advantage of Bart and Wren's kindness, but she would talk to them about it tonight. Surely they wouldn't mind.

Mr. Linder extended his business card. "Here. Why don't you call me sometime Monday afternoon?"

"Yes, I will. Thank you."

He held her gaze a breath longer than necessary, but she brushed aside the twinge of discomfort it caused. She had a job. She felt sure of it. She practically skipped back to the inn. She'd gone from dark discouragement to hopeful elation in the space of a conversation on the street.

She pushed open the front door and nearly toppled Wren, who was perched on a wobbly ladder washing the tall windows over the front door. A mixture of lemon wax and Windex tickled her nose.

"Hey, kiddo." Wren spooled out a length of paper toweling and spritzed the glass. "You're back awfully soon. Is that a good sign or not?"

Maggie ducked under the ladder and looked up, excited to share about her morning. "Maybe good news. The guy that runs that gallery in the next block up might have a job for me."

Wren's vigorous circles with the wad of paper towel stopped abruptly. "Jackson?"

"Yes. Jackson Linder." She practiced his name. "Do you know him?"

Wren hesitated. "I know him." Without meeting Maggie's eyes, she handed down the spray bottle and started descending the ladder. "Have you had lunch?"

"Trevor is picking me up at eleven-thirty, remember?"

"Oh, that's right. Well, I have a nice soup on the stove and Bart wound up going down to the senior center for a workshop, so he's not here to eat it and I'm not really hungry. Guess I'll save it for tomorrow."

"Sorry."

"Well, goodness, it's not your fault." Wren twisted the soggy paper toweling through her fingers. "Meg . . ."

The hesitation in her tone drew Maggie's attention.

"I'm not sure it would be a good idea for you to work for Jackson."

"But . . . why not?"

Wren breathed out a quiet sigh. "Listen, Bart and I don't mind putting you up for a few days. You don't need to get in a big hurry about a job. You haven't even tried out on the highway yet. There are several good businesses out there."

"I thought, for now—until I can afford a car—it'd be best to stay here . . . downtown." She studied Wren. "Is there a reason it wouldn't be good to work for Mr. Linder?"

Wren's weary sigh made Maggie think there was a story coming. Wren smiled, but it didn't come easily the way it usually did. "Well, it's none of my business, but . . . for one thing, I don't think he'd be able to keep you busy full-time."

"Yes, he said that, but maybe I can find something else to fill in."

"Maybe." Wren seemed suddenly preoccupied. "I'd better go put that soup away."

"Let me help."

She trailed after Wren—no small effort, as the woman scurried between the stovetop and the counter, where a plate of little cheese and cracker sandwiches sat.

"Here." Wren handed her the plate and met her eyes for the first time since Maggie had mentioned the possibility of working for Jackson Linder. "Why don't you take these and put them in the fridge in your room? They'll make a nice midnight snack tonight."

"Oh, I shouldn't." Maggie patted her stomach. "I think I've gained five pounds since I got here."

"Nonsense." Wren clicked her tongue and reached to pinch Maggie's forearm. "You could stand to put on a few pounds, sweetie."

Despite all the walking she'd done, she'd been eating like the proverbial pig. But what a treat it had been to eat guilt free, without Kevin as her constant watchdog.

The clatter of bells on the front door saved her from having to argue with Wren. She looked through the archway to the clock in the lobby.

"It's almost eleven-thirty. That'll be Trevor." Wren beamed as if she'd abandoned her earlier concern. "You two enjoy yourselves." She held Maggie's gaze, a softness moving in behind her eyes. "Trevor Ashlock is the nicest man you could ever meet."

Maggie was beginning to suspect that very thing. But the thought of seeing him again sent a little shiver of nerves through her. She only hoped she could keep her stories straight through an entire lunch.

Maggie placed her
hand over his, for one
brief moment, but it
was long enough to
feel the warmth and
strength there.

Chapter Twenty-Six

Trevor stood by the fireplace in the lobby, wearing a subdued smile. "You ready?"

He looked cool, refreshed, and—well, wonderful—in his navy polo and Dockers.

Maggie glanced self-consciously at her outfit. "Am I dressed okay?" Immediately she laughed at her own question. "Not that it matters. I don't really have much to change into."

"Oh, no, you're fine." He peered through the side window now polished to a shine through Wren's efforts. "I got stuff for a picnic, if you don't mind eating outside. It's clouded over a little, and the park is fairly shady this time of day anyway." He eyed her, then quickly moved his gaze away.

She got the impression he was making excuses. "A picnic is fine. Sounds like fun."

"Okay then." He indicated the door with a nod. "I'm parked out front."

The sun played peekaboo with fluffy white clouds, and it had cooled off some, but it was warm inside Trevor's pickup. He cranked up the air conditioner—which spit out a stream of cold air, then immediately turned warm. He rolled down the windows.

In the short time it took them to drive to the edge of town to the roadside park, Maggie felt like a wind-blown, wilted daisy.

Trevor parked in the sandy lot near an empty playground and came around to open Maggie's door. While she climbed down, he lifted a small cooler from the bed of the truck.

"Here." He pointed to a picnic table under a massive tree. The old cottonwood's roots crawled down the bank to drink from the muddy waters of the Smoky Hill River. "Does that look okay?"

"Perfect. Can I carry something?"

"I've got it." He patted the cooler. "Everything is in here. It's nothing fancy, but I thought you might like to see the park."

"It's beautiful." It wasn't Central Park by a long shot, but it did have its own charm. Mostly that it was peaceful and quiet, save for the whispering of the cottonwood trees and the occasional splash of a fish or frog in the river. There was a teenage girl playing with two toddlers on the swings a distance away, and an elderly man fishing on the riverbank, but other than that they had the place to themselves.

Previous picnickers had left broken potato chips littering the table and benches. Trevor brushed them off with his free hand. "I guess I should have brought a blanket to sit on. Sorry. This was kind of a last-minute idea. Maybe it wasn't a very good one."

"Oh, no, it's fine." Maggie didn't know whether to be suspicious of his polite sweetness or to just swoon and be done with it. A bolt of guilt surged through her at that thought. She had no right to be thinking romantic thoughts. If Kevin knew she was here—on something strongly resembling a date—he would be livid. Though she realized now that

Kevin had cared little for her, she had been his possession and woe to the man who dared interfere. She shuddered at the thought of what his reaction might be.

"Are you cold?" Trevor eyed her with surprise.

She rubbed away the goose bumps that pebbled her bare arms. "No. I'm just . . . hungry."

"Well then, let's get this show on the road." He opened the cooler and took out a bag of purple grapes and two fat ready-made subs bundled in cellophane. A bag of pretzels and cans of soda completed the feast. "Have a seat." He threw a leg over the bench seat across from her, straddling it.

She sat down and arranged the things he set in front of her, waiting to see if he'd pray a blessing over them as Bart had at the inn yesterday. Trevor bowed his head. His lips moved slightly, but he didn't pray out loud.

She waited until he looked up, then busied herself with unwrapping her sandwich. "Mmm . . . this looks good."

"Well, I hope you don't mind that I didn't actually take you out for lunch like I promised."

She spread an arm to encompass the riverside park. "Hey, this *is* out."

He laughed. "That it is. At least it's not so warm this afternoon. They say we're supposed to get some rain tonight."

"You say that like it's a good thing. It wouldn't be in New Yo—" She caught herself. "It-it does make everything *new*. The rain."

Had he noticed her clumsy cover-up?

If he did, he didn't show it. "When you live in farm country, rain is usually a good thing. Well, unless it's harvest. But look how low the river is." He ripped off a healthy bite of his sandwich and pointed toward the river's edge with what was left of it.

She took a sip of her Coke. "You must've had the soda in the freezer. It's still nice and cold."

"*Soda*?" He grinned. "That must be California-ese."

Her breath caught. Even her language was giving her away. But she recovered quickly, flashing a smile. "Why? What do you Kansas hayseeds call it?"

He narrowed his eyes and glared at her, as if her hayseed comment had deeply offended, but almost instantly the grin was back. He popped the top on the Coke can, took a swig, and blew out an overlong sigh of satisfaction. "We call this here stuff *pop*," he drawled.

She laughed. "Pop, huh?"

He winked. "Or if we wanna be real formal-like, we call it sody pop."

"Ah, that would be *soda* pop. Hence, soda." As soon as the words were out, she bit her lip. Did Californians call it *soda*? She was weary with having to analyze every word in even the most innocent exchange.

She concentrated on her lunch, and they ate in silence for a few minutes. Yet it wasn't an uncomfortable silence. The birds twittered in the treetops overhead, the leaves whispered in the breeze, and Maggie reveled in this world that was so different from the prison of Kevin's apartment in New York.

Trevor unwrapped the grapes, tore off a sprig, and handed them to her. He popped two in his mouth. "So, do you want to talk about—" He shrugged. "You know, the whole thing with . . . California."

Maggie bowed her head, embarrassed and a little bit frightened. She'd never thought about how much of her life was a lie. At the Mannings, where she'd spent most of her growing-up years, she'd been taught that lying was wrong. But with Kevin, she'd learned that it saved a lot of arguments and kept his temper at bay. So it had become a bad habit. Mostly what she told were little white lies.

No, Kevin, nobody called today.

Yes, I'm happy here with you.

Sorry, I forgot to stop by the liquor store.

Her fibs were nothing that really hurt anyone.

But it had escalated, of necessity, when the gift of escape had been handed to her Tuesday morning on the streets of New York. She'd been living a lie since that morning. For almost five days she'd pretended to be someone she wasn't—inventing her past, making her life up as she went along.

Trouble was, she liked where it had gotten her. Were it not for the lies she'd told, she wouldn't be sitting here in this idyllic setting— safe with this kind, generous man and the hope of a fresh start in this little town. But when would she crash back to reality?

"Meg? Are you okay?"

His voice nudged her from her reverie. Trevor was leaning across the table, his palm inches from her cheek, as if he wanted to touch her. Or maybe slap her?

But one look into his eyes and she knew it wasn't the anger she was so accustomed to seeing in a man's eyes. It was concern—and something more.

"I really don't want to talk about it."

"Okay. I understand." He snatched back his hand and held it palm up, as if he were apologizing for even asking. Or was he apologizing for wanting to touch her?

"What about you?" She tried to deflect his question.

"What about me?"

"Wren said you . . . were married."

His expression—like she was accusing him of having a wife at home while he romanced another woman in the park—made her rush to explain. "She told me your wife died in an accident. And your little boy."

When the muscles in his jaw tensed, Maggie instantly regretted bringing it up. She'd wanted to get it out in the open. To not have to pretend that she didn't know when she did. The irony wasn't lost on her when she was still pretending about so many things.

He nodded. "Amy. Her name was Amy . . . and our son, Trev. It was two years ago." He took sudden interest in the rough-hewn top of the picnic table. "On a Saturday morning."

Saturday. Maggie wondered if he was still counting anniversaries. If so, today was one.

A far-off look paled his blue irises. "They were on their way to Salina. He was only three, but Amy was going to buy him his first bicycle. One of those little ones with training wheels." He inhaled a deep breath. "Someone . . . a car pulled out in front of them out on Old Highway 40. They never had a chance."

His hands were palms down on the splintered top of the picnic table . . . like he was ready to push off and escape at a moment's notice.

Maggie placed her hand over his, for one brief moment, but it was long enough to feel the warmth and strength there. "I'm so sorry, Trevor."

He worked his jaw. "Thanks."

She hesitated, nervous about where their conversation might go. But she truly wanted to know. "Tell me about her."

"Amy?"

She nodded, waiting.

A soft smile curved his mouth. "Amy was sunshine. Always laughing, always being silly. Everybody adored her. She didn't have a mean bone in her body. And open . . . like a book. You always knew what she was thinking. She was honest to a fault."

Maggie squirmed on the hard wooden bench, feeling rightly chided, even though she doubted Trevor meant anything by it. If he *was* trying to make her feel guilty, trying to make her come up short by comparison, he was doing a pretty fine job. She put the thought aside and tipped her head, waiting for him to go on.

His eyes misted over. He swallowed hard. Maggie felt his pain as though it were her own.

At that moment the sun slipped from beneath a cumulus cloud, and its rays streamed below the canopy of trees that had shaded them. Trevor squinted and turned his head, so that Maggie saw him in profile. His Adam's apple bobbed in his throat.

Again Maggie wished she hadn't brought the painful subject up. "I'm so sorry . . . about your wife. It sounds like she was a wonderful person."

He looked up at her. "Thank you. She *was* a wonderful person. Trev too."

"He was named after you?"

Trevor nodded. "He would have started school this year."

"Is that why you read to the kids . . . at the day care?"

A spark of mischief lit his eyes. "Actually, it's to fulfill my community-service requirement."

At the arch of her brows, he burst into laughter. It was contagious. She joined in once she realized he was teasing her again.

But the seriousness returned to his face an instant later. "It's mostly because of Trev. But my mother loved books, too—still does."

"Oh? Do your parents live close?"

"They used to. I grew up in Clayburn. I inherited the print shop from my dad. My folks retired to Florida a couple years ago. The cold winters here really messed with Mom's arthritis. They considered California, but Florida won out over the land of fruits and nuts."

Maggie tensed. *Please change the subject. Please change the subject.* She chanted it to herself like a mantra. She was too weary to make up any more stories.

Trevor nudged her arm across the table, a tentative grin on his face. "Hey, that was a joke, okay? Just something stupid my dad used to say. I didn't mean anything by it."

"It's okay." She forced a smile, her mind racing. What would she say if she really *were* from California? "It's just . . . I get that all the time."

His grin turned sheepish. "Sorry. Bad joke. I won't bring it up again." The spark returned to his eyes. "*If* you'll promise never to call me a hay-seed again."

That made her laugh . . . then wonder if he was serious. But one look at his face told her he was anything but. Teasing seemed to be the way of people here. It took some getting used to. Kevin had never teased her—at least not like this. If he made a joke, it was cruel . . . or vulgar. And she was usually the butt of it.

But Trevor's good-natured banter made her feel . . .

She shook herself back to the present, afraid to allow the thought to fruition. But then something let loose inside her and she gave it full rein.

Being here like this, with Trevor, made her feel something she'd never felt before. And she didn't ever want that feeling to end.

How far could
she go trying to get
into Kevin's account
before she set off a red
flag somewhere?

Chapter Twenty-Seven

T hanks for lunch. I enjoyed *every-thing*." Maggie felt suddenly shy. She reached for the door handle.

Trevor wrestled the pickup's gearshift into park but stayed put behind the wheel. "Do you mind if I don't walk you to the door?"

"Oh, no. I didn't expect . . . I'm fine." Pushing the heavy door open, Maggie climbed down from the high seat and started to close the door behind her.

Trevor reached across the bench seat. "I've got it. Maybe I'll see you this afternoon. I'm coming back to work on the remodel later."

"Oh. I'm not sure I'll be here. I thought I'd visit some more stores, fill out some more applications."

"Uh-oh. You're not going to find very many places open. Clayburn closes up tighter than a clam after lunch on Saturday."

"Really? Wren mentioned that, but I thought she was exaggerating. But why on Saturday afternoon? That's one of the biggest shopping days."

He shrugged. "I guess I never thought about it. I suppose people are just too busy. Getting ready for church, doing family stuff. A lot of people head to Salina to go shopping or to the movies. A small town like Clayburn can't supply everything."

"Oh." Her shoulders sagged. "I suppose that means nothing's open on Sunday either?"

"'Fraid not. But bright and early Monday morning things will be hopping. You might as well take advantage of the quiet and relax this weekend."

She resisted the urge to inform him that she'd have no place to relax if she didn't get a job soon.

Distracted, she thanked him again and turned to the inn's front door.

At the bell's jangle, Wren came from the dining room. "Meg! How did it go?"

Maggie laughed at the woman's wide-eyed eagerness. "It was nice. You were right. Trevor is a very nice man."

"Oh, that he is. I've never met a—" Wren threw her hands up mid-sentence. "My sauce!" She waddled back to the kitchen as fast as her short legs would allow.

Maggie followed. Fragrant steam rose from a huge stockpot on the back burner of the old range, spicing the air. She inhaled. Spaghetti sauce. The stove was parked out in the middle of the floor, a heavy-duty extension cord connecting it to the kitchen wall. Wren turned down the fire and grabbed the pot handles with the corners of her apron.

"I thought you were going out for dinner."

"This is for tomorrow, after church. I prefer not to cook on Sundays." Wren stirred the bubbling sauce for a minute before plopping into a chair and wiping her forehead with the same apron corners. "You're invited, of course," Wren added.

"Oh, I still have the sandwiches you made for the bus. They're in the fridge in my room. Don't worry about me."

"No, no, those sandwiches will keep another day. You'll have spaghetti with us tomorrow."

Maggie opened her mouth to protest. She'd developed a conscience over the last few days, and she didn't want to mooch from the Johannsens. But Wren cut her off before she could make a squeak.

"You'll eat with us tomorrow, and I don't want any arguments." Her face brightened. "That is, unless you've already made plans with Trevor."

"Oh, no. But I think he's coming to work on the kitchen later."

"Well, *that* news is music to my ears."

The bells jangled in the lobby, and Wren and Maggie both turned toward the door.

"Is that you, Bart?" Wren hollered.

No response. Wren's brow knit, and she frowned at Maggie. "That man is deafer than a post. Bart? Bart!" The bells jangled again, and Wren started for the lobby, but her scolding changed to a musical greeting as she disappeared through the arch. "Good afternoon, folks. Welcome to Wren's. How can I help you?"

Maggie listened from the kitchen as Wren checked guests in. From the conversations, she gathered it was a rather large family group. They'd planned to stay in Salina, but a youth basketball tournament had filled the hotels there and someone had recommended Wren's Nest.

"Well," Wren said, "we're glad they did. We'll get you squared away in no time." "Give that sauce a stir, Meg, would you?" she yelled into the kitchen.

Maggie went to stir the sauce but tuned one ear to the lobby as Wren explained the situation with the kitchen to the guests. "We apologize for the inconvenience, folks, but don't worry. You'll be served a lovely breakfast right here in the lobby."

Maggie inched to where she could see the noisy party of seven as they followed Wren down the hall to their rooms. She returned to her post at the range and watched over the spaghetti sauce.

When Wren returned a few minutes later, she looked worn out but happy. "Well, how about that? We rented four rooms tonight!"

The unspoken message in Wren's words struck fear in Maggie's heart. For the first time, she realized there might come a night very soon when there would be no room in the inn for Meg Anders from California. She dared not dwell too long on the possibility.

"But now I've got to put a breakfast together for them! *Acck!*"

Wren's comical shriek made Maggie forget her dark thoughts.

"I could help. I'd be glad to. I'm a pretty good cook."

Wren eyed her, as if considering her offer. But then she brushed her hands together. "You know what? I've got some homemade cinnamon rolls in the freezer. I can heat those up in the morning and frost them. Whip up an egg casserole. I'll need to get some bacon and some fruit juice, but I think we've got it covered. There's no need to get in a tizzy." She waved a hand. "Never mind me. I'm just talking to myself."

"Well, tell me what time to get up in the morning. I'd be glad to help."

Wren patted Maggie's hand. "Thanks, sweetie. I just might take you up on that. Bless you." She untied her apron and hung it up on a magnetic hook on the side of the refrigerator. "For now, I'm going to go take a little nap. You ought to do the same. You've had a big day, and it's barely afternoon."

"Well, if you don't mind, I thought I'd go to the library for a little while and then walk over to the park."

"You don't need my permission, honey. But if you're going, you'd better hurry. And you might want to go to the library first. They close at three on Saturday afternoons. Going to get something to read, huh?" Wren brightened. "Oh, hey, would you mind returning some books for me when you go?"

"Sure. I'd be glad to." Maggie didn't tell Wren that her real reason had nothing to do with the library. She wanted to see if Jenn had replied to her e-mail yet. Maybe she could find out what Kevin knew. Whether he was looking for her.

Wren searched through the bottom cupboards. "Now where did I put the lid to that pot?" She finally found it in a drawer and waved it in the air, huffing out a breath of frustration. "This remodeling project is going to be the death of me."

Maggie put a hand on Wren's shoulder. "Your kitchen will be done before you know it. And I bet it'll be so beautiful it will make you forget all about what a hassle it's been."

Wren looked contrite. "Oh, I've been a big baby about it. I'm sorry, honey. I should be counting my blessings, and instead I've been a crabby old crank."

"No you haven't."

Wren laughed. "Trust me, sweetie. I have. And if you don't believe me, just go ask Bart." She put down the wooden spoon. "Let me go get those library books so you can get going."

✳ ✳ ✳

Zigzagging her way to the library and searching for patches of shade on the sidewalk, Maggie composed a new letter to Jenn in her head. By the time she got inside, perspiration was rolling down her face, and the cool, dank air was a sweet relief. She put Wren's books in the drop and walked back to the carrels where the computers were located.

All four of the machines were in use, so she browsed the nearby stacks, keeping an eye out for one of the desks to open up.

When she finally got online, she accessed the e-mail account she'd set up. Immediately thirteen e-mails poured into her box. A chill of alarm snaked up her back until she saw that all but two of the messages were spam. One was a welcome to Hotmail and the other was from Jenn.

Maggie opened it and leaned in to the screen.

Maggie,

Where are you??? I've been worried sick. K called Tuesday night and told Mark the police found his car by the side of the road somewhere in Connecticut. He said he didn't know why you'd gone out in the middle of the night, but that you called him, so he knows you're alive.

Why didn't you tell me you were trying to leave him again? I'm sure it's no surprise to you that K is furious. Mark won't let me out of his sight. He's afraid K will try to come after you through us.

I hope you know what you're doing. I'm worried about you and wondering why you haven't e-mailed again since I got this. Please answer this e-mail and tell me where you are. And be careful! I know you always said he wouldn't hurt you, but I'm afraid of what he's capable of when he's angry.

Please let me know what's going on! It's not safe for you to stay here, but if you need someplace to go, we'll help you find a place. Mark lost his job again, so money's a little tight, but we'll do what we can to help.

                    I love you, Maggie.
                    Jenn

Maggie placed her fingers on the keyboard, longing to put her sister's mind at ease. But what could she say? Finally she settled on a brief reassurance—and a warning.

I'm fine, Jenn. Please don't worry. I'll let you know more the minute I can. But please listen to Mark. Until things blow over and K realizes I'm not coming back, you need to watch your back. Do not trust him. No matter what he says.

She was surprised to find tears close to the surface. She missed her sister. Baltimore had always seemed a thousand miles away because Kevin never wanted her to go visit Jenn, but now that Jenn truly was halfway across the country, the ache of missing her grew deeper.

It had taken over two days of traveling almost constantly to end up here in this tiny Kansas town. That meant it was at least two days back to Jenn.

Maggie sighed and closed her eyes. The ache in her heart was more than mere homesickness for Jenn. In a strange way she missed Kevin too. Not the Kevin she'd run away from, but the man she once thought Kevin to be—the attentive charmer she'd bumped into at the gym after work one night. He'd given up his spot on the treadmill for her and asked her out to dinner the next night. She'd accepted, and their courtship had been like something out of the movies for the first two weeks. How desperately she'd wanted him to remain the man she thought he was that night.

Sadly, she was beginning to recognize that even before Kevin became physically abusive, he had been abusive and controlling in a different way. He was possessive—overly so, she realized now. At first it felt good to belong to someone. To have someone care where she was every minute and whether she was his one and only. Reality punched her as she remembered her old suspicions: while she had been *his* one and only, she wasn't sure he had always been faithful to her.

But she had always thought deep down that Kevin needed her, so she exchanged that feeling of belonging for her freedom. Her mind told her it was a good thing, but her heart wasn't altogether sure about the trade-off. She could die tomorrow, and there would be no one at her funeral. Oh, sure, Wren and Bart might come—and even Trevor. But they wouldn't even have her real name to put on a gravestone.

A psychedelic screensaver popped up on the computer—stars twinkling on a midnight field. Maggie sat staring at it. She thought of a scene from a movie she'd once seen. An astronaut, tethered to his spaceship, ventured out to make repairs. But the line snapped, and the poor man drifted away, watching his spaceship—and his chance of being rescued—grow smaller and smaller until it disappeared and he was an insignificant dot in the universe.

That's how she felt right now. There were very few people to whom she mattered, and not one of them even knew where she was right now. It hurt to remember back to a time when she and Jenn and Mom were a family. She'd thought about God then. Even prayed to Him sometimes. She rubbed her temples, trying to dismiss the thoughts. It hurt too much to think about those days.

Maybe she should go back. To New York. This was too hard. Unless she got work at the gallery—and that would only be part-time—she had struck out with the job search today. Wren had warned her that Saturday wasn't a good day to look for work in Clayburn, but Maggie couldn't help feeling anxious. Wren said she didn't need to worry about paying for her room, but they weren't going to let her stay here for free indefinitely. And by the time she bought a few days' worth of groceries, she'd be flat broke. She could make Wren's sandwiches last a couple of days. She was used to eating light, thanks to Kevin's fear that she might put on a pound or two. But eventually she'd have to have some way to support herself.

Though she knew the odds were slim of Jenn's answering immediately, she checked e-mail one more time. Last she'd heard, her sister didn't usually work on Saturdays, but if Mark was without a job, maybe Jenn was putting in some extra hours. She felt a twinge of disappointment when her e-mail box was empty this time.

She may as well go back to the inn. Maybe she could come up with a game plan. Or at least arrange some way to stay on at Wren's until she could check out other job possibilities on Monday.

She started to log out of the e-mail program, but before she clicked the mouse, a bank ad popped up on the sidebar of the Hotmail page. It wasn't the bank Kevin used, but it gave her an idea. What if she could access his bank account online? She thought Kevin had transferred money that way from time to time, but though he was happy to have her pay the bills and balance the checkbook, he'd never trusted her with actual transactions.

On a whim, she typed the name of Kevin's bank in New York into the browser's search field. A complex Web site opened, and she navigated through a labyrinth of links, her mind churning. If it weren't for Kevin, she would still have her job and access to her own bank account. What a fool she had been to merge what little savings she'd accumulated into his retirement fund. How easily he'd convinced her it was the right thing to do.

The more miles and hours that separated them, the more clearly she saw the ways he'd manipulated and coerced her into things that seemed utterly foolish now. If there was a way to somehow get into his account, she could almost justify withdrawing funds. She wouldn't take more than the amount she'd turned over to him. She didn't want his money. But the funds from her savings were rightfully hers. It was only eight hundred dollars, but right now that seemed like a small fortune. She calculated how many nights she could stay at Wren's with eight hundred dollars, then laughed at herself. She could pay a whole month's rent somewhere with that amount—and have money to spare. That would give her plenty of time to find a job.

Her hands trembling, she clicked on a link titled *Security.* How far could she go trying to get into Kevin's account before she set off a red flag somewhere?

She shoved down the fear that crawled up her throat as she skimmed the text on the screen in front of her. It was all about encryption and firewalls and a complicated network of other terms that might as well have been Chinese for what she understood of them.

There was a toll-free number listed to call with questions. But the account was in Kevin's name alone. She didn't even have the authority to sign his checks for the apartment bills. Every month she'd written out checks for the bills and turned them over to him to sign. He didn't trust her to stay within his budget.

Or had he somehow known the day would come when she would need access to this account? Had he known she would someday find a way to escape his grasp?

She stared at the link labeled *Log in.* Holding her breath, she clicked on it. A series of boxes appeared, asking for a User ID and a password. She put his name in the field labeled *User ID*.

She had no idea what his password was. She typed in the numbers of his birth date. Her hand hovered over the keyboard before she summoned the courage to click *Submit*.

A new page started to load, but it contained a message in red letters: *User ID and password are invalid. Please try again.*

She tried again with a different password—*her* birthday—and got the same message, with a link to have the password sent. Of course if she did that, it would be sent to Kevin's office and he would know what she was trying to do.

She knew Kevin's e-mail address at work. Maybe that was what was supposed to go in the User ID space? She tried that. This time the message merely said the password was invalid. She must have the User ID right. She tried other passwords. The anniversary of the day they met. The day she moved in with him. It was crazy, trying to pull a password out of thin air. They'd never celebrated these dates. She doubted Kevin even knew them, but she couldn't think of any other combinations to try.

On the fifth try, a new message appeared, printed in larger letters over a triangular warning symbol. *For security purposes, this account has been temporarily suspended. Call the number below to reactivate your account.*

Her blood ran cold. Could the bank detect when someone was trying to access an account? Might they flag her attempts to access Kevin's account and report it to him? She'd read news accounts of criminals being tracked by their computer usage.

Her pulse revved. She shoved away from the desk, almost toppling the chair in the process. At the commotion, a nearby library patron looked up from his book to glare at her.

She hurried from the building, stopping at the bottom of the steps to catch her breath. Forcing herself to walk at a normal pace, she headed back to the inn, but it was all she could do not to break into a run. She stole a glance over her shoulder at each crosswalk, feeling almost as though she were being tailed. Kevin Bryson still had a hold on her, even a thousand miles away.

Trevor's truck was parked in front of the inn when she got back. The lobby felt like a sanctuary after worrying all the way home. All desire for a walk in the park was gone. All she wanted to do now was escape to the safety of her room.

She heard Trevor hammering in the kitchen, but she wasn't in the mood to talk. She tried to escape down the hall, but he appeared in the arched doorway. "Oh, I thought you were Wren. Do you know where she is?"

"Bart took her to the movies in Salina. Said she needed to get out."

"He was probably trying to get her off my back."

She grinned back. "I'd say that was a good move on Bart's part."

He chuckled in agreement. "Hey, would you mind giving me a hand for a minute? Real quick?"

"Sure." Maggie followed him into the kitchen, which looked more like a demolition site right now. He once again had all the appliances unplugged and scooted away from the walls. If anything, he appeared to be losing ground on this project. She scanned the room and shook her head. "Man, I don't want to be here when Wren sees this."

He propped his fists on his waist and trailed her gaze. "I know. That's why I was hoping you could help me out. I need to measure for some trim." He held out a bulky tape measure. "Can you hold one end for me?"

"Okay." She gripped the end he handed her, and they worked together measuring, Trevor stopping to jot numbers down on a little notepad.

"Thanks," he said when they were finished. "If I can get this one wall finished, I can at least move the appliances back until I can get around to painting."

"Is it ready to paint?"

"The kitchen part is. But I need to tape everything in here first." He indicated the dining area.

She looked around the room. "Do you have the paint?"

He crossed the room in half a dozen easy strides and hoisted a left-over sheet of drywall, revealing two gallon pails of paint on the floor. He leaned the bulky Sheetrock against the wall they'd just measured.

"If you're ready, I'd be glad to help paint. It's been awhile, but my sister and I painted her whole apartment a couple of years ago, and it turned out pretty good."

He seemed to be considering her offer. "You really wouldn't mind?"

"Not at all." She rolled her eyes. "I'm bombing out finding a real job, so I may as well pitch in here. We could probably do this wall in an hour or two and get everything moved back before Wren gets home."

His eyes lit. "Hey, if you're serious, I'll take you up on that. Wren will kiss the ground you walk on if she comes home tonight to a kitchen she can actually work in."

"Let's do it." She looked down at her clothes. "Hang on. I'd better go change. This is the only decent thing I have to wear to job interviews Monday."

"Here." Trevor grabbed a rumpled flannel shirt that was draped over the stepladder. "You can wear this. Doesn't look like much, but it's clean." He touched a splotch of dried Spackle on one sleeve and gave a sheepish smile. "Well, it's not sweaty anyway."

She reached for the shirt. "Thanks."

He grinned. "You're on your own in the pants department though. Sorry."

"I'll be right back." She trotted down the hall to her room with renewed purpose.

Kicking off her shoes, she hurriedly grabbed the capris Wren had given her. She changed into them and stretched Trevor's shirt over them as far as it would go. She'd have to take her chances that she wouldn't get paint on her good clothes.

A strange elation welled within her chest. It felt good to be able to help someone. Especially someone who appreciated it so much. Trevor— and Wren too. Maggie smiled, imagining the glow on the woman's face when she came home to a freshly painted kitchen with all her appliances plugged into the proper outlets and in working order.

Sitting on the side of the bed to retie her shoes, Maggie leaned in to read the alarm clock on the nightstand. Maybe Bart would take Wren out to a nice sit-down restaurant and buy them another hour. Maybe there was a way to call him. She'd ask Trevor, but she somehow doubted Bart was the type to carry a cell phone.

It was almost four o'clock. They'd have to hurry to be finished before the couple got home, but it could be done. She ran into the bathroom and gathered her hair into a ponytail, then hurried out to the dining room. Adrenaline pumped through her veins as she ran. It was a sensation she remembered from being on a tight deadline at the design firm. It was a good feeling.

She stopped painting
in midstroke, a
gleam of curiosity
in her eyes.

Chapter Twenty-Eight

Trevor pried open the paint can with a screwdriver and set it on a canvas tarp on the floor in front of Meg.

"Ooh, what a gorgeous color." Meg peered into the bucket of paint as if she were gazing into a wishing well.

He watched her face, enjoying the excitement in her expression, and trying not to notice that she managed to make his ratty flannel shirt look like a million bucks and then some.

She dipped a paint stick into the butter-colored paint and stirred for a minute, then held the stick up to the light. "It's perfect for this room. The way the sun comes through those windows in the morning, it'll just glow."

She must have sensed his amusement. Head tipped, she crinkled her brow. "What?"

"Oh . . . nothing."

"No, what? You were thinking something."

He grinned. "It's just that . . . well, not too many women get that worked up over a can of yellow paint."

"I love color," she said simply. "And this is a great shade. Is this the only brush you have?" She picked up a brush with a rusted ferrule and examined the bristles.

"Hang on." He went to Wren's supply closet behind the check-in counter and rummaged around until he found two other paintbrushes.

"Are these better?"

She took them from him and swished the bristles against her palm. "Ah . . . much. Thanks."

"And you're right, this is a good color. It'll catch the sunlight in the morning, but it won't be too gaudy in the evening either." He affected a swagger. "I picked it out myself."

"Really? Where did you learn about color?" She studied him for a second, then answered her own question. "Oh . . . the print shop."

"Well, yes. There. But I took a couple of art classes in junior college too. But mostly trial and error." He stripped off a length of painter's masking tape that hadn't adhered tightly enough to the baseboard and wadded it into a tight ball. "My dad and my uncle started the shop thirty-some years ago, and I worked there all through high school— when I wasn't playing basketball."

She rolled her eyes comically. "Don't tell me you're one of those jocks?"

He lifted his shoulders. "Okay, I won't tell you."

"But you are," she deadpanned.

"Was." He aimed the balled-up tape at the trash can in the corner and swished the shot.

"Nope." She shook her head and pointed at the trash can. "See there. Once a jock, always a jock."

Conceding her point with a wry smile—and a healthy dose of pride—he grabbed the roll of masking tape and redid the baseboard.

"There. That should do it in here." He ripped the end of the strip from the roll and stood back to look for any other spots he'd missed. Satisfied, he turned to Meg. "Paint away."

She rubbed her hands together like a ten-year-old at the front gates of Disneyland. He smiled and put aside the twinge of guilt he felt for allowing her to help with *his* job.

He carried the smaller stepladder over from the dining area. "Here, you'll need this."

"Thanks." She climbed to the third rung and situated the paint can on the ladder's shelf.

He watched for a minute while Meg stroked the creamy paint along the line where the wall met the ceiling. Her work was meticulous. Reassured, he went back to taping off the windows and doorways in the dining area across the room. He kept a watchful eye on her as they each worked their way around respective sections of the wall, but it didn't take him long to see that he'd negotiated a good "hire."

Jasper wandered into the room and made a beeline for Meg's ladder. The cat stood under the bottom rung looking up at her. When she ignored him, he pawed the air and gave a series of short mews.

"Hey, kitty." Paintbrush aloft, she peered down and cooed at him. "Where have you been hiding? You'd better go on if you don't want paint on your tail. Go on, buddy. Go on now." She tried to dissuade him with baby talk, but Jasper ignored her and plopped down on the drop cloth directly under the ladder.

Meg gave a soft sigh and climbed down from her perch. She scooped up the cat and nuzzled her nose into his fur. "Come here, kitty. You could get into all kinds of trouble in here."

As she carried him out to the lobby, Trevor heard her talking to him, explaining why he couldn't be in the kitchen and trying to convince him to lie down on the love seat in the lobby. "See, buddy. It's nice and sunny here. Come on now. That's a good kitty cat."

He smiled even as a memory pricked his consciousness. *Amy, trying to coerce Trev to lie down for his afternoon nap.*

She appeared in the doorway, brushing off her hands.

"How long do you think that will last?"

She shrugged, then looked away quickly. But not before Trevor noticed her eyes were red rimmed and teary.

"Are you allergic to cats?"

"No." She picked up her paintbrush.

Had she been crying? He scrambled to fill the awkward silence. "So you didn't have much luck on your job search, huh?" His voice echoed through the open space, louder than he intended. And only after the words were out did he realize how they sounded. Good grief! Was this his idea of comforting a tearful woman? He was seriously out of practice.

But Meg climbed the ladder and resumed painting, as if nothing had passed between them. Maybe he'd only imagined the tears.

She painted for a minute before she turned to him from her perch on the ladder. "I have one job possibility," she said, seeming perfectly composed again. "It's only part-time though. Wren said I might have better luck looking on Monday."

"That's probably true. Did you try the Dairy Barn?"

She laughed. "Boy, that must be the hot place in town to work. I think everybody I talked to today suggested I apply there."

"Probably because everybody knows they need good help. It's the only place in town to get a decent cheeseburger, and right now they've got a bunch of irresponsible high-school kids working there. It takes them fifteen minutes to dip an ice-cream cone and twice that long to figure out how to make change for a ten."

She laughed. "Hey, if it's good ice cream, it might be worth the wait."

"Oh, it's good all right. Otherwise they would have been out of business a long time ago."

She bit her bottom lip and fidgeted with the paintbrush handle. "You don't need help at the print shop, do you? I have some graphic-art experience."

"Really?" He stalled for a minute, pretending the strip of masking tape in his hand was taking all his concentration. He didn't want to tell her that they could barely make payroll with the skeleton staff they had. "Where did you work in graphics?"

She didn't answer for a minute but climbed down from the ladder to switch to the smaller brush. He was starting to think she hadn't heard him.

But once she climbed the ladder again and resumed painting around the edges of a kitchen cabinet, she started talking as if no time had passed. "I've worked a couple of different places. My degree is in design, but I've done a little of everything. If you have *any* kind of opening, I'd be interested. I'll answer phones or file or whatever. I'll even clean the toilets if that's what you need." She giggled. "Do I sound desperate?"

"Maybe a little." His grin melted to a sigh. "I wish I *could* hire you to clean the toilets because, right now, that's my job."

She laughed again. It had been a long time since he'd known the pleasure of making a woman laugh.

He frowned. "Unfortunately, we don't have the money to hire anybody right now." Then, without prompting, an idea materialized in his mind. "You know what?"

She stopped painting in midstroke, a gleam of curiosity in her eyes.

Why hadn't he thought of this before? "Listen, Bart and Wren are paying me a pretty decent wage to do this remodeling job. But I need to finish it up before the back-to-school jobs start coming in at the print shop. If you could keep on and just do the painting for me, and maybe help out with some finishing work later, I'd pay you."

Meg's face lit like a jack-o'-lantern. "Seriously?"

The idea took on a life of its own, and his enthusiasm gave his words steam. "Yes, I'm dead serious. I can only work in the evenings, but if you can get the painting done during the day, I'd be able to get to the other stuff a lot quicker. It would help us both out. Have you ever hung wallpaper?"

She shook her head, and her expression revealed she was afraid her negative answer was going to cancel the whole deal.

"Hey, neither have I. But Wren talked about putting up a border of some kind out here." He spun on his heel, panning the walls, trying to imagine. "I don't know that I'm crazy about the idea, but Wren thinks she wants one."

"What about stenciling—or a painted border? I did an ivy vine sort of thing in my sister's bathroom, and it turned out great . . . if I do say so myself." She balanced her paintbrush across the can of paint. Leaning out over the ladder, she pointed at the arched doorway. "Can't you see something with vines twining over the doorway—morning glories maybe? Lavender would look wonderful against this sunny yellow."

He could envision what she suggested, and it sounded nice. If she were any good, the artistic element could add a unique flair to the décor. But what if she was terrible? He had a vision of the wall of drawings the day-care kids did. He'd better give himself an out before he got in too deep. "I think it's a great idea, but I don't know how set Wren was on wallpaper. We'll talk it over with her when she gets back. Maybe you could do a sketch for her first. But I know she'll do backflips over the idea of you helping with the painting."

They both laughed at the image he'd created of Wren, and Meg clapped her hands together at his idea, making him think again of that little girl at Disneyland.

"This is fantastic," she said. "How long do you think it'll take to finish all this?"

He did some quick calculations in his head and spread his arms to encompass the dining area. "I'll finish taping and drag all this extra drywall and stuff out of here tonight so you can start painting first thing Monday."

"Oh, no need to wait until Monday. I could start first thing tomorrow morning!"

He wagged his head. "Huh-uh. That'll never fly."

A quizzical look came to her eyes. "Because they have guests?"

"It's not that. Bart and Wren would never go for you working on Sunday."

"Oh, I don't mind. Honestly."

He puffed up his cheek, trying to think how to explain. "I don't think you understand. Sunday is the Sabbath. A day of rest. Bart and Wren are sticklers about that."

She nodded slowly, but he could tell from her expression that she didn't really understand.

"But even so, if you can get it all painted in a couple of days— say by Tuesday night, I can do the trim work in two evenings, maybe three, while you work on the border. I don't know how fast you paint, but we could have the whole thing done and cleaned up before next weekend."

"Oh. That soon?" She deflated a bit. "Well . . . sure. Count me in."

He studied her. Obviously her expectations had been very different from reality. And he hoped she wasn't expecting California wages for this job. "Sorry. I wish it was more hours, but I'm just being realistic. And Kansas wages might be a bit of a shock to you after living on the West Coast."

"Oh, no . . . I didn't expect . . ." She became preoccupied with a hangnail. "I didn't mean to seem ungrateful. I'm very glad for the work. And maybe by the time we're finished, I'll have heard from the gallery."

Trevor's hand stilled on the wall he was taping. "The gallery?"

She nodded. "That's the possibility I was talking about. The owner said he might have work for me. Of course, it would only be part-time, but at least—"

"You mean Linder's?"

"Yes." She pointed to the north. "Just up the street."

He nodded. "I know where you mean."

Old feelings came roaring back. He tried to push them down, but they left a bitter taste in the back of his throat.

"Mr. Linder didn't promise anything but said he might have some part-time work."

Trevor swallowed hard and turned back to his taping. Was this some kind of test? He'd squared things with Jack a long time ago. He truly had. And maybe Meg really could make a difference with the gallery. Coming from a metropolitan area, she'd probably have some fresh ideas. And maybe this was a chance for Jack to get his life straightened out.

But didn't he owe it to Meg to at least caution her? Yet what kind of friend did that?

And then there was Wren. He wouldn't hurt her for the world. Still, Meg had become a friend too. And if she was going to be helping him out here . . .

He raked a dusty hand through his hair. Meg Anders hadn't been here a week, and she was already tying his life in knots.

She'd invented a whole new background for herself, but it was getting harder and harder to keep her stories straight.

Chapter Twenty-Nine

here was something about Jackson Linder that wasn't being said. Maggie had wondered at Wren's reaction earlier, and now Trevor had that same sour-lemon expression. What was it they weren't telling her?

"What . . . what would you be doing . . . in the gallery?"

Trevor kept his back to her, but Maggie didn't miss the ferocity in his motions as he ripped a length of masking tape from the roll.

"I don't know yet. Maybe cleaning toilets." She waited for the laugh she'd hoped to elicit, but it didn't come. "I'd be helping out with the business stuff so he can concentrate on his painting."

Trevor gave a noncommittal grunt and turned back to the window sill he was taping.

"So you know Mr. Linder?"

"Oh, I know him."

He and Wren were reading from the same script. Maggie laid her brush on the top of the ladder and climbed down. Trevor was on his knees taping the wide woodwork beneath the window sill. She crossed the room and stood behind him until he glanced up at her.

He rocked back on his heels. "Do you need something?"

Arms akimbo, she studied him. "Is there something I should know about Mr. Linder?"

He rubbed the bridge of his nose. "What do you mean?"

"You tell me. You and Wren both started acting weird when his name came up. Like there's some reason you're not too thrilled with me taking that job at the gallery."

"You said it wasn't for sure."

"No. But if it was, is there anything you'd be telling me?"

He rose to his feet. "Jack is a friend of mine, Meg. We go way back. I don't know if it'd be right for me to—"

"What? What is it?"

"It's just . . ." His work boot rubbed a trail through the layer of dust on the floor. "Jack's had some rough times in recent years. He's . . ."

She waited while he gnawed the inside of his cheek and shifted from one foot to the other, painting in the dust with the other foot now.

"Jack went through some bad times, and he hasn't handled it well. He . . . drinks too much and . . . well, I've said enough." He lowered his voice. "The thing is, I don't know where he'd get the money to pay you. As far as I know, he hasn't sold a painting since before—let's just say business isn't booming at the gallery, and what money he has gets spent on booze."

So she *had* smelled liquor on his breath. "Is that his only business?"

"It is now."

She wasn't sure how to interpret that, but before she could ask him what he meant, the bells on the front door jangled. Trevor looked to Maggie, as if she would know who it was.

"Wren got guests this afternoon. A big group. That's probably them."

"Really?" Trevor pushed off the floor and stood. "I don't think they had reservations. At least Wren didn't say anything. Well, hey, that's great."

Maggie started toward the door. "I'll go see if they need anything."

Out in the lobby, she stopped short when she saw Bart and Wren bent over the front counter, sorting through a jumble of Wal-Mart bags. "Oh, it's you. You're home early, aren't you? I thought you were going to see a movie."

Wren looked up. Her eyes were puffy and her cheeks ruddier than usual. But she offered Maggie a smile, and her voice came out as chipper as always. "We decided not to. We're not really movie people."

Bart rubbed the palm of his hand in circles on his wife's back. Wren smiled up at him and leaned into his caress, all at once looking like she might cry.

"Is everything okay?"

"Everything's fine," Wren said, suddenly intent on digging in a shopping bag.

Maggie took a step forward, wishing she could think of something to say or do. "Can I help put things away?"

"Heavens, no!" Wren was instantly herself again. "You're a guest, sweetie. You go on now. Relax."

"Well, um . . . I'm sort of helping Trevor out."

Bart and Wren exchanged looks, and Maggie ducked back into the dining room without explanation.

But she was barely ensconced on the ladder again when the older couple peeked in through the doorway.

Wren clapped a hand over her mouth. "For land's sake! Look at you two!"

Trevor winked at Maggie before turning to Wren. "If you'd gone to the movies like you were supposed to, you might have come home to a fully painted *and* plugged-in kitchen."

Wren crowed and spun on her heels. "I'm not here," she said over one shoulder. "You just pretend you don't see me. For all you know, I'm sitting in the Dickinson with a big tub of popcorn in my lap. Come on, Bart. Let's go find an old video to watch." She grabbed her husband's arm, and they disappeared through the archway, giggling like young lovers.

At the sound of their footsteps on the stairway in the lobby, Trevor came to the ladder and reached up to give Maggie a high-five. "Let's pretend they never came home," he whispered. "We can do this."

She nodded agreement and made a show of slapping paint on the next portion of the wall. They worked in silence to the *whish whish* of Maggie's paintbrush and the rhythmic *zip* of Trevor unrolling and tearing off the painter's tape as he worked his way around the room.

When he finished taping the dining area, he came over to the ladder with an empty roller pan. "Hey, that's looking good. If you don't mind doing the trim work along the baseboard on this wall, I can start rolling where you've already been."

"Sure, that's fine."

He held out the roller pan, and she tipped the can and poured paint into the pan. They moved the ladder to the other wall, and she climbed up and went to work trimming the largest wall of the kitchen while Trevor worked the roller brush in long, even strokes on the walls Maggie had trimmed. Even as the light outside the windows faded to dusk, the kitchen began to take on a sunny glow.

Jasper sauntered into the room and swept by Maggie's ladder. His tail knocked off a paintbrush that had been balanced across a can. Thank goodness Trevor had seen to it that the floor around the edge of the room was covered in canvas tarps. Maggie shooed the cat away again.

Half an hour later, she took a bathroom break and brought back two Cokes that someone—probably Bart—had put in the miniature refrigerator in her room.

"You want a soda?" She held out the chilled can to Trevor.

He flashed a knowing grin.

"Excuse me! A *pop*." She dragged out the word in a hayseed drawl. "I'd like to give you a pop all right," she mumbled under her breath but loud enough to be sure he heard.

He laughed and held out his hands in surrender.

Maybe it was time she came clean about the whole West Coast thing before she dug herself any deeper. She opened her mouth to speak, but Trevor was standing there grinning at her with that appealing sparkle in his blue gray eyes, and no words would come out. She felt heat rise to her cheeks.

He seemed not to notice and went back to work. But Maggie's stomach churned. With her lies, she'd invented a whole new background for herself, but it was getting harder and harder to keep her stories straight. A little ditty her mother had often quoted ran around in her head. *Oh, what a tangled web we weave, when first we practice to deceive.* The words wove themselves over and under one another, until the web was tangling up her brain. She had to come clean.

But if she told the truth, what would he think of her? What would any of them think of her? There was something different about these people. She'd never met anyone as sweet as Bart and Wren Johannsen. After only a few days with them, she somehow knew that everything about them was genuine. They put on no airs. Their kindnesses weren't performed to impress or to call in favors at some later date.

Trevor was cut from the same cloth. She had suspected his motives at first. Of course, he had every right to suspect her too. She'd used him, really, because she'd needed to get to the bus. But then he'd stayed to make sure she was safe and invited her on a picnic. She was pretty sure he had no ulterior motive for doing those things. They were purely kindnesses, helping out someone in need.

She looked over at him, and a foreign emotion flooded her being. It was a feeling she couldn't identify, but it drenched her with possibility, with hope. And with an emotion she dared not entertain.

Trevor seemed not to notice that her brush had stilled, that she was watching him. How could she ever be a part of the life she saw here—in the town, the inn, and in the life of the man working beside her? They had something she wanted desperately. But she didn't have the first clue what it was. Or how to get a handle on it.

She resumed the comforting rhythm of painting, but her heart felt all out of kilter. And for once, it had nothing to do with Kevin Bryson.

Trevor stood there,
waiting, as if he
~~thought she might~~
change her mind if he
~~stared at her~~
long enough.

Chapter Thirty

"Ta-da!" Trevor's shout caused Maggie to pivot on the ladder. He waved the long-handled roller in front of the finished wall with a flourish and took a courtly bow. Only the first of three walls, but it looked lovely, and already Maggie could begin to picture how the room would look when it was finished.

Would she be here to see it for herself? Or would she have moved on by then? She shook off the question and forced herself to climb out of the funk she'd been buried in. "What time is it anyway?"

Trevor wiped a paint splatter off the face of his watch. "It's almost six o'clock. You want to call it a day?"

It was all she could do not to laugh at the puppy-dog eagerness in his paint-splotched face. It was obvious he was nowhere near ready to call it a day.

"I have nothing else to do. But if you need to go, I can clean up here."

"Oh, no. I can stay all night."

"Well, I don't know about that, but I'm good for a couple more hours anyway."

"Great!"

"How about a bite to eat first?"

"I am kind of hungry, now that you mention it."

She went and got the sandwiches from the fridge in her room. They were starting to be a little on the soggy side, but they'd do. Trevor gathered chairs around a table in the lobby, and they sat down across from each other.

Maggie watched him wolf down three of the half dozen little sandwiches Wren had made her for the bus. She'd counted those sandwiches as "security" against hunger, intending to make them last several days. But tonight she was happy to share them with Trevor, and she watched him wolf them down without a twinge of anxiety over where her next meals might come from.

She ate two of them and offered Trevor the last one. He accepted with a grin. A few minutes later he put the last bite in his mouth, brushed the crumbs from his hands, and pushed back from the table. "Ready?"

"Ready when you are."

He followed her to the kitchen and helped her refill the roller pan from her bucket. For the next two hours they worked. And they talked. Mostly Trevor talked. And she preferred it that way. He regaled her with the colorful history of the unincorporated town of Clayburn and his boyhood stories of growing up here. Trevor's childhood had been one Maggie could only imagine—one full of love and a whole town of supportive mentors. His memories were built around simple adventures that she could sense grew more precious with every recall. His telling of his one and only climb to the top of the Clayburn water tower with two of his buddies the summer he turned ten had her rolling with laughter.

"But scared as we were climbing those eighty-seven rungs to the top, we didn't know the meaning of fear until we got up there and looked down to see our mothers glaring at us from the ground. We seriously considered camping out up there . . . until Mom told us the police were on the way."

A faraway look shadowed his smile, but Maggie watched him shake it off and turn to her, a winsome spark lighting his eyes. "So, can Meg Anders top the water-tower story? What was it like growing up in California?"

She shook her head, her mind whirling. "Can't top that." But Trevor's story had reminded her of a story she hadn't thought of in a long time—maybe since it happened. Her mom . . . trying to teach her how to make pancakes. She smiled, unspooling her memory for Trevor. "I read the recipe wrong and only used half a cup of flour when it called for two cups. I didn't know the batter wasn't supposed to be thin as glue."

"Oops," Trevor said, obviously knowing where this was headed.

"They came off the griddle thin as cardboard and full of holes—like lace. Mom picked one up and saw that I was about to cry from humiliation. So she announced that I'd just made a lovely batch of *crepes*."

"Those fancy French pancakes?"

She nodded. "She spread orange marmalade on them, rolled them up, sprinkled them with powdered sugar, and you know what? They were pretty good."

"That was quick thinking on your mom's part."

Maggie swallowed over the lump in her throat. Why had she spent so much time dwelling only on the times after they'd put Mom in the hospital? She laughed as a new memory rose to the surface. "Mom made some jam once that never jelled. She opened a jar and it was like syrup. She said, 'We need to make some of your famous crepes to pour this over, Magg—'" She caught herself and dropped her voice. Trevor seemed not to notice, so she hurried on. "We made crepes every Saturday morning after that. Mom called them *faux crepes* and made us all speak with thick French accents while we ate them." She lifted her chin and dem-onstrated. "Jennifuh, dahling, would you pahss the cr-r-repes, *s'il vous plait.*" She trilled her *r*s and struck a haughty pose.

Trevor roared, and his laughter washed through Maggie, filling up a place inside her that had been empty and dry.

Her story reminded him of another, and he launched into his tale. They traded memory after memory, and by the time the clock in the lobby chimed nine o'clock, Maggie had quit worrying that she would slip up and say something that would give her charade away.

By ten, when the noisy guests came in and sat out in the lobby laugh-ing and talking, Maggie and Trevor were having their own party in the kitchen.

All three walls of the kitchenette area were painted, and they had a good start on the wall the archway was on. Maggie had figured out a design for a border in her head and she could hardly wait to start sketch-ing it out on paper to show Wren.

"Is there anyplace in town to buy art supplies? My fingers are itch-ing to hold a paintbrush," she told Trevor when they talked about the border again.

He chuckled and pointed to the wide paint-caked brush in her hand. "You can *say* that after tonight?"

She laughed. "I was thinking of something a mite smaller . . . and a mite more artistic."

"I doubt Alco has the kind of paints you need, but we'll find them. I might even have some stuff in the print shop that would work."

As a burst of laughter wafted from the lobby, Trevor checked his watch. "I don't know about you, but I'm plumb tuckered out. What do you say we move the appliances back and call it a day? I think Bart and Wren are down for the count."

They hadn't seen hide nor hair of the couple since they'd gone up to their apartment earlier to watch a movie. Maggie smiled, picturing them together on the love seat in their little living room sawing logs while a soundtrack droned in the background. She made a mental note to set her alarm so she'd be up when Wren came down in the morning. She could hardly wait to see the look on the sweet woman's face when she saw how much they'd accomplished. She and Wren would be able to fix breakfast for the guests in a nice, neat kitchen. They'd still have to move the tables out to the lobby to serve the meal, but a few more work nights like this one and the dining room would be finished too. Maggie couldn't remember the last time she'd felt such a sense of accomplishment.

She helped Trevor plug in the heavy range and scoot it back into place, likewise the refrigerator. While she swept the floor and wiped off countertops, Trevor moved three of the four small tables out into the lobby, ready for breakfast guests in the morning.

Maggie took the paint rags to the laundry room and found Wren's kitchen knickknacks stored away on a shelf there. She arranged them on the kitchenette counters, which worked wonders for the overall effect.

By the time they finally stood under the archway surveying their handiwork, the guests had retired to their rooms for the night.

Trevor smiled down at her. "Not bad for a day's work, huh?"

"It looks so good, I'm tempted to go wake Wren up."

He laughed. "I think she'll enjoy it more in the morning."

"Fine, but I'm setting my alarm so I can be here when she sees it. Want me to call you?"

"Ha! You do and all deals are off." The glint in his eye made her laugh.

"Chicken."

"You do know that Wren gets up around six a.m. when she has guests?"

"No way!"

"Oh, yeah."

"Even when she's just thawing out cinnamon rolls?"

"That I don't know. But I am not answering my phone before nine a.m. Speaking of which, are you going to church with Bart and Wren in the morning?"

"Church? I wasn't planning on it."

He looked at the floor before meeting her eyes. "You want to go with me?"

"To church?" Her voice quavered.

He nodded. "I could pick you up a little before ten."

"Um, I don't know." She squirmed, rummaging for an excuse. She hadn't been to church since the Tarkans had taken her and Jenn to Sunday school every week. A very long time ago. With the path of lies she'd strewn from New York to Clayburn, the very thought of all that righteousness terrified her. "I promised Wren I'd help her get breakfast. And besides, I don't have anything to wear."

Trevor held up a hand. "Hey, it's okay. Just thought I'd ask. What you wore yesterday would be fine though."

His hopeful smile made a part of her long to say yes, but common sense won out. "Thanks anyway."

Trevor stood there, waiting, as if he thought she might change her mind if he stared at her long enough. She looked at the floor, then stooped to pick up a tiny clump of fuzz off one of the wood planks. The clock on the mantel seemed to hammer in her ears. Maggie wished the evening had ended ten minutes earlier on the high note of their triumph with Wren's kitchen.

"Well, I think I'm going to shove off. Thanks for all your help. You'll have to tell me what Wren says."

She gave a little nod. "I will."

"I'll be back Monday afternoon to work on the dining area. Wren gave me a check for part of the job, so I'll bring you a check then—for the work you did today. And I'd welcome your help again . . . if you can."

"Okay." She touched the sleeve of the flannel shirt he'd loaned her. "I'll get this washed and back to you Monday."

"Keep it." He stared at the floor. "You'll need it. At least I hope so."

He gathered his tools and went out through the front door.

She turned off the lights in the kitchen and dining room and checked the front door. Trevor had apparently locked it on his way out.

Her room was quiet. The freshly made-up bed invited her to crash. It was tempting, but she was too grimy and paint-splattered to seriously consider it. But she nearly fell asleep under the warm shower spray.

She set the alarm clock for six a.m. and was asleep almost before her head hit the pillow.

Trevor's pillow felt cool against the back of his neck. He lay staring up at the ceiling, hands clasped behind his head. His hair was still damp from the shower. He was dead tired, but it had been a good day. With Meg's help, he'd gotten more done than he'd thought possible, and her company had made the hours fly by.

He sobered a little, remembering Meg's possibility of working for Jack. But maybe he'd bought them both a reprieve. The remodeling job for Wren would take at least a few more days . . . longer for Meg if Wren agreed to let her do the decorative painting. It was obvious Wren liked Meg. She'd taken her under her wing from that first morning she'd come squawking down the hall shushing him because Meg was sleeping—in the middle of the day. He had a feeling Wren might have other jobs up her sleeve when the painting was done. Especially if Meg mentioned Jack's job offer to her. Maybe Wren would talk to Meg and save him the trouble.

He doubted it though. Wren had been awfully quiet on the subject of Jack Linder lately. He understood. It hurt to see what Jack was doing to himself. Trevor understood the man's pain, but couldn't Jack see that it only made everything that had gone before that much worse?

He drew in a deep breath. In the darkness his thoughts always seemed bleaker and more overwhelming than he knew they would be in the light of morning. Still, it angered him that pondering Jack's situation forced him to deal again with the question of forgiveness. He knew he'd forgiven Jack. A long time ago. But sometimes the temptation to pick up that burden again was more than he could endure.

"I forgive him completely, Lord. You know that. Help me to keep on forgiving." He spoke the words aloud, perplexed at their contradiction, yet knowing his prayer had been accepted.

Think about something else. Something good, he told himself. *Whatsoever things are true, whatsoever things are honest, whatsoever things are just, whatsoever things are pure, whatsoever things are lovely . . .*

Meg. Now there was something lovely. He thought of her smile, her genuine laughter at his corny jokes. Until tonight, he hadn't heard her laugh much. He intended to change that. Meg's laughter was musical. He longed for her to have a reason to make music. To know how much God loved her.

He smiled to himself in the dark. It had been a good day. For the first time in ages—maybe the first time since that terrible day—he'd come home feeling happy, looking forward to what tomorrow might bring. He wasn't going to let anything spoil that.

He plumped his pillow and rolled over to face the other side of the double bed. The empty side. And he dared to hope that space might someday be filled again.

If she were going
to survive here, she
had to remember to
forget everything about
her old life.

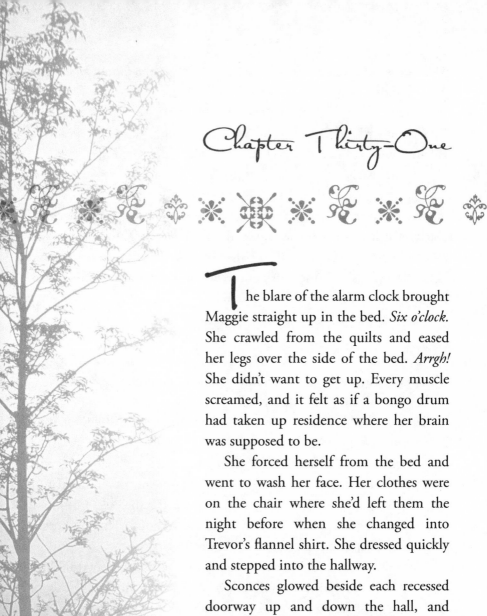

Chapter Thirty-One

The blare of the alarm clock brought Maggie straight up in the bed. *Six o'clock.* She crawled from the quilts and eased her legs over the side of the bed. *Arrgh!* She didn't want to get up. Every muscle screamed, and it felt as if a bongo drum had taken up residence where her brain was supposed to be.

She forced herself from the bed and went to wash her face. Her clothes were on the chair where she'd left them the night before when she changed into Trevor's flannel shirt. She dressed quickly and stepped into the hallway.

Sconces glowed beside each recessed doorway up and down the hall, and when she entered the lobby, she saw light streaming from the kitchen. Wren must already be up.

Maggie hurried across the lobby and through the archway but stopped short when she saw Wren sitting at the lone table left in the dining area, head in her hands.

"Wren?"

The snowy head came up and Wren gave a little gasp. Her eyes were red and puffy, her hair disheveled. "Oh, child, you scared me!"

"Wren?" Maggie hurried to her side and crouched down beside her, resting her elbow on the table. "What's wrong?"

Wren smiled through her tears. "You sweet, sweet kids. Look at this!" She spread her arms to encompass the kitchenette. The room looked especially cozy and charming in the dim glow of the undercounter lights. "You finished! And you put everything away for me." She sniffed and blew her nose on a crumpled tissue.

"But why are you crying?"

Wren's tears seemed like anything but tears of joy.

She sniffled into the tissue again. "Don't you worry about me. I'm just a little overwhelmed right now. And what are you doing up so early?"

"I want to help you with breakfast."

Wren scooted her chair back and pushed herself up. "Well then, we'd best get started. Do you know how to make coffee?" She didn't wait for an answer but bustled about the kitchen, opening a cupboard door and handing a coffee canister to Maggie. While Maggie measured the grinds into the basket, Wren pulled ingredients from the shelves. "Oh my! I can't tell you how nice it is to be able to work without having to hurdle an oven every time I want to open a drawer."

Wren obviously didn't want to talk about whatever was troubling her, so Maggie played along and followed her instructions, scrambling two dozen eggs, slicing sweet red peppers and mushrooms, frying bacon to crumble into the egg casserole. By seven o'clock, the casserole was baking, cinnamon rolls were warming in the toaster oven, and the coffee was wafting its heavenly aroma down the hallway.

"That'll wake 'em up," Wren declared. She seemed her jolly self now.

"Did you hear all the noise down here last night?"

"Honey, Bart said I was asleep before the previews were over on that video. He woke me up and made me get in bed. I didn't hear a thing until the alarm went off this morning."

"Well, good. Between the party in the lobby and Trevor and me crashing around down here, I thought for sure we'd wake you."

Wren patted Maggie's arm. "I wouldn't have cared if you did. Thanks again, Meg. You're a dear." She tipped her wrist and checked her watch. "I think everything is under control here. Our noisy guests said they probably wouldn't be out for breakfast until around eight. Why don't you go back to bed for a little while? Your body is probably still on California time."

There was that dagger to Maggie's heart again. Her lies coming back to haunt her. She was growing to love these people. It seemed impossible, but in a few short days, they had become like family to her. Yet every time someone made reference to her history—the one she'd made up—she felt like a traitor. She had to come clean. And soon.

But if she told the truth now, they might put her out on her ear. And she wouldn't blame them if they did. What else could they think but that she'd tried to take advantage of them?

She would find a job here. Get settled in her own place. Pay Wren and Bart back every penny for all they'd done for her. She'd do it first thing, even before she bought her art supplies. Then she'd make things right with them, tell them the whole truth. They would understand that she'd lied to protect herself. That she hadn't known who she could trust at first. That she'd never intended to let the deception go on this long. But if she were going to survive here, she had to remember to forget everything about her old life.

And they would understand, wouldn't they? All of them?

Trevor's smile flashed through her mind. Would he forgive her?

It surprised her how very much she cared about the answer to that question.

By nine o'clock the inn was eerily quiet. All the guests had checked out, and Bart and Wren had gone off to church. Main Street outside the windows was like a ghost town—every window bearing a Closed sign, and not a car in sight on the street.

Nothing had changed about her room with its cheery blue and white prints and sunshine streaming in her window, but Maggie was overcome with loneliness. She felt it even more than in the apartment in New York. Here in Clayburn, Kansas—instead of the usual city traffic and the wail of sirens that was background music to her solitude—the only sounds were the twittering of birds outside her window. Even though Bart and Wren had done their best to coax her into attending church with them this morning, she felt somehow abandoned by them. As much as it terrified her to think of setting foot inside a church building, she almost wished she'd accepted their invitation.

She wondered if Trevor was in church right now. She felt certain he was. And it struck her that, for him, she might just be persuaded to darken the door.

Monday morning dragged on forever with more than the usual wrenches in the works of the print shop. It seemed to Trevor that a hundred little jobs had popped up overnight. He might have been happy for the work, except that none of it was big-ticket stuff, and most of it was mere busywork—collating a printed-in-office manual for a manufacturing firm in Salina, corrections on a poster Mason had fouled up in the press, and other odds and ends of the business.

Trevor was anxious to be done with his day here and get to the inn. He felt like a high-school kid, worrying that Meg might have finished her part of the painting and quit for the day. But he didn't want to miss her. Besides being a big help to him, she made the hours fly by. And the laughter they shared seemed to extend into his evening, keeping his emotional metabolism burning long after he'd left her presence.

He remembered that she'd planned to continue her job search this morning, and he hoped it would take her the better part of the day. But then she might be too tired to paint tonight.

He couldn't quit thinking about her. Wondering what her story was. He was certain now that she wasn't being up front with him—or with anybody in Clayburn for that matter. But she'd been hurt. She'd admitted that much, and he was willing to give her an out while she healed. He'd spent the last two years in similar shoes. He knew all too well how painful the healing process could be. Yet, though Meg admitted to lying, he didn't think of her as a liar. He sensed that Meg's stories served to make her feel safe. To protect her from whatever it was that threatened her. He found himself fiercely protective whenever he thought about whoever or whatever had caused her to run away from wherever home was.

Finally the clock in the front office ticked to four, and he extricated himself from the pressroom and drove across the street to park in front of Wren's. He hauled his toolbox out of the back and headed inside.

Meg was already on a ladder in the dining room. She was wearing his flannel shirt, sleeves rolled up, and her hair was tucked into a navy bandana he recognized as Bart's. She had her back to him, and the wall she was painting was two-thirds finished.

"Hey you. You're making some serious progress there."

She twisted on the ladder to face him, and her pleased smile reminded him why he'd been looking forward to this job all day. "I hope you don't mind if I took over your job."

"No problem." He grabbed a paintbrush and started trimming in the corner of the wall adjacent to the one she was working on.

Wren appeared in the doorway. "How's it going in here? Do you two need to take a snack break? I baked cookies this morning."

"I just got here," Trevor said. "But Meg's apparently been here for a while. I guess, if forced, I could take a snack break for her sake."

Wren affected a chastening, motherly glare. "Watch it, buster."

He winked at Meg and dipped his paintbrush in the can, laughing with her.

Wren steepled her hands beneath her chin and turned 360 degrees, surveying the room. "It's looking great in here."

"Did Meg talk to you about the border, Wren?"

Meg's paint roller stilled. She looked from him to Wren and shook her head. "Not yet."

"What's this?" Curiosity sparked in Wren's eyes.

"Meg suggested instead of wallpaper, you might like a hand-painted border—something similar to stenciling."

Wren's eyes narrowed.

"Who would do the painting?"

Trevor studied the misgiving in her expression. Did she think he was suggesting Jack could do the painting? He hastened to put her mind at ease. "Meg worked for a graphic-arts firm. She's done this type of thing before."

"Well, I've only tried stenciling once," Meg demurred. "But I was thinking of doing this freehand. I did some sketches last night, and I think they turned out pretty nice."

Wren's face softened. "Well, let's see them."

"I don't want you to feel obligated. They're only sketches. Bart gave me some colored pens from the front desk, but they're not exactly the colors I was thinking would look best in here, so you'll have to use your imagination."

Trevor moved to take the paint roller from her hand. "Go get them. Let's take a look."

She climbed down and practically ran through the lobby to her room.

Wren eyed him. "You put her up to this, didn't you, Mr. Ashlock? You never did like the idea of me putting up wallpaper."

He held up a hand in defense. "It was the idea of *me* putting up wallpaper that I wasn't crazy about."

Wren chuckled.

"But this was Meg's idea . . . honest." He gave a guilty shrug. "I might have encouraged her a little."

Meg returned with several sheets of copy paper. She spread them out on the lone table that remained in the room after they'd moved the others to the lobby for Saturday's guests. Her face was lit up with joy. Her hands flew over the paper as she showed Wren what she had in mind.

Trevor was relieved to see she had real talent. The simple, scrolled floral design she proposed fit the inn's quaint architecture perfectly. And her craftsmanship was meticulous.

Wren looked from the papers to the archway, squinting. "I like it. I like it a lot. How long do you think it would take to finish?"

Meg rested her chin on her fist, thinking. "Probably three or four days. I'll need to let the paint dry on a couple of different layers before I can finish. And it'll depend on how many hours Mr. Linder can give me."

Wren gave Trevor a look that said, "Do something!"

He cleared his throat. "You're going to work for him for sure?"

Meg smiled. "I talked to him after lunch, and he wants me to start first thing in the morning. It's a good thing. I bombed out everywhere else I went. But that's why I wanted to get as much done here as I could this afternoon."

Wren gathered Meg's sketches and tamped them into a neat sheaf. "Why don't you take these back to your room so they don't get ruined? I love your idea, and I'd like to commission you to do the work."

Trevor tensed. Money was tight for the Johannsens, especially with business slower than it had been in years. He'd been hesitant to even accept the remodeling job until he realized Bart and Wren were determined to have it done. At least he could charge them a more reasonable rate than the exorbitant amount Buddy Rollenmeyer up at the lumberyard had quoted.

Wren went on, her hand on Meg's arm. "I don't know what you charge for a job like this, but you'll stay here for free until it's finished."

Meg's eyes grew round. "Really? Oh, that's wonderful!" She gave Wren a spontaneous hug, then backed away, seeming embarrassed by the show of affection. "The room will be more than enough pay, Wren. I can't thank you enough."

"You already have. You tuck those drawings safely away now."

As soon as Meg was out of earshot, Wren turned to Trevor, her voice wobbly. "I feel like I need to say something to her, Trevor. Jack is . . . well, he's just Jack. But for Bart's sake, I don't want to go into all the . . . well, you know. Still, I don't feel right letting Meg get involved in that mess." Wren nodded in the general direction of Jack's gallery.

"Have you said anything to Jack?"

He was sorry the minute the words were out. Of course she hadn't. As far as he knew, Jack hadn't darkened Wren's door for almost two years. Wren could have blamed him—Trevor—for that. Jack probably *did* blame him. But Trevor had made his peace with his place in Bart and Wren's lives long ago, and he wouldn't rehash that now.

"I'm sorry, Wren. You do what you think is right. But maybe this will be a good thing. Meg seems rather worldly wise."

"She's been hurt. She hasn't talked to me about it, but I see the signs. I know she needs a job—heaven knows I wish Bart and I could give her one—but I don't want her to be hurt again."

He shook his head slowly. "I know. I know."

He didn't want to see Meg get hurt either. But there was enough trouble between Wren and Jack, and this situation wasn't going to make it any better. And Jack—well, he'd been hurting for a long time, and he didn't seem ready to find any relief for it.

Trevor huffed out a sigh. He'd faulted Meg for being evasive about her past, for hiding behind what he suspected were flat-out lies. But the truth was, he and Wren harbored their own secrets. Innocently, each lovingly protecting the other—and Jack. But Meg would walk into a potential catastrophe if they didn't clue her in and soon.

An old heaviness invaded his heart. He was glad Amy would never know all the sorrow that had seeped into the world because her car had just happened to be on that particular stretch of highway at the wrong time.

Had Wren and Trevor been wise to her lies all along?

Chapter Thirty-Two

When Maggie walked back into the dining room, an awkward silence pervaded the room. Trevor was suddenly preoccupied with putting a third coat of paint on the corner he'd been trimming, and Wren darted over to the kitchenette and started swabbing already-spotless countertops.

Maggie looked from one to the other, but both refused to make eye contact. They'd been talking about her, that much was obvious.

Had she said something earlier that gave her away? Or had Wren and Trevor been wise to her lies all along? She suspected as much. She'd tripped up too many times. Even though, since Trevor had brought her back from the bus stop, she'd tried to make her lies ones of omission only, she'd become too practiced at the art of falsehood. Maybe Wren had decided she couldn't trust her living and working under the inn's roof.

Wren hurriedly gathered linens from pegs in the kitchen—towels Maggie knew were clean that morning—and backed from the room. "I have laundry to do," she said. "You two holler if you need anything."

No mention of the snack she'd offered a few minutes ago.

"So . . . what was that all about?" She felt brave because Trevor's back was to her. "My ears were itching."

"Huh?"

She shrugged. "Just an old wives' tale. If your ears itch, someone must be talking about you."

"Oh." He went on painting.

"So were you?"

He bent to balance the paintbrush across the rim of the can, then straightened to face her. His mouth turned down in a thoughtful frown. "I need to talk to you about something." He came a step closer.

Uh-oh. Here it comes. She stood, waiting.

"It's about Jack Linder."

"Yeah, you told me. Believe me, Trevor, I know how to handle a drunk."

Trevor's eyebrows shot up, but she was glad she'd said what she did. It was true. Maybe she could ease gradually into the truth. It would be less painful that way. "Is he like the town drunk or something? Wren was upset, too, when I told her I might start working at the gallery. Does she know about this guy's problem?"

He rubbed the space between his eyes, as if staving off a headache. "Wren knows." Trevor lifted his head and studied her for a long minute.

Maggie got the impression he was trying to decide how much to reveal to her.

Finally he blew out a hard breath. "Wren knows better than most, Meg. Jack is her son."

"What?" Hadn't she met Jackson Linder's mother at the gallery that day?

His expression grew somber.

"But—I *met* his mother."

Trevor nodded again. "That's Twila . . . Linder. It's a long story, Meg, and it's not all mine to tell."

Maggie waited, hoping he didn't plan to stop there.

He glanced past her to the lobby and craned his neck, listening, she knew, for Wren.

The muffled tremor of the washing machine agitator apparently gave him license to continue. "John and Twila Linder adopted Jack as an infant. John died a few years ago, but they were a great couple. I spent a lot of time at their house when we were kids. Jack always knew he was adopted—it never seemed to be a big deal. But he had a girlfriend in high school who convinced him he should search for his birth mother. With Twila's blessing, Jack did a search when he turned eighteen and . . . well . . ." Trevor eyed Maggie. "It turned out his birth mother had been living in Clayburn all along."

Maggie released the breath she'd been holding. "Wren?"

"Yes. Wren was . . . well, let's just say she wasn't the Wren we know and love now. I don't know all the details, but apparently Jack's birth father wasn't exactly"—he cleared his throat meaningfully—"*available* to marry Wren."

"But Bart?"

"Bart and Wren just celebrated their tenth anniversary last summer."

Meg leaned back against the table, stunned, trying to wrap her mind around the things Trevor just revealed. The situation was so different than she'd imagined. She'd assumed Bart and Wren had been together forever. That they were nearing retirement after being high-school sweethearts. Of course she hadn't bothered to ask Wren about her life. She'd been too immersed in her own problems. Problems that paled now, in the light of Trevor's story. It seemed she wasn't the only one with problems, with a past she was ashamed of.

Her heart melted with tenderness toward Wren. It all started to make sense to her now. Wren's odd reaction when she'd mentioned the gallery owner. Her concern about Maggie working there . . .

She stared up at Trevor. "Do people in town know? Does Wren have a relationship with Jack?"

He shook his head. "Not lately. People know—the newspaper ran a story years ago, when Jack first found Wren. For years they were close. Wren was careful not to try to take Twila's place—not that she ever could—but it was good for both of them to know the truth. And they got along great."

Maggie wrinkled her nose. "So what changed that? Jack's drinking?"

"Not exactly."

Trevor's tremulous sigh made Maggie wonder why he seemed to have a stake in Jack's story. It seemed to be deeper than their high-school friendship.

He glanced at his watch, then picked his paintbrush back up. "Let's finish this last coat and grab some supper. Then I want to show you something."

※ ※ ※

From her perch in the passenger seat of Trevor's pickup, Maggie watched the telephone poles sail by on Old Highway 40—the highway she'd walked into town on. She'd spent four days in Clayburn now. By some strange trick of her mind, this place—this tiny, humble town on an ancient prairie—felt more like home than anywhere she'd lived before.

She was curious where Trevor was taking her now. He hadn't spoken a word since they'd cleaned up their painting mess and climbed into his pickup.

The chill of the air conditioner blew across her bare arms, and she wished she'd left Trevor's flannel paint shirt on. She glanced at him across the truck's cab. She had known him such a short time, but she didn't feel an ounce of fear toward the gentle man who sat with tanned wrists lopped over the steering wheel, eyes on the road ahead, Vivaldi on the CD player.

The sun balanced atop a hedgerow that stretched across the horizon behind them in the distance, and a band of puffy purplish clouds lined up for what promised to be a spectacular sunset. Ten minutes east of town, where the road crossed the Smoky Hill River, Trevor slowed the truck and turned onto a gravel road just past the bridge. He made a U-turn on the side road, pointing the pickup back toward Clayburn. He shifted the truck into park and switched off the radio.

The intersection seemed vaguely familiar, but Maggie didn't understand why he'd brought her here.

Trevor cut the engine and opened his door, leaving the keys dangling in the ignition. "Careful climbing down. The ditch is steep on that side. Here. Hang on." He ran around to her side and gave her a hand down.

The ditch was lush with tangled weeds and tall grasses. Clumps of sunflowers were scattered at haphazard intervals. The air was musky with damp soil.

She followed him along the edge of the dirt road, their shoes crunching on the ridge of fine sand the passage of rural traffic had created. A few yards behind the truck, Trevor stopped and stared off across the pastureland. She paused beside him, following his gaze, but the low buttes and the copse of gnarled trees beyond the stone post fence gave her no clue as to why they were here. A mourning dove cooed somewhere behind them. A pair of the doves had a nest under the eaves of the inn, and Bart had identified their call for Maggie one evening. It was the loneliest sound she'd ever heard.

And now the haunting birdsong seemed to reflect Trevor's demeanor.

He stood straight and somber, seeming someplace far away. Maggie stood a step behind him, respecting his silence with her own. After a minute, Trevor bowed his head, as if trying to compose himself. She waited, growing steadily more uncomfortable.

But then he turned to her, his eyes glistening with unshed tears. "This is where my family died . . . Amy and Trev." He swallowed hard, looking away. "The accident happened right here."

She inhaled a shuddering breath, finally understanding. "Oh, Trevor." Her voice rushed out in a whisper. This made it all seem so real. She tried to imagine this peaceful spot swarming with emergency vehicles, paramedics, shattered glass. A chill went through her. "I'm so sorry."

Staring at the dirt beneath his feet, he nodded a silent acknowledgment. A long minute passed. "Come over here." He walked around the pickup to the other side of the ditch. He climbed down the grassy embankment and held out his hand to help her down behind him.

When she was on solid footing in the ditch, she looked around her. Trevor was bent, wading through the high grasses as if searching for something. And then she knew why this intersection seemed familiar.

He parted a tall curtain of plumed grass to reveal the hewn crosses she'd seen in the ditch the day she'd walked from the bus station. A deep sadness came over her as the meaning of the crosses became clear. She swallowed the lump in her throat and waited for Trevor to explain.

He knelt on one knee in the ditch, a hand resting on the larger cross as he yanked out some of the grasses and tossed them aside, clearing the space. She waited, not knowing what to say, aching for this man and all he'd been through.

Finally he rose. The sun had fallen below the hedgerow, casting his face in shadow. "These crosses . . . Jack made them. For Amy and Trev. For a year—maybe longer—he put fresh flowers on them every single Saturday. It's been awhile now." He bowed his head again.

"I don't understand."

"Jack pulled out in front of Amy. Plowed into her car, probably going about fifty. The police said chances are . . . she never knew what hit her."

Maggie's breath caught. "Was he . . . drunk?"

"No." Trevor gave a humorless laugh and wagged his head. "No, that's the ironic thing. Jack *never* drank—not even that teenage rebellion thing in high school. He was stone sober the day of the accident."

"Oh, Trevor." She tried to fathom how much this must have cost him. "How can you ever forgive something like that?"

Trevor stared at her. "No, Meg. I forgave Jack. The day it happened. I truly did."

Maggie shook her head. She didn't understand how anyone could possibly forgive such an incredible mistake.

"It could easily have been you or me, Meg. We've all done it. You're in a hurry, you think you checked traffic, but you're distracted . . ."

"So . . . his drinking . . . ?"

"Guilt over what happened drove him to the bottle. He can't seem to get over it."

She stared at him for a minute, unable to comprehend the kindness she saw in him. "But you forgave him."

He nodded, the dim light eclipsing his expression. "I think I understand how he feels. If the tables had been turned, I might have struggled with a similar temptation." He hung his head, then looked up at her, sorrow clouding his eyes. "I've done everything I know to help release him from the guilt. But he can't seem to forget. It's out of my hands now. Until he can forgive himself, there's nothing I can say or do."

He panned the dusky sky and nodded toward the pickup. "It'll be dark soon. We should probably go." He led the way around to her side and opened the door for her.

When they were back in the truck, Trevor put his hand on the keys, then hesitated. "Would you mind if we just sat here for a while?"

Maggie wanted to tell him she would've sat there with him all night. Instead she managed a nod.

He rolled down his window, and she did likewise, letting a breeze move through the stuffy cab. They sat in silence, her mind reeling with everything she'd learned. She thought again of Trevor's claim that he'd forgiven his friend. She ran a finger along the edge of the window, trying to muster the courage to ask the question burning inside her. "Please . . . don't take this the wrong way, but . . . I don't see how you could possibly forgive what he did."

He smiled softly. "I love Jack, Meg. He's my friend."

"But what if he *had* been drunk when he hit Amy's car? Could you still have forgiven him?"

Trevor bit the corner of his lower lip and bent over the steering wheel for a moment. But when he straightened and met her eyes, his own were clear. "Even then I hope I would have chosen to forgive. But Meg, it's not by my own will. I couldn't do it without His help." He gestured heavenward, then looked pointedly back at her. "None of us can do it without Him."

She averted her eyes, wanting to change the subject. "It must be so hard. This whole thing with your friend, on top of losing your family."

He gripped the wheel, a rueful smile curving his lips. "It pretty much stinks. But what are you going to do?"

"I'm so sorry, Trevor." Why could she never think of the words that might hold true comfort?

He shifted in his seat. "The worst of it is what it's done to Wren."

"I don't understand why he distanced himself from Wren."

"I'm not sure I understand it either. But then liquor doesn't do much to put sense into a man's head."

She nodded slowly. She understood more than Trevor could possibly know.

"I think Wren saw Jack throwing his life away and tried to intervene. That didn't sit well with Twila, and somehow it got all messed up, and Wren became a place Jack could unleash his anger."

"Poor Wren."

"So now maybe you can understand why Wren"— he reached across the seat to pat her hand—"and me, too—are uncomfortable with you working for Jack. The gallery was thriving a few years ago. Jack had so much promise. He's a very talented man. But I don't know if he's even finished a painting since that day. Or sold much of anything." He shook his head. "In case you hadn't noticed, Clayburn isn't exactly a cultural mecca with people lining up to collect original art."

She smiled at his sarcasm.

His gaze moved out to where the crosses poked up through the grasses in the ditch. "Maybe he *does* need help at the gallery. It's not my business—or Wren's, for that matter—what you do. We just don't want to see you get hurt. And most of the time, Jack has a full-time job just trying to stand up straight."

Sincerity softened his expression. Maggie saw in his face how much Trevor cared for his friend. And for Wren.

"What happened to Jack wasn't fair." Trevor's voice was far away for a minute. He stared out the front windshield into the encroaching darkness, his Adam's apple bobbing. "I don't have to tell you how much I hate it that it was my friend driving that car that terrible day."

Maggie watched him, feeling strangely privileged to be here with him right now. She shook her head. "It seems like a cruel joke—if there is a God—to play tricks like that."

Trevor's gaze bored a hole through her soul. "I've never doubted God's providence, His care for a minute, Meg. Even after that awful Saturday. I think His heart broke over Amy and Trev, and I think it's broken for Jack. I don't claim to understand why any of it happened the way it did, but I know God didn't stop being God the day Amy died."

Maggie wanted to argue with him, tried even, to find the words that would dispute his claim. But the truth was, she envied him, longed to believe in something—Someone—the way he did. She fingered the frayed edge of her seat belt. "I'm so sorry for everything you've been through. It makes my life seem like a piece of cake." She wanted to snatch back the words the minute they left her mouth. What she'd said was true, but with one sentence, she'd given him an open invitation to inquire into her life.

And from the look on his face, and being the gentleman he was, he was graciously taking the bait. He stretched his arm over the back of the truck's bench seat and touched her shoulder briefly. "So tell me about Meg. What are you looking for?"

The question startled her. "I'm not sure what you mean."

"What do you hope to find here in Clayburn?"

She tipped her head, thinking, intensely aware of his eyes on her. What *was* she looking for? Interestingly enough, she felt as if she were on the verge of finding whatever it was, yet she didn't know how to answer Trevor's simple question. He didn't push, he didn't make her feel uncomfortable. He simply waited.

"I'm not sure what I'm searching for. But I know I've needed to get away for a long time. I wish I could tell you that I finally found the courage to leave—Kevin." She cast a quick look at him, then away again. "His name was Kevin. But that's not what happened." She shook her head slowly and a scornful laugh bubbled from her throat. "I got carjacked."

Trevor's eyes grew round, his brows rising in unison. "Seriously?"

She told him what had happened that morning. "It's not that unusual in . . . where I'm from—where I used to live. When I finally got away from the guy, I was a long way from the apartment where we lived."

"You lived with him?"

She looked at her lap and nodded. No hint of accusation hardened Trevor's tone, yet she felt one inside her. A week ago she'd never given her and Kevin's living arrangements much thought. It hadn't been a big deal in New York. Most people she knew got married when they were ready to start a family—if then. Before that, they tried on the shoes before they bought them, as Kevin liked to put it. But something about the people of this small town made her rethink so many of her decisions. Made her feel embarrassed even.

She risked a glance at Trevor's face, expecting to see traces of judgment there. Instead genuine concern was written in his kind eyes. And something else. Something she couldn't quite define.

She contemplated how much to say, and finally spoke, slowly, hopping from one phrase to another, as if she were navigating steppingstones across a pond. "That day, when that guy took my car, I was sitting there with a gun pointed at me, and it struck me that I was more terrified to go home to Kevin than I was to stay in that car." She hung her head, finding pain in remembering.

Trevor's brief, tender touch on her shoulder acted as a balm, and her throat tightened.

"It sounds to me like what you did took a great deal of courage. More than you realize maybe." His voice was soft in the graying evening light.

She'd never thought about it that way. Maybe it was true. Maybe she *was* stronger than she knew. Maybe she wasn't doomed to repeat her mother's history. Maybe she really could start all over again, here in this quiet little town. Trevor Ashlock made her want, with everything in her being, for that to be true.

A breeze threaded through the windows. She heard the doves call to one another again.

"Meg, you need to understand that I love Jack like a brother, but I don't think working for him is the best thing you could do right now. For anybody—Jack included. I hope it doesn't seem like I'm being disloyal to my friend."

She tensed slightly, trying to weigh her words. "And I hope it doesn't make me seem ungrateful to say that I think I can handle it."

He held up his palms in surrender. "I'm not telling you what to do. But I'm thinking of Wren here, too. I know you probably don't plan to stay at the inn forever, but Wren thinks a lot of you, and it would make things uncomfortable for her, too, if you were working for Jack."

Maggie wanted to kick herself. Was she so thoughtless that she hadn't seen that Trevor's deeper concern was for sweet Wren? He must think she was a first-class jerk. Well, she was. She pressed her lips into a hard line, wishing the floorboards would swallow her up. "I'm sorry, Trevor. I didn't even think of that. I'm an idiot."

That coaxed a smile to his mouth. "No you're not. You're a woman who *needs* to worry about her own life right now. I think I understand."

But he couldn't understand. He didn't know what kind of person she was, how selfish she'd been, the mistakes she'd made, the good people she'd deceived and taken advantage of in order to get to Clayburn. Not to mention the lies she was still perpetuating in order to stay there. She'd dug herself so deep a trench, she wasn't sure how she could ever climb out.

Even if she were
safe now, she had
a new reason to
keep her secrets.

Chapter Thirty-Three

The telephone poles blurred past again as they drove back into town, and Maggie's mind played a tug of war with itself. Something in her—some foolish, self-destructive part of her—wanted to tell Trevor everything. Come clean. Get it over with. Be free once and for all from all the secrets she harbored.

But she couldn't do that. She knew she couldn't. Even if she were safe now, if Clayburn really was far enough away from Kevin that she'd never have to worry about him again, now she had a new reason to keep her secrets.

Trevor. It hadn't taken her a week to know that Trevor Ashlock was a decent man. A man of honor and integrity. She'd never known anyone like him. But if she told him the truth about herself now—that she wasn't the woman he thought her to be, that even her very name was a lie—he would be out of her life so fast her head would spin.

And if he was the kind of man she thought him to be, maybe he would even warn Bart and Wren and Jackson Linder about her. He wouldn't let his friends be duped by a woman like her. She could never convince him that she'd changed. Not when she still held so many secrets from them. They would all send her packing faster than she could say "Greyhound," and who could blame them?

How could it matter so much to her—this little town that she'd never even heard of a week ago? And these people who'd somehow made her care for the first time in ages. She didn't understand it. She had changed. She was different somehow. She had a hope inside that she'd never before dared to entertain. She even found herself wondering if God had something to do with it all. If maybe He knew who she was and cared what happened to her. It frightened her in a way she couldn't explain.

She sensed Trevor's eyes on her, but she couldn't face him with these thoughts snarling her brain.

"Hey." His voice was low and gentle. "You okay?"

She kneaded her temples. "I have a lot to think about right now. I'm sorry if I'm not the best company."

"Are you worrying about . . . him? About Kevin?"

She nodded. "I'm scared." That was true, but it was so much more.

"I'll look out for you. If you hear from him, if he gives you any trouble, we'll go to the authorities. He has no rights to you whatsoever if you don't want him in your life anymore. He needs to know that."

She shook her head. "It's not that simple."

"What is it then? I know you don't really know me, but I want to help you. You don't have to be afraid. You're safe here."

Oh, how she wanted to believe that. If only it were true.

"What can I do to help? If there's anything I can do, you only have to call me. I want you to believe that."

She took a deep breath and took a plunge into trust. "Trevor, I need that job . . . with Jackson. I'll wait to talk to him for a few days. I promised Wren I'd help get the painting finished at the inn. I've got a place to sleep until then, and I can keep looking for other work in the meantime. But I—" She swallowed hard. "If I don't find anything else, I just can't run anymore. I'm too tired."

※ ❈ ※

The weariness in Meg's eyes, in the hunch of her shoulders, touched Trevor. He'd been there . . . too recently. Not for the same reasons, of course, but he thought he understood. At least in his own sorrow and seeking, he'd been surrounded by people who loved him. Meg was alone. Completely alone. How terrible that must be.

He remembered she'd mentioned a sister. Maybe that was a way he could help. Surely it would be a comfort to have family here. He turned to her, nervous about broaching the subject. "Meg, have you talked to your sister since you got here?"

She gave him a wary eye. "I sent her an e-mail. Why?"

"Could she maybe come and help you find a place to live? Help you get settled in?"

She opened her mouth, then hesitated. He could almost read her mind as she tried to decide whether to confide in him. *Please, let her trust me, Father.*

"My sister—Jenn—doesn't know where I am. Kevin is . . . not a nice person. I'm afraid of what he might do if he thought Jenn knew where to find me."

Trevor whistled under his breath. "I didn't realize it was like that. But maybe she could come here for a while? Until Kevin . . ." He wasn't sure how to fill in the blank. Did a man like that give up?

Meg shook her head. "Jenn's happy. She had a rough start, but she's married to a decent man. They struggle. For some reason, Mark has a hard time holding a job. But I think she's truly happy. After all she's been through, I wouldn't dare mess up her life. I'm happy for her, I really am." Meg's voice cracked.

"She knows you're okay though, right?"

Meg laughed, but it came out stilted and unconvincing. "*Am I okay?*"

Her sad smile tugged at him. At a place so deep he hadn't dared explore for a long time. Not since Amy.

"Only you can know that, Meg. I think you're going to be fine. But can I make a suggestion?"

She shrugged.

"Don't hide who you are. Be honest. People around here will love you for who you really are. That's one thing you don't ever need to be afraid of."

The tears came then. She tried to gulp them back, but they rolled down her cheeks in torrents. If he hadn't been driving, he might have been tempted to take her in his arms and try to soothe away her silent sobs.

Probably best he was driving.

When they got back to the inn, he hopped out of the pickup and ran around to open her door. "You gonna be okay?"

She swiped at a damp cheek, then nodded and gave him a wobbly smile.

"Why don't you go to your room and—"

She giggled. "Are you sending me to my room?"

It was good to see a little sunshine back in her smile. "I didn't mean it that way." He grinned. "Just take a little break. Take a nap or wash your face or whatever. I'll get started painting later on, and you can help when you're ready."

"Thank you, Trevor. If you don't mind, I think I'd like to go to the library before they close. I want to e-mail Jenn."

He smiled. "Good for you."

✳ ❈ ✳

Maggie hesitated, her finger hovering over the mouse, cursor pointed at the Send button. She was tempted for a split second to erase everything she'd written and crawl back into her cocoon of fear. But she made herself click the button and whispered the closest thing she knew to a prayer as she watched her e-mail disappear and the telling words pop up on the screen. *YOUR E-MAIL HAS BEEN SENT.*

She sat in front of the computer at the study carrel for several minutes, wondering if she'd done the right thing. She kept hearing Trevor's encouraging words. *Good for you. Good for you.* It seemed like a blessing.

She hoped so. She'd asked a lot of her sister. Not only did she tell her where she was staying, but she sent Jenn the information she would need to get a copy of her birth certificate and Social Security card. As soon as she had the details taken care of and the papers in her hands, she intended to come clean and start living an honest life. As flawed and confused as she was, it was too hard trying to be somebody else.

She logged off the e-mail program and pushed her chair back, vaguely aware of whispering behind her. She turned to see a tow-headed boy of about four pointing at her.

"See, I told you, Mommy." He stuck out his chin in defiance.

The woman with him balanced a toddler on her hip and reached to put one hand on the little boy's head, shushing him. Then her eyes widened. "Oh! It *is* you!" The woman had a little boy and two small girls close beside her. "You probably don't remember, but we gave you a ride last week out east of town. I'm Kaye."

"Of course." Maggie recognized the woman Trevor had called Kaye

DeVore. "I'm Meg. Thank you again. I don't know what I would have done if you hadn't come by that night."

"Oh, hey. There's always room for one more. Glad we could help." Kaye studied Meg for a minute. "You must have family in town. At least I can't imagine any *other* reason to stay in Clayburn this long."

"No . . . no family. Actually, I'm thinking of . . . moving here. I'm helping with the remodeling at the inn right now and looking for a permanent job. You don't know of anybody who needs help, do you?"

Kaye laughed her bubbly laugh. "Honey, if I could afford it, I'd hire you myself in a flash." Her gaze corralled her herd of children, and the slight bulge under her loose-fitting blouse confirmed what Trevor had said about another one on the way. Kaye shook her head. "Sorry, I don't know of anyone. I'll keep my ears open though. Are you still staying at the inn?"

Maggie nodded.

"Oh, you lucky woman." Kaye heaved a sigh. "That sounds like heaven. And don't think I haven't dreamed about checking myself in to Wren's for a few days just to get a break." She winked. "I might even let my husband come along for one night. We could get, *ahem*, reacquainted."

Maggie felt her cheeks flush, but an unfamiliar joy rose inside her. Like she'd made a new friend. Except for her infrequent phone calls to Jenn, she hadn't had a close woman friend since Kevin made her quit her job.

"Well, I wish I could help. Maybe after I get settled, I could baby-sit some night while you and your husband go out?"

Kaye brightened. "I just might take you up on that."

Before Trevor came to paint again the following afternoon, Meg slipped away for a walk in the roadside park by the river. It was peaceful there and a good place to think. As she walked under the shade of the cottonwood trees that grew along the uneven riverbank, Meg thought about her conversation with Kaye DeVore. An idea began to percolate. What if Wren had a special open house to celebrate the inn's new look, and what if she invited people from right here in Clayburn to stay the night? Advertise it as a sweethearts' getaway or whatever.

The idea wouldn't let her go, and she was still brainstorming that afternoon while she and Trevor finished putting on the last coat of paint in Wren's dining room. If they held an open house, they could lower the room prices enough to make it an affordable date for community couples. According to Trevor, the way gas prices were, a trip to Salina for dinner and a movie cost more than a night's stay at the inn.

Her roller moved faster over the walls as the ideas came until, finally, she excused herself to run and get a notepad and pen off the front desk. She brought it back to the lone table in the dining room and started scribbling furiously.

Trevor leaned out over the top of the ladder. "You writing the great American novel over there?"

She gave a smug smile. "No. But I think I just came up with a pretty good idea."

"Oh? What's that?"

"I'm not sure it's the kind of thing you'd get excited over, but—" She snapped her fingers. "But you *could* help. Would you have time to print some posters?"

"What kind of posters?"

She glanced up at him but waved a hand, dismissing him. "Never mind. I need to talk to Wren first, but I'll get back to you."

"Ohhhkay."

She ignored his feigned scowl and returned to her list. For all she knew, Wren had already tried something like this to boost business at the inn. But she couldn't help feeling more than a little excited. It just might work, and then she wouldn't feel like such a moocher staying here.

She jotted down a few more notes, folded the paper, and tucked it into her pocket. She pushed back her chair. "You want me to take over there?"

Trevor looked down at her from his perch on the ladder. "I'm fine, unless you want to trade." He surveyed the room. "We're almost finished, you know it? Another day like this and you could start on your border while I put up the trim and get the baseboards back on."

She trailed his gaze. "It's looking good, isn't it?"

"It really is. I know Wren's happy as a cat in a barn full of mice. She said you offered to help her with the decorating too."

Maggie nodded. But part of her felt a rising anxiety. The painting was nearly finished. She would probably finish the border in a couple of days. Then what?

She looked up at Maggie. "A lot of people got hurt because of my foolishness."

Chapter Thirty-Four

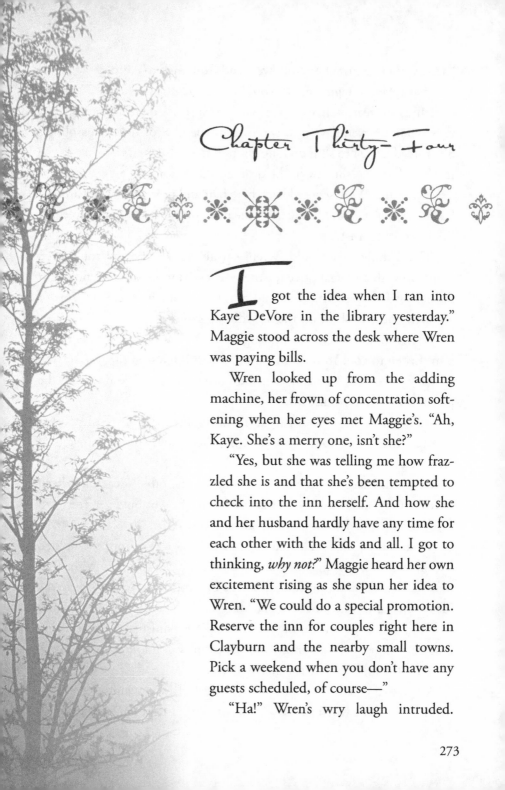

"I got the idea when I ran into Kaye DeVore in the library yesterday." Maggie stood across the desk where Wren was paying bills.

Wren looked up from the adding machine, her frown of concentration softening when her eyes met Maggie's. "Ah, Kaye. She's a merry one, isn't she?"

"Yes, but she was telling me how frazzled she is and that she's been tempted to check into the inn herself. And how she and her husband hardly have any time for each other with the kids and all. I got to thinking, *why not?*" Maggie heard her own excitement rising as she spun her idea to Wren. "We could do a special promotion. Reserve the inn for couples right here in Clayburn and the nearby small towns. Pick a weekend when you don't have any guests scheduled, of course—"

"Ha!" Wren's wry laugh intruded.

"That would be just about any weekend from here to eternity."

That egged Maggie on. "It would be a romantic getaway—a way for husbands to treat their wives, or wives to surprise their husbands. And they wouldn't even have to leave town or spend a fortune on gasoline." She forced herself to shut up long enough to study Wren's face across the front desk. What she saw in the dear, crinkled eyes encouraged her.

"Hmmm." Wren scooted back her chair and retied her apron around her ample waist. "You, know, with the price of gas right now, people just might consider that."

"Oh, I think they would, Wren! I really do. Maybe you could even come up with a special price for the weekend and include a candlelight dinner on Friday night. We could bill it as a romantic retreat—sort of an open house to show off the new dining room."

Wren's shoulders shook with laughter. "Oh, Meg, I like your enthusiasm. Listen to you! You'd think you had part interest in the inn."

Maggie colored, realizing that she'd been using "we" as if she ran the place. "I'm sorry. I didn't mean—"

"Oh, honey, no!" Wren patted her arm. "It tickles me to pieces that you feel that way about the inn. This place could use an infusion of creative energy."

Relieved, Maggie launched into some of the other ideas she'd been daydreaming about since yesterday. "And maybe we could get Trevor to print up some fliers, put them up around town?"

Wren slid the desk calendar closer and took a pen from the holder. "Well, let's look at some dates and see what we can come up with. Bart may fuss a little about putting on such a big to-do, but he'll warm to the idea eventually." She looked up at Maggie. "How long did Trevor think it would take to get the dining room completely finished? The last thing I want to do is plan this thing and have him still fiddling around with the trim the night before the guests arrive."

Maggie laughed, imagining what a kick Trevor would get out of Wren's comment when she told him tonight. "I think he's planning to be done with his part in the next couple of days. And if you're sure you don't mind letting me stay here while I'm working on the border, I can probably have it done in two or three days."

Wren snapped her fingers and started paging through the calendar. "I've got it! We'll make it an after-harvest celebration. If we get a few more of these warm days in a row, the wheat harvest will be finished in a couple of weeks. The farmers will be ready for a break, their wives will be beyond ready, and everybody will have a little money in their pockets to play with."

"That's perfect." Maggie gave a sharp clap.

Wren glanced toward the dining room. "Oh, but I've got curtains to hang and that drywall dust is all over everything—"

"I'll help, Wren. I'll be happy to help. We can make centerpieces for the tables and—" She looked around the lobby, and inspiration struck. "It'll be too hot for a fire, but we could fill the fireplace with candles. Dozens of candles! That would make such a romantic setting."

She turned to find Wren watching her with an odd smile. "What's got Miss Meg cooking up romance, I wonder? It wouldn't have anything to do with our resident carpenter, now would it?"

Maggie took in a sharp breath. "No. Oh, no. Not at all. I mean . . . Trevor's nice and all, but, well, I barely know him. We barely know each other."

Wren winked. "I knew Bart Johannsen for three whole weeks before I knew he was the one and only man for me. Sometimes you just know."

Maggie wondered if Wren knew that Trevor had told her about Jack, and Wren's youthful indiscretion. She didn't feel right asking, but—as if Wren had read Maggie's mind—she offered her story.

A shadow crossed her face. "Now don't get me wrong. Bart and I didn't rush to the altar. We took our time to really get to know each other. To make sure God had the same idea we did about our getting married. Once upon a time I didn't check it out with God."

She shook her head slowly. "No, that's not exactly right. I knew what

God thought about it from the beginning. I . . . I just didn't want to pay attention. Wanted to go my own way. I was too stubborn for my own good."

She looked up at Maggie. "A lot of people got hurt because of my foolishness."

Wren's confession nudged at Maggie's conscience. "Wren"—Maggie dropped her eyes, hoping she wouldn't get Trevor in trouble. "Trevor told me a little. He didn't think you'd mind. He said Jack . . . is your son."

Wren nodded, averting her eyes. "He's my son. But I didn't get to be his mother. Not until he was already grown. I watched him grow up from afar, and you can't know what a joy and anguish that was all at once. We were friends for a while. Until Amy—Trevor's wife's accident."

The shadow upon her countenance deepened. "It was devastating for him. And I lost him—we all lost him—over it. It's one of the sorrows of my life, Meg. It was bad enough Trevor losing Amy and Trev. Jack doesn't seem to see that he's only made Trevor's grief worse. He's become a selfish shell of a man. But of all people, I can't judge a man for being selfish. It was the root of my own mistake. I'd give anything to undo it."

"Wren! You don't have a selfish bone in your body."

"Oh, honey I do. We all do, truth be told. Only by God's grace—" She shook her head. "I've grown, I've grown." Wren seemed to be far away.

Maggie wanted to touch her, to offer some comfort. But she hesitated, not wishing to intrude on Wren's private thoughts.

After a moment, Wren came to herself and put on her old, familiar smile. "And you, Meg. I apologize if I pushed a little—you know, with you and Trevor. I fancy myself a matchmaker sometimes." She gave a musical chuckle. "That's gotten me into a bit of trouble from time to time, but I've had a little success too. Don't think I haven't. In fact, you can talk to Kaye and Douglas DeVore about that."

Maggie laughed, relieved to have Wren back to her cheerful self. "Really?"

Wren winked. "Those kids of theirs—I think there's half a dozen of 'em now—they practically think of me as Grandma."

Watching Wren, Maggie's whole being was bathed in warmth. Knowing that this wonderful, kindhearted woman had made mistakes in her past—the same kinds of mistakes Maggie had made—yet managed to find such joy in life . . . it gave her hope.

And look how people loved Wren. It was enough to make Maggie believe she might someday unearth the same kind of grace Wren found.

Wren moved around the desk, the open calendar in hand. "Well, let's go find Bart and see if we can sell him on your little idea."

Maggie laughed. "Oh, it's not little, Wren. I haven't told you the half of it yet."

Wren chuckled, and Maggie followed her up the stairs, feeling happier than she could ever remember.

Meg and Wren
whirled around and
glared at him like
a couple of crabby
schoolmarms.

Chapter Thirty-Five

revor balanced a knee against the ladder and nailed another section of molding into place where the wall met the ceiling. He worked to the background music of Wren and Meg chattering below him in the dining room. If their banter didn't tickle him so much, it might have annoyed the life out of him. They cackled away like two keyed-up hens, and they'd been at it for almost a week—ever since Meg had come up with the idea for some kind of after-harvest celebration at the inn. A romantic getaway for couples.

"We could make little centerpieces for each table," Meg was telling Wren. "Something simple, but maybe with little sprigs of wheat, to go with the harvest theme."

Wren squealed her approval. "Oh, yes, Meg! Bart's flower garden should have some good things blooming by then.

Daisies for sure and maybe some zinnias for color." Wren sounded more excited than Trevor had heard her in a while. Meg was good for Bart and Wren.

She was good for him too. He couldn't remember when he'd last enjoyed someone's company the way he did Meg's. He raked a dusty hand through his hair. Well, of course he could. *Amy.*

But Meg made him feel alive again. Ready to go on with his life. He'd started waking up in the morning looking forward to the day and coming home at night to sleep like the proverbial log. He had watched her, day by day, move closer to the truth, closer to understanding God's love for her. How he longed for her to finally take that step into the Father's arms.

Meg twirled around, eying the room as if she were planning to remodel. "Could we get a few more tables? So we could have romantic little tables for two."

"Good grief, child! How many people do you think we're going to rope into this event?"

"I think you're going to have to turn people away and plan for a second weekend."

Wren let out a belly laugh. "Well, I doubt that, Miss Meg, but I sure like the way you think." She went to the windows that overlooked Main Street. "We'll get the curtains back up as soon as Trevor's done in here, but it's going to be dark outside when we have the dinner. I wonder what we could do with the windows?"

Trevor hollered down from his perch on the ladder, "You could put up Christmas lights."

Meg and Wren whirled around and glared at him like a couple of crabby schoolmarms.

"You know, the little colored lights that twinkle." He made a twinkling motion with his fingers. "Like you put on the Christmas tree?"

As if on cue, Wren and Meg exchanged identical looks—expressions anyone else would have taken to be contempt—or worse. But he knew better and fought back a smile.

Wren propped her hands on her hips and bored holes in him with her eyes. "Listen, buster, you stick with the construction and let us girls handle the decorating."

He reined in his laughter and offered a sharp salute. "Yes ma'am."

Meg dissolved in giggles, and Wren chuckled along with her. They lowered their voices, whispering together.

He stopped hammering to catch Meg's comment.

"You know . . ." She glanced his direction.

He pretended to be preoccupied with fitting a piece of molding flush with the ceiling.

"Don't tell Trevor I said so"—Meg put her head close to Wren's— "but the Christmas lights aren't a half-bad idea."

"Hey," he shouted, feeling triumphant. "I heard that!"

More giggling. More whispering. He rolled his eyes—not that anyone noticed—and went back to work. These two were on a mission, and apparently he wasn't invited.

※ ⚛ ※

Maggie woke to a low rumble on Main Street outside her window. She squinted at the clock, rolled out of bed, and hurried to the window. A parade of mammoth machines—some type of monster tractor—rolled past, followed by several dump trucks and the usual weekday traffic of pickups bringing up the rear. Must be the harvest crews she'd heard so much talk about.

She dressed quickly and went out to the hall to see what was going on but stopped short of the lobby when she saw Bart and Wren, heads bent over the desk where Wren had been paying bills yesterday. They seemed oblivious to the commotion outside. At first Maggie thought they were praying, and she back-pedaled quietly out of sight. But she listened to their low voices for a moment before she became aware they were discussing business matters.

Maybe Wren was still trying to win Bart over to the idea of the open house. Bart had listened politely when she and Wren talked to him about it last week, but Maggie could tell he wasn't completely convinced.

She turned and started quietly back to her room, but her ears pricked when she heard her name. She stopped and paused in the hallway, just out of sight.

"It makes no difference to me, Wren." Bart's newspaper rattled as he unfolded it. "You're the one who's always wanting to do things by the book. I don't know . . . does the IRS recognize the bartering system?"

Maggie listened to the tinkle of the spoon in Wren's tea, a morning melody that had become as familiar to Maggie as the clock ticking on her nightstand.

"I don't know, and I'd just as soon not find out." Wren lowered her voice, and Maggie had to strain to hear her next words. "And don't you go looking it up either, Mr. Encyclopedia. The IRS can say what they like, but if I want to have a sweet young woman as a guest in my home, I'll have her, and I'll have her for as long as I please."

Wren meant her! Maggie was touched almost to tears.

"Suit yourself, Wren. She's a sweet girl, and I have nothing against her staying here. I just don't want you second-guessing yourself if you have to fudge a little when it comes time to do our taxes."

"You know I obey the law to a T, but the government has no business telling me who I can or can't have as a personal guest in my own home."

Maggie could picture Wren, puffed up like a banty hen, hands on her hips, elbows flapping like wings.

"That may be," Bart said, "but you may think otherwise if your suspicions are correct and this girl is on the run from the law. Or worse."

Maggie stifled a gasp at that. Wren thought she was some kind of criminal . . . and still was defending her right to have Maggie as a guest in her home? It didn't make sense.

Maggie slunk back to the door of her room, deeply troubled at the thought that poor Wren might be losing sleep worrying that she was harboring a fugitive.

Maggie stood with her hand on the doorknob, feeling guilty that she'd overheard, and now feeling the need to hide out for a while. She'd have to come out to breakfast and act as if she hadn't heard words that weren't meant for her ears. More pretending. She pushed the door open.

Jasper meowed behind her and zipped into her room before she could close the door. Meg started to shoo him out but instead lifted the big tabby into her arms and snuggled against the softness of his fur. A wave of longing for her own cat overwhelmed her. She wondered if Kevin had gotten rid of Buttons by now. Maybe she could find a way for Jenn to get the cat out of the apartment.

No. Of course not. She dismissed the idea as quickly as it had come. She wasn't thinking straight. If Jennifer came to get the cat from Kevin, it would be a dead giveaway that she knew where Maggie was. She couldn't risk it no matter how much she missed Buttons. Besides, she didn't have enough money for her next meal, let alone to transport a cat all the way to Kansas. And where would she put him if she got him here? Jasper had the run of the inn, and Maggie was already pressing her luck with Wren and Bart. Especially now.

She thought again of the conversation she'd overheard. A heavy realization washed over her. She *had* to tell Wren and Bart the truth—before she buried herself so deep in lies that she couldn't find her way to the surface.

Whole hog? She was
even starting to think
like a hayseed!

Chapter Thirty-Six

The Fourth of July was just around the corner, but Maggie barely had time to notice the town gearing up for celebration as she and Wren worked tirelessly on the plans for the open house they'd dubbed Operation Wren's Nest. Bart was apparently on board whole hog now.

Whole hog? Maggie gave a little laugh. She was even starting to think like a hayseed!

She sobered quickly, though, remembering she'd promised herself to find an opportunity to confess her situation to the elderly couple. But as busy as things were, it seemed more and more unlikely that this would happen before the open house.

Wheat harvest was in full swing around the countryside and, in the midst of all the planning, Wren's Nest put up a crew of wheat harvesters—custom cutters, Bart called them—in the inn for three nights.

"Those guys are the salt of the earth," Wren said of the harvest workers who came up from Texas. It was the crew's second night to stay, and she and Maggie had just put two huge pans of cinnamon rolls in the oven for the next morning's breakfast. "But I'm none too happy about all the dirt and stinky sweat they tracked in with them last night. Did you see them? They were filthy."

Before Maggie could answer, Bart appeared in the arched doorway. "The dirt on those boys smells like money to me, Mrs. Johannsen, and you'd best not let the good Lord hear your griping." He ducked away as quickly as he'd popped into the doorway.

Maggie laughed at his impromptu speech.

But Wren's face fell, and she wiped her hands on her apron and went out to the lobby. Maggie heard her give Bart a kiss, and then their whiffling breaths as they embraced. "You are right as usual, Bart. And forgive me, Lord. I take back every word."

From where she was cleaning up in the kitchen, Maggie couldn't see the couple, but she knew from experience that Wren was looking up at the ceiling, as though God were perched in the rafters, waiting to hear from her.

Maggie was still getting used to Bart and Wren's open affection for each other and their easy way with God. They didn't talk to the Almighty as if it were some hocus-pocus superstitious thing, the way some of her friends in New York did. Bart and Wren treated God as if He were right there in the room with them. Sometimes she was almost convinced He was. It gave her pause.

Since the day she'd overheard Wren's suspicions that "Meg" was running from the law, she'd determined that while she may be withholding the whole truth from them, she was not going to stack any new lies on top of her old ones. She'd had to use some creative diversion tactics to change the subject a few times, and she'd slipped up a time or two—old habits weren't easy to break—but she was learning to be honest with these people who had been so kind to her. And to be honest with herself.

She'd done her best to extend her new honesty-is-the-best-policy motto to Trevor as well, but it proved a little more difficult with him. Maybe because, as the days went by, she found herself caring more and more what Trevor Ashlock thought.

Trevor had finally completed the remodeling job—about the same time she finished painting the border. Wren seemed pleased with both their efforts, and the newly finished dining room did look beautiful, especially as Wren and Maggie gave it the finishing touches.

She'd been sad to see Trevor's work on the room—and thus, her excuse to spend time with him each night—come to an end. But she'd worried for no reason. Trevor continued to report to Wren for duty almost every evening after he got off work at the print shop, helping with whatever projects Maggie and Wren managed to come up with for him.

In the evenings, just before dark, she and Trevor took walks along the banks of the Smoky Hill River in the roadside park. He regaled her with stories of his boyhood growing up along the river, and through him, Maggie got to know the people of Clayburn.

Somewhere in the midst of all the hours they spent together, Maggie began to be convinced that Trevor Ashlock was exactly who he appeared to be. Unlike Kevin, Trevor seemed to have no need of controlling her or dictating her plans. Twinges of guilt overtook her when she realized how open and honest he always was with her.

Though she'd adopted the same policy of "no new lies" with Trevor that she had with the Johannsens, she had yet to tell him her whole story. She shared brief memories of her childhood, the happier times, testing the waters of Trevor's acceptance. He hadn't let her drown either. For the life of her, she couldn't understand what was holding her back. She suspected Trevor knew that she hadn't been honest with him about who she was. Still, he was ever patient with her, never pushing her to tell more than she chose to reveal.

She felt certain Kevin had all but forgotten about her by now. And she longed for—and at the same time, dreaded—the day when she could knock on his apartment door, pick up her belongings (including Buttons), and sever all ties to that part of her life.

She had happily taken on the job of cleaning the inn's guest rooms top to bottom. At Wren's insistence, they did a spring cleaning that Wren said was long overdue. Despite the "filthy" custom cutting crew, Maggie couldn't see that any of the rooms had a speck of dust in them. But she wasn't about to argue. Bart and Wren insisted she was earning room, board, and a little spending money, and Maggie was in no position to dispute them.

Yesterday afternoon Bart had taken Wren and Maggie to Salina to shop for supplies, and today Wren was stitching new curtains for the dining-room windows on her little black Singer sewing machine. One set was finished and hanging inside the freshly trimmed window sills. The red-and-white-toweling fabric looked crisp and fresh against the golden walls. Maggie's gaze panned the room, remembering what it had looked like before.

Now, the room simply oozed charm. The twining border she'd painted over the archway and across each transom picked up the pattern in Wren's antique transferware dishes. Newly framed hen and rooster prints on the walls completed the décor.

At Trevor's suggestion, Jackson Linder had done the framing on the prints. Wren had been the one to talk to Jack, and by her jovial humming the morning she'd brought home the framed pieces, Maggie guessed Wren was pleased with the outcome of her visit with her son. But Wren hadn't offered any details, and Maggie hadn't felt right asking.

Maggie had called Jack after they'd begun planning Operation Wren's Nest in earnest and told him she was working full-time at the inn for now. Not another word had been said about her going to work at the gallery. She was grateful, not wanting to interfere with the tentative peace that seemed to be under construction between Wren and her son.

The front doorbells clanked in a way that Maggie had come to recognize as Trevor's. She smiled. The man never just opened a door. He made an entrance. And it always made her heart turn a funny little flutter.

"Where is everybody?" Trevor's voice was followed by the sound of the ceramic cookie jar lid being lifted.

"Where do you think?" Wren hollered, giving Maggie a knowing wink. "I told you I shouldn't have left those cookies out."

Trevor appeared in the archway munching on a cookie. Maggie touched Wren's arm, then pointed at Trevor. "I have dibs on him this afternoon, okay?"

Wren looked up from her sewing machine. "What do you have up your sleeve?"

"I want to get everything sketched out for the poster. If we don't get those printed and distributed this weekend, it's going to be too late for anyone to make plans."

"You're probably right about that." Wren winked again. "Okay. He's all yours."

Trevor's eyes bounced from Maggie to Wren and back. "Um . . . excuse me? Do I have nothing to say about my own fate?"

"Nope." Wren and Maggie spoke in unison.

Trevor burst out laughing and made a show of skulking off to the lobby for another cookie, but Maggie saw the smile that quirked his mouth. It warmed her to her toes.

He was back in a few seconds, cookie crumbs sticking to his lower lip. Maggie wanted to reach up and brush them off but stopped herself before she embarrassed them both.

He gave her a smile that almost made her think he knew what she'd been thinking. He pulled a chair out from one of the tables and straddled it backward. "So what did you have in mind for this poster?"

Maggie ran to get her sketchpad and sat down across from him at the table. She showed him the design she had drawn up. "I couldn't remember the names of a couple of fonts I was thinking about. It would look better if I could have done it on the computer."

"Well, hey, we can go over to the print shop if you want to."

"Really? That would be great."

"Sure." He rose and returned the chair to its rightful place in one smooth motion. "If we get it done tonight, I can put it on the press tomorrow. I've got a couple of jobs that have priority tomorrow, but we can get this on after lunch. It shouldn't take long."

A little thrill rose in her. She remembered what it had felt like back when she was working and had a fun project on the board.

She put a hand on Wren's shoulder. "We're going to abandon you. Is that okay?"

Wren looked up from her sewing and waved them off. "You go on. I've got my work cut out for me here."

Maggie started for the door, but Wren swiveled her chair and abandoned the curtain on the sewing machine. "Now don't forget to say that we're serving dinner *and* breakfast."

"I won't."

Wren held up a finger. "Oh, and be sure and put that it's a *candlelight* dinner."

Maggie tapped the sketchbook under her arm and hid a smile. "It's all right here, Wren. Everything we talked about."

"Don't wait up," Trevor called, opening the lobby door with a conspiratorial grin and steering Maggie out with a hand on her back.

"Now don't you keep her out too late, Trevor. I've been working her too hard as it is."

Trevor rolled his eyes and Maggie smiled up at him. She had never felt so much like she belonged. Like she had a place that was truly home.

If only this feeling could last forever.

Trevor realized that whatever news Meg had received might be the thing that took her away from Clayburn.

Chapter Thirty-Seven

Trevor flipped the light switch in his office and fired up his computer. "You want something to drink?"

Meg stood by the door, arms folded around her sketchbook, hugging it to her as if it were a security blanket.

"Maybe later." She gave a nervous laugh. "Knowing me, I'd probably spill it on the keyboard."

"Oh, no." He grinned. "That's Mason's job."

"Mason?"

"The college kid who works for me. He's a klutz with a capital K. No machine is safe if Mason Brunner is within fifty feet of it." He pulled out his desk chair and patted the seat. "Here, have a seat. I'll get you started."

She slipped into the chair while he grabbed a stool and brought it over to perch beside her. He leaned across her and clicked to open the Photoshop program and set up a new document. "You've worked with this program before, right?"

She looked up at him over her shoulder with a little cringe. "It's been a while."

"It'll come back to you."

She spread her sketchbook out on the desk to her left and tentatively copied the first lines of information onto the computer file. "Let's see . . . I choose fonts here?" Her finger hovered over the mouse.

He peered over her shoulder so he could see the screen. "Yep. And if you want to change the size, go here." He pointed.

"Oh, yes. I remember." She typed, glancing from her notes to the screen. After a few minutes, she glanced up at him, beaming, wonderment in her voice. "You're right. It *is* all coming back."

"All right if I go take care of a couple of things in the pressroom?"

"I think so."

"Holler if you get stuck."

She gave a distracted nod, and sat with head hunched over the keyboard, clicking, repositioning the cursor.

When he came back ten minutes later, he stared at the impressive graphic design on the computer screen. She'd somehow created a whimsical, geometrical likeness of Wren's Nest, artfully arranging the lettering around it. Her choice of fonts was perfect, and the result was eye-catching and colorful. "Hey, that looks great!"

She rolled her chair back and squinted at her work. "It turned out pretty nice, didn't it? I haven't forgotten as much as I feared. It's kind of like riding a bicycle." She giggled. "Well, I guess it is. I haven't done that for a long time either. This is kind of fun though."

"Well, let me know when you have something ready to go to the printer. We'll run a couple of tests on the printer in here before we fire up the big dog."

"I'm just about finished. Let me tweak a couple of things, then would you take a look and see if I missed anything? Or if you want to change any of the colors?"

He held up both hands, palms out. "No way. You're the artist. I'm just the grease monkey here."

Forty-five minutes later, she slid back from the desk and moved aside so he could see the results of her labor.

"Incredible. Let's print out a copy and see what we've got."

She moved aside to let him into the desk chair. Once he was seated, she slid onto the stool beside him, watching him work. Her closeness disturbed him—in a very pleasant way. She smelled of paint, and Wren's, and something wonderfully flowery and feminine. Her shampoo? He was struggling to resist the urge to get close enough to breathe in a whiff, when the printer clunked on and chugged through its warmup.

She followed him to the printer in the corner, and they hovered above the machine, waiting to see the first poster roll out.

They stood, not speaking for several minutes. The printer churned and whirred, but the paper moved through at a frustratingly slow pace. "It takes awhile to print color," he explained, moving away from the printer. "Hey, do you want to use the Internet? Check your e-mail or anything?"

Her face lit. "I can get online here?"

"Sure. I'll show you." He studied her for a moment. "Have you . . . heard back from your sister?"

Meg shook her head, the light dimming in her eyes.

He was instantly sorry he'd said anything. "Well, maybe there'll be something there tonight?" He prayed he wasn't offering her false hope.

He connected to the Internet and opened a browser, then offered Meg his chair. She sat down and typed something. He walked back to the printer to give her some privacy.

After a minute, he saw her eyebrows lift. She sucked in a short breath and a soft smile illuminated her face.

"Did you get something?"

Her smile widened as she looked his way. "Yes. It's from Jenn."

"Great."

He watched the expressions on her face change like a sunset—from expectant, rosy glow, to dim uncertainty, to something he couldn't quite interpret. "Is everything okay?"

She looked up as though she'd forgotten he was in the room. "I-I think so."

She didn't offer more. He pointed toward the front of the shop. "I'm going to the other office for a minute. I'll be right back."

He left his office door slightly ajar and let himself in the front of the shop. With the front office darkened, he could see Meg's silhouette through the glass that separated the spaces. The blinds were down, but canted at an angle that made the interior of his office visible. He noticed that Meg's shoulders had slumped a bit. She must have heard from the sister she obviously loved. Had the e-mail held bad news?

With a start, Trevor realized that whatever news Meg had received might be the thing that took her away from Clayburn. Away from him.

He inhaled the scents of the office—ink, paper, dust. They usually invigorated him.

He'd only known Meg for a few weeks, but somehow she'd come to feel like a lifelong friend. That, in spite of the fact she had yet to share her deepest thoughts with him. In truth, their relationship had been rather lopsided, with him doing most of the talking and her, well, keeping secrets from him. He knew that, yet was confident she would reveal the truth to him in due time.

Oddly, spending time with Meg these last few weeks, he'd thought a lot about Amy. He didn't dare tell Meg that, of course. Not exactly the way to a girl's heart. And he could probably never make Meg understand that it had been a good thing—his thinking about Amy.

He'd done some letting go over the past few days that he should have done a long time ago. Even though Amy had been gone for two years, he hadn't said good-bye until now. Not really.

Funny. As much as he anguished over losing his son, he'd finally allowed room in his heart for the possibility of another child—another little boy or girl—to love someday. He'd opened his heart to the kids at the day-care center.

But until Meg, he hadn't been able to clear a space in his heart for another woman. How Meg Anders had managed to do just that, he wasn't sure. It scared him a little because he couldn't say for certain that she would still be in his life a year from now—or even a week from now. It wasn't easy to wait. To be patient while God worked in Meg's life.

But he had a certain feeling . . . a good one.

He'd forgotten what this peace felt like. This overwhelming sense of well-being. He prayed that someday soon he could share it with the woman sitting in his office chair. He wanted her to know how wonderful it felt.

Maggie prepared to pull away, ready to face the verdict she knew she deserved.

Chapter Thirty-Eight

eg?" Maggie heard Wren's voice through the door of her room and hurried to open it. Wren stood there with a funny look on her face.

"Wren? What's the matter?"

"There's someone on the phone asking for a Maggie Anderson. You wouldn't . . . know anything about that, would you?"

Maggie's breath caught and heat seared her cheeks. She avoided Wren's eyes. "Who is it?"

Wren shook her head. "She wouldn't say."

Maggie followed Wren to the lobby and picked up the receiver from where Wren had laid it on the desk.

"I'll be in the kitchen," Wren mouthed, pointing through the archway.

Maggie put the phone to her ear. "Hello?"

"Maggie!"

"Jenn! Is everything okay?"

"Yeah, everything's fine. But why did that woman call you Meg? She almost hung up on me."

Maggie sighed. She'd never told Jenn that she was living under an assumed name. It was only the other night at Trevor's office that she e-mailed Jenn the address of the inn so she could write to her and, hopefully, send her replacement identification. Jenn must have looked up the inn's phone number.

Oh, what must Wren be thinking right now? Maggie had some serious explaining to do when she got off the phone.

Turning her back to the dining room, she lowered her voice. "Why are you calling, Jenn? You're sure everything is okay? Oh, it's so good to hear your voice."

"You too. What's going on, Maggie? What are you doing there? You said you were safe. But why are you—"

"I *am* safe, Jenn." Maggie could tell her sister was near tears, and she was afraid she might break down too. She twisted the phone cord around her wrist. "It's too much to explain right now. But I'm fine. I really am. Bart and Wren are wonderful. But they don't know . . ." Where did she begin to untangle her lies? "I haven't told them everything yet. I'm sort of . . . going by a different name now."

"Why?" Jenn's voice rose an octave, and Maggie held the phone away from her ear for a second.

"I was scared. I just wanted to start over." She moved as far away as the phone's cord would allow. "I was afraid Kevin would find me and—"

"I think he's trying, Maggie."

Her blood went cold. "What? What makes you think that?"

"Mark went to try and pick up your stuff."

Maggie gasped. "He did? Oh, Jenn, you should both stay away from him. It's too dangerous. What happened?" She held her breath, waiting for Jenn's response.

"Mark said Kevin tried to trick him into telling him where you were."

"He didn't say anything, did he?" She held her breath.

"No. Of course not. He doesn't have a clue. But he practically threw Mark out of the apartment. Said he got rid of your stuff. Mark didn't believe him, but he didn't want to push it."

Maggie let herself exhale. "Stay away from him, Jenn. I mean it. There's nothing there I can't live without."

"What about your ID? Aren't you going to need your license and birth certificate and all that for your job?"

"I'll worry about it when I have to. The only thing Kevin has that I even care about is Buttons. And it's not worth—"

Jenn squealed. "I *have* Buttons, Maggie! He's here!"

"You do? But how?" She didn't dare to believe it was true.

Jenn gave a little laugh. "Kevin followed Mark to the car and tossed Buttons in the backseat."

"No!"

"Yes. And you know how much Mark loves cats. You're lucky he didn't dump him on the freeway on the way home."

Maggie smiled at the sarcasm in her sister's voice, then beamed as the realization came over her. *Buttons is safe.* She wanted to hug someone. "Oh, Jenn, thank you! And tell Mark I owe him big time."

"Oh, believe me, he knows. To tell you the truth, I think the little guy is kind of growing on him." Jenn's giggle was contagious.

They talked for a few minutes until Maggie heard Wren in the kitchen. "I really have to go now, Jenn. But I'm glad you called. It's good to hear your voice."

"You too. Stay safe." Silence stretched across the miles of wire connecting them. "I love you, Mag."

Maggie touched a hand to her heart. "I love you, too, Jenn."

She placed the receiver in its cradle and squeezed her eyes shut against the tears. She and Jenn had never spoken those words to each other before—not as adults anyway. She'd written it in letters and had always known Jenn loved her . . . and assumed her sister knew she returned her love. But it felt good to say it.

Maggie took a deep breath. Now. To deal with Wren.

She went to the dining room and stood under the archway, wondering if Wren would even want to talk to her. "Wren?"

Wren turned from the sink where she was up to her elbows in suds. Was that disappointment in her eyes?

Maggie hung her head. "Can I talk to you?"

"I wish you would, honey." Wren dried her hands and came around the counter to the dining area. She slid out a chair at one of the tables and patted the chair beside her.

"Oh, Wren." Maggie melted into tears and slumped against Wren's softness. "I'm so sorry."

Wren put her arms around her, the way she had the day she'd come back from the bus station, and let her cry. "There, there." She cooed as if Maggie were a little girl again. "There's nothing so bad you can't tell me about it."

"I'm a big fake! A big fat fake."

Wren chuckled in a way that made Maggie feel loved rather than chastised. "Fat is one thing you're not. Now what is it, Meg? What are you running from?"

She collected herself and sniffed, not even knowing where to begin. "My whole life here in Clayburn has been a lie, Wren." The words trickled out at first, one confession at a time, as she told Wren about the carjacking and her escape from Kevin Bryson. "This sweet old woman gave me money . . . a lot of money. And I took it. It's how I paid for my first night here. I don't even know how to find her to pay her back."

"Maybe we can find her," Wren said softly.

"You don't understand. It's not just her. I lied my way across the country. I told people whatever I thought would get me a ride, or a meal. I didn't mean to lie, Wren. It sort of *happened,* then I couldn't stop. I've lied to you! And Bart . . . Trevor . . . *everybody*! About so many things. Everything, really." She dissolved in tears again.

She told Wren about fleeing the convenience store, running out on the Blakelys, and spending the night on the playground in Kansas City, terrified the police were after her, but more terrified that Kevin might find her.

The trickle of her confession became a torrent and, one by one, her lies were exposed and washed away. When all Maggie's tears had dried, Wren knew everything. *Everything*. Taking in a deep breath, Maggie prepared to pull away, ready to face a verdict she knew she deserved.

But Wren wouldn't let her go. Her arms only tightened around Maggie. And in that moment, Maggie understood the old adage about the truth setting a person free.

She doubted he
would ever want to
see her again after she
told him what a lie
she'd been living.

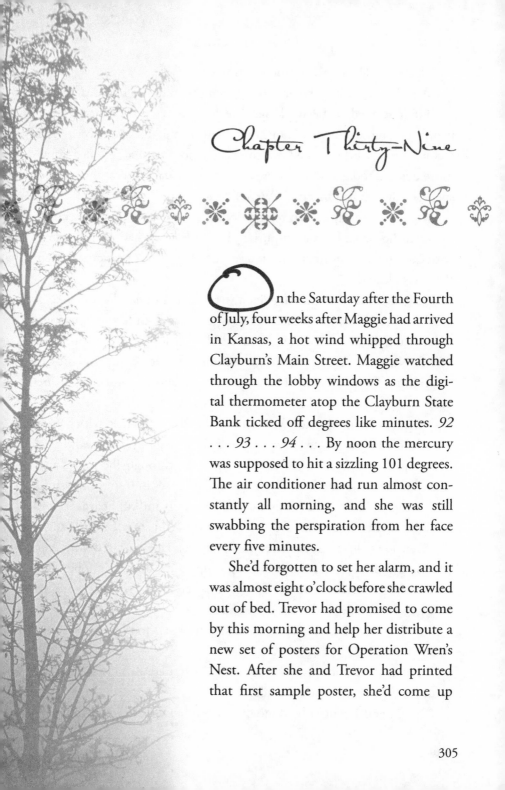

Chapter Thirty-Nine

On the Saturday after the Fourth of July, four weeks after Maggie had arrived in Kansas, a hot wind whipped through Clayburn's Main Street. Maggie watched through the lobby windows as the digital thermometer atop the Clayburn State Bank ticked off degrees like minutes. *92 . . . 93 . . . 94 . . .* By noon the mercury was supposed to hit a sizzling 101 degrees. The air conditioner had run almost constantly all morning, and she was still swabbing the perspiration from her face every five minutes.

She'd forgotten to set her alarm, and it was almost eight o'clock before she crawled out of bed. Trevor had promised to come by this morning and help her distribute a new set of posters for Operation Wren's Nest. After she and Trevor had printed that first sample poster, she'd come up with a clever idea for an all-out ad campaign.

"A real blitz, huh?" Trevor teased when she told him her idea.

But it seemed to be working. The first week's posters had gotten people talking, wondering about this event coming to Wren's Nest. The second week, she'd switched out the posters for one that revealed a few more details. Today's posters were a carefully guarded secret that would spell out the whole Operation Wren's Nest event.

Wren had already gotten reservations for five rooms the weekend of the open house and many inquiries. The little town had been buzzing with questions about the mysterious event. Wren was ecstatic, and even Bart was pleased.

Now, at nine o'clock, Maggie was rushing around the inn like a cyclone. They'd had guests last night—the tail end of the wheat-harvest crews—and Bart was checking out the last group at the front desk. Wren's Nest had taken reservations for another two rooms tonight—a vacationing family of six. That meant lots of laundry and beds to be made.

Maggie went looking for Wren to see what she could help with before she left to hang the posters. *Please, please, Trevor, don't get here early.*

She gathered dirty coffee cups as she went through the lobby and carried them to the kitchen. Wren was on her knees in front of the sink, working to replace the old knobs on all the drawers and cupboards. "Hey, those look nice, Wren. Can I finish up for you? I'm sorry I overslept."

Wren looked up, screwdriver in hand, her face beet red with her efforts. "I think I'm just about to wrap it up. Some of these old handles are practically rusted through." She gave the cupboard she was working on a good *thump* with the flat of her hand.

"Well, please don't make yourself sick working too hard. You look tired."

Wren laughed and waved Maggie off. "I *am* tired. But I've been tired before and survived to tell the tale."

"Trevor and I should be done by noon or so. I'll make up the beds when I get back. How about if I run by the café and bring home some salads for lunch? My treat."

Wren had handed her a fifty-dollar bill yesterday morning— payment for her work on Operation Wren's Nest—and Maggie was feeling a little guilty. She had protested that room and board was more than enough for what she'd done, but she hadn't pushed the argument too far. It felt good to have a little money in her pocket again—money she'd earned by the sweat of her brow.

It continued to amaze her how she'd managed to live for almost a month with barely any cash. With her cozy room here at Wren's, her meals paid for, and small-town life providing all the entertainment she could have hoped for, she had everything she needed.

She'd picked up another outfit and a pair of sandals at a second-hand store in Salina last week and had even splurged on a set of cheap watercolors the last time she and Wren were in Salina for groceries. She felt wealthy. "What do you think . . . salads? And will Bart be here for lunch?"

"No, he's eating with his buddies at the senior center today. And you save your money, Meg. There's leftovers in the fridge from last night. If you don't mind, we can just eat that chicken cold. Won't even have to turn on the oven. There's plenty, so tell Trevor to stay if he wants."

Maggie smiled. "We'll see. Now why don't you take a break and let me finish that?"

Wren clutched the edge of the counter and hauled herself up. "Why don't we both take a break? When's Trevor coming by?"

Maggie glanced at the clock. "Any time now."

"Then sit." Wren pointed to the table.

They plopped into chairs at the small breakfast table and sat in silence for a few minutes, truly resting. Maggie let her gaze wander around the room, enjoying its charm, remembering how she and Trevor had gotten to know each other as they painted these walls. She was amazed at the transformation the space had undergone in the weeks she'd been living at the inn. It somehow made her feel at home here, to have been a part of the process.

Her gaze came to rest on Wren, and she smiled across the table, remembering the other night when she'd spilled all her secrets. "I love this room." Somehow she couldn't quite say the words yet, but what she really meant was that she loved *Wren*. And Bart. And her new life here in Clayburn. What a burden had been lifted from her that night she'd confessed everything to Wren.

Now if only she could get up the courage to come clean with Trevor. Wren had assured her that he would understand. That he would forgive her.

Maggie thought he probably *would* forgive her. But she also doubted he would ever want to see her again after she told him what a lie she'd been living. That was a possibility she simply couldn't face right now. She'd used the open house as an excuse, promising herself she'd tell him afterward. Things were too hectic now. Especially with guests in the inn.

As she did every week, Wren invited Maggie to church the next day. Wren never pressured her or made her feel guilty when she declined the invitation, but now that she'd confessed to Wren, she felt even guiltier— or maybe *convicted* was a better word. She really should go, out of respect for Bart and Wren. But she couldn't seem to muster the courage. She didn't think God struck people with lightning for sins like she'd committed, but she didn't exactly want to put Him to the test either.

She frowned and rubbed her temples as another twinge of fear nipped at her subconscious. *Jenn.* She and Jenn had exchanged several e-mails since the day her sister had called Wren's. Jenn seemed genuinely happy for her, and the two of them had even started dreaming about Jenn and Mark making the trip to see her in Clayburn. She dared to dream that she might be able to get Buttons to Kansas after all.

But it had been five days now since she'd heard from Jenn. She checked her e-mail every day—either at the library or at Trevor's office, and there hadn't been anything but junk in her in-box. But Jenn had mentioned in her last e-mail that they were having some problems with the computers in the office where she worked and were having to revamp their security systems. That was probably why she hadn't heard anything.

Movement outside the dining-room window shook her from her reverie. Trevor's pickup pulled into a parking space on Main Street. His athletic form climbed down from the cab.

Wren flashed a smile. "I'd say by the look in your eyes that Trevor Ashlock just drove up."

Maggie returned her smile.

Wren patted Maggie's hand. "Have fun, sweetie."

"Thanks, Wren. Be back in a couple of hours."

Hand me that tape, will you?" Trevor pinned a poster to the window with his forearm and reached behind him, hand outstretched.

Instead of handing him the tape, Maggie gave him five, then laughed at the goofy look he threw her over his shoulder. She ripped off a piece of the clear tape and handed it to him.

He secured the upper corners of the poster to the glass. "Does that look straight to you?"

She took a few steps back and squinted. It was hard to tell with half a dozen other posters hung all helter-skelter and vying for space in the café's front window, but she gave Trevor a thumbs-up.

He smoothed the paper and taped the last corner in place before turning toward her with a weary sigh. "Okay . . . where to next?"

"What's the matter?" She put her hands on her hips and winked, doing her best "hayseed" imitation. "Are you plumb tuckered out again?"

He flashed a grin and rubbed his fist over the top of her head as if he were polishing it.

"Hey, you! Cut it out." She ducked out from under his hand and fished her list out of her pocket, laughing. This was turning out to be a fun job.

They'd driven out to the businesses on the highway that had allowed them to post the ads, and now this side of the street was finished. She checked off the names on her list and pointed up the street, feeling like a guide on an African safari.

They crossed Main and walked past the inn. Seeing Wren inside, Trevor tapped on the window as they went by. Wren waved from the dining room.

Maggie waved back. "I sure hope we get a good turnout for Wren's sake."

"Didn't you say you already have a bunch of reservations?"

"Seven now. To fill the inn, we'd need four more couples—five if you count my room."

Trevor looked askance at her. "You might have to give up your room?"

She shrugged. "I guess if we get enough reservations."

"Where would you go?"

"I don't know . . . but it would almost be worth it to have a sell-out crowd."

They walked past two vacant storefronts and an antique shop that had declined the posters. Before Maggie realized it, they were standing in front of the door to Jackson Linder's gallery. Maggie turned to look up at Trevor, not sure how he'd feel about seeing Jack.

"Jack let you hang a poster?"

She nodded. "I think maybe things have simmered down a little between him and Wren. Do you want me to take care of this one?"

He shook his head. "No. I'll go with you."

Jack hadn't been in the gallery the first week the posters went up, and last week he'd been there, but a customer came in at the same time Maggie brought the poster, and he called his mother out to talk to

Maggie. Twila Linder seemed a little cool toward Maggie, and she had wondered if the woman was upset because she hadn't come to work for Jackson. Or maybe it was because she was a friend of Wren's.

Today Jack was behind the counter. He looked up when they came in, and a shadow darkened his face when he saw Trevor. But he stood and came to greet them. He seemed altogether sober.

Trevor put out his hand. "Hey, Jack. Good to see you, man."

Jack took his hand, and Trevor drew him into a brief embrace.

Jack stiffened, Maggie noticed, but he didn't squirm away. When they'd stepped apart, Jack nodded at her, but didn't make small talk as he had before when she'd come in. Maybe this was the real Jack, and it was the liquor that made him so friendly before.

The tension was thick in the space between the two men, but Maggie sensed that Trevor's affection for Jackson Linder was genuine. It still amazed her, knowing what had happened between these two men, that Trevor had managed to forgive Jack.

"You have another poster to hang up?" Jackson nodded toward the stack of posters lopped over Trevor's arm, but his question was directed at Maggie.

"Well, we're replacing the old ones." She explained the campaign briefly to him. "This is the last one though. After next weekend you can toss it. Or we'll come in and take it down if you like."

"It's a nice-looking piece."

Trevor put a hand lightly on her back. "Meg designed the series."

She ducked her head. "Thanks."

Jackson eyed Trevor but addressed Maggie. "If you change your mind about work"—he pointed back toward the studio—"give me a call. I could really use an assistant."

"Meg's been working pretty much full-time at the inn." There was no trace of animosity in Trevor's voice, but his hand pressed more firmly into the small of her back.

Jack seemed to ignore Trevor's comment and stared pointedly at her.

"You have my number, if you change your mind." He nodded toward the posters Trevor held. "It's obvious you have some strong artistic skills."

Maggie's gaze ping-ponged from Trevor to Jack and back again, wondering how she'd gotten caught up in this odd tug of war between them. The way his hand slipped from her back to her waist made her wonder for a minute if Trevor was jealous. Kevin had been an insanely jealous boyfriend. She hadn't been able even to look at another guy's photo in a magazine—never mind innocently chatting with a male clerk at the grocery store—without him blowing up and giving her the third degree.

But this was something different. Trevor's possessiveness didn't seem to be about *his* insecurities so much as it was about watching out for her best interests. Still, it gave her pause. She'd been in one relationship with a man who thought he owned her. Did she want that again? Not that Trevor had made any claims on her. She was very aware of that. In fact, he'd seemed careful to offer merely friendship and a brotherly shoulder to lean on.

She took a step away. Trevor's hand left her back.

"Thank you, Jack. I appreciate the offer. I'll let you know if anything changes." She reached to take a poster off the dwindling stack Trevor held. "I'll go put this up."

Leaving the men to mentally duke it out, she hurried to the front of the store and took down last week's poster.

"Are you ready?" Trevor stood behind her, close enough for her to feel his breath on her neck.

She finished taping up the new poster, then turned and nodded without meeting his eyes. Her mind raced, still trying to sort out her conflicting emotions. She wanted to belong to Trevor. The realization startled her. She'd never felt this way about any other man. But now that she'd come to know Trevor, know his selfless care for her, she knew she would feel somehow incomplete without him in her life. If he ever opened his heart to her, she was a goner.

But the old fears niggled at her. Trevor didn't know of her deceit yet.

Wren had promised to keep quiet until Maggie had a chance to tell him everything. Maggie lived in fear that Wren would forget and call her by her real name.

Sometimes she wondered if the barriers her lies had erected between her and Trevor were for the best. After all she'd been through with Kevin, maybe it was wrong to let her life become entwined again. Would that be fair to Trevor, who deserved so much more?

She left the gallery and started down the street toward the small hardware store that was next on their list. She heard Trevor tell Jack good-bye, then the thud of his shoes on the pavement, running to catch up with her. She didn't look back.

"Hey, you. Slow down, will you?"

She slowed her pace but kept her eyes straight ahead.

"Meg?"

She took the six steps to the hardware store's entry two at a time.

"Wait up, Meg."

She turned, one hand on the door, to study him. What she saw in his eyes scared her to death. Because what shone there she didn't deserve.

"Did I say something wrong?"

She shook her head, not knowing how to explain to him the torment she was experiencing. But she hadn't imagined it. Looking head-on into his eyes now, she saw his love for her. His compassion. Clear and bright as his blue eyes. Yet how could this be? How could he possibly love her? Maybe she was fooling herself.

"Meg?"

Hearing him speak that name, she came to her senses. Trevor Ashlock *couldn't* love her. He didn't *know* her. Didn't even know her real name.

She stopped short
when she spied a gaily
wrapped package lying
on the end of the bed.

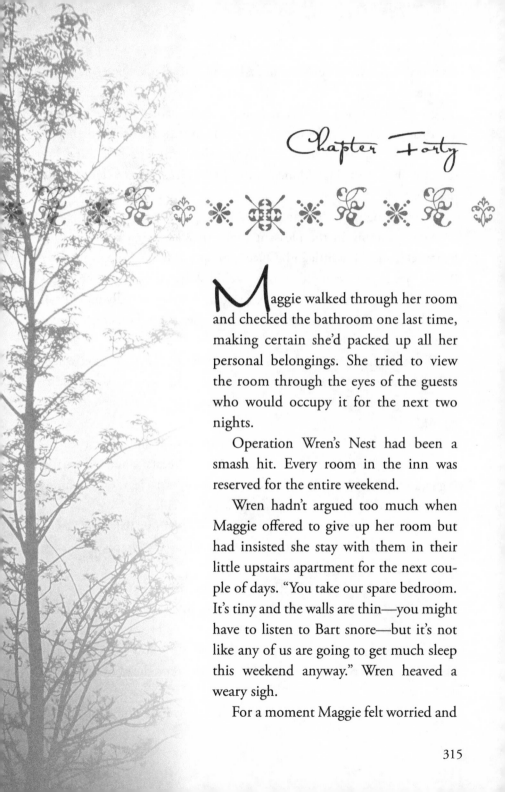

Chapter Forty

Maggie walked through her room and checked the bathroom one last time, making certain she'd packed up all her personal belongings. She tried to view the room through the eyes of the guests who would occupy it for the next two nights.

Operation Wren's Nest had been a smash hit. Every room in the inn was reserved for the entire weekend.

Wren hadn't argued too much when Maggie offered to give up her room but had insisted she stay with them in their little upstairs apartment for the next couple of days. "You take our spare bedroom. It's tiny and the walls are thin—you might have to listen to Bart snore—but it's not like any of us are going to get much sleep this weekend anyway." Wren heaved a weary sigh.

For a moment Maggie felt worried and

responsible for Wren's exhaustion. After all, this whole open house was her idea.

But Wren seemed to sense her guilt and immediately launched into a chorus of praise for the idea's success. "I won't deny that I'll be happy when this crazy weekend is over. And believe me, the first thing I'm doing with our earnings Monday morning is hiring you to clean up the place."

Maggie laughed at that and promised to pitch in.

Now, standing in the pleasant room that had been her home for five weeks, she felt a little sad. Once again, she'd packed the sum of her belongings into a small canvas bag. A chill skittered between her shoulder blades where the strap of the bag rested. Would she really move back into this room Sunday night after the last guest went home? Or would it be time to move on?

Clayburn had become home for her. She couldn't imagine where else she would go. Except maybe to Jenn and Mark's. But she couldn't intrude on their life. With Mark out of work, they had enough to worry about.

No time to think about it now. She brushed her palm across the bedspread, smoothing out a nonexistent wrinkle. Guests would start arriving in an hour, and there was still much to do, not the least of which was to shower and try to make her hair look presentable.

She carried her things up to the spare bedroom in Bart and Wren's apartment and stopped short when she spied a gaily wrapped package lying on the end of the bed.

She stooped to inspect it. The tag said simply, "Meg."

Curious, she slipped off the ribbon and carefully removed the wrapping paper. Lifting the lid, she caught her breath. Inside was a simple, flowing summer dress in a tiny red and yellow print. She giggled. She would coordinate perfectly with the remodeled dining room and kitchen.

She shook the dress out and held it up. It was feminine and pretty and looked like a perfect fit. She inspected the tag. *Made especially for you by: Wren Johannsen.*

Tears stung Maggie's eyes. How in the world had Wren found time to sew her a dress amidst all the preparations for the open house?

She hummed through her shower and, twenty minutes later, dressed, and with her hair swept up on top of her head, Maggie practically floated down the stairs and into the kitchen.

Wren was removing a heavy pan of lasagna from the oven. Maggie twirled in the cramped space between two linen-clad tables. "Thank you, Wren! It's beautiful. I love it."

Wren slipped off her oven mitts, brushed a wisp of white hair from her forehead, and looked up. "Oh, honey. *You* are beautiful. Does it fit all right? I could take it in if you think—"

"Oh, no, it's perfect! I don't know when you ever had time to work on it without me knowing."

Wren wriggled her eyebrows Groucho Marx style, and Maggie laughed. "Oh, I pulled a couple of late-nighters, don't think I didn't. But it was worth every minute. You look *lovely.*"

"Thank you, Wren." Maggie crossed the room, arms outstretched. She wrapped Wren in a hug, her throat too full to speak.

Wren hugged her back, then waved her off. "It was fun to make. Did you notice how pretty you look with the décor?"

Maggie trotted over to stand between a set of new curtains and the archway she'd painted to match. She struck a comical pose. Wren rewarded her with a gleeful laugh. Her life was so different here that sometimes she forgot who she used to be. She wanted only to remember the now . . . not what happened before.

✳ ❊ ✳

At Wren's strict instructions, Trevor parked around back, leaving plenty of room for guests to park on Main Street and along

Elm on the south side of the inn. He let himself in the back door and walked down the long hall to the lobby. Several of the rooms along the hallway were open, showing off crisply made beds and small vases of flowers on each desk—specially arranged for this occasion. A couple of closed doors already had Wren's whimsical DO NOT DISTURB signs hanging on the handle, an indication that some guests had already checked in.

He entered the lobby and stood in awe of the transformation. The sofa had been moved in close to the fireplace, and four small table-and-chair sets were placed strategically around the room. Through the arched doorway, he could see half a dozen more tables for two, each layered with white linens and set with the fancy red and white dishes that had been Wren's mother's. Unlit candles and vases of bright flowers decorated the center of each table.

Meg's dozens of candles glowed in the fireplace, and he chuckled to see white Christmas lights twinkling in the windows throughout the lobby and the dining area. He'd have to give her a hard time about that.

She chose that instant to scurry around the corner. When she saw him, she stopped short, perfectly framed beneath the archway.

Trevor could only stare. All thoughts of razzing the woman evaporated, and the only word filling his mind at the moment was . . . *stunning*.

Careful, Ashlock. She's not yours.

Meg smiled, obviously unaware of his emotions. "Oh. Trevor. It's you. Hey, can you come help Wren and me move this table?" She whirled and disappeared back into the dining room.

He stood, transfixed, until she appeared in the doorway again. "Hey, you coming or not?"

He stared. Meg, in a dress that hugged her form in all the right places. She moved, and the hem swished against shapely calves that led to dainty ankles and sandal-clad feet. Her hair was swept off her neck with tendrils brushing her cheeks in a style that was most becoming.

"Wow. You look . . . stunning."

Her cheeks flushed pink, making her look prettier than ever. He half expected her to run back to the kitchen, but she surprised him by taking his hand and pulling him into the kitchen.

"Good grief." She muttered under her breath. "You'd think the man had never seen a woman in a dress before."

He laughed. "I've never seen *this* woman in a dress before." He gave a low whistle.

She rewarded him by twirling around and dipping in a little curtsy. "Wren made it for me. Isn't it great?"

He could only nod and grin like the village idiot. "Wren did an extremely nice job," he finally stammered.

Wren and Meg laughed at him.

"You look pretty spiffy yourself." Meg nudged him toward the table where Wren was standing. "We want to move this table about a foot this way." She pointed to the window at the back of the room. "But we'd like to do it without taking everything off. Doable?"

He studied the table with its pressed linens, vase of flowers and candlestick, accessing the situation. "If we each take a corner and go slow, we can do it. Ready?"

Wren and Meg each claimed a corner and he took the side opposite. "One . . . two . . . three." They lifted and headed toward the window. For one breath-holding moment the water glasses swayed and the dishes rattled, but everything righted itself and Wren stepped back to survey the room.

She nodded her approval and brushed off her hands. "Okay, I'm headed to my room to change and get Bart on the ball. Can you two handle any early arrivals and make sure nothing burns down here?"

"Got it." Trevor gave a sharp salute. "What else needs doing?"

Wren bit her lip, obviously clicking off her mental list. She checked the clock. "It's probably not too early to light the candles on the tables. If you guys would do that. Oh, and Trevor, put some nice music on, would you? Some of that elevator music you're always listening to."

He chuckled. "Wren, those are the great masters of music you're talking about . . . the classics. C'mon . . . elevator music?" He shook his head and harrumphed.

Wren waved him off. "Whatever. And in ten minutes or so you can ice and fill the water glasses. I started the coffee, but you might keep an eye on it."

Meg laughed and put her hands on Wren's shoulders, steering her toward the door. "Go, Wren. You obviously have everything under control here. I don't think we can goof anything up in the next twenty minutes. Go."

"Okay, okay. I'm going." She started out of the room, then pivoted to face them. "Thanks for everything, you two. I couldn't have done this without you."

Trevor winked at Meg, then told Wren, "I have a feeling you would have done just fine."

Wren waved him off again with a "pshaw" for good measure, then hustled up the stairs to the apartment.

"The place looks nice," he said, once he and Meg were alone.

She followed his gaze around the room and out to the lobby. "It does, doesn't it? I'm just glad we filled the rooms. I have a feeling Wren spent all her profit putting this together."

"Yes, but maybe it will get some word of mouth going. Maybe even start some traditions for some couples. Let people know they don't have to leave town to get a little vacation."

"Exactly."

He went to put on some music in the CD player in the lobby. When he came back, Meg was rummaging through kitchen drawers. She came up with a couple of propane lighters and handed one to Trevor. "Here,

I'll do the lobby if you'll light the ones in here. And don't forget the candles on the window sills."

"Got it."

He watched her sail out to the lobby and bend to light the candle centerpiece on a table there. He shook himself a little and forced his mind to the task Meg had assigned him. He was falling for her. And hard.

"Hello, Maggie.
Or is it Meg?"
She fought for
enough air to
breathe his name.

Chapter Forty-One

Through the front lobby windows, Maggie watched two sets of headlights pull up to park in front of the inn. She thought she heard car doors slam out on Elm Street too. Her heart beat a little faster. It seemed everyone was arriving at once.

She lit the last candle and tucked the lighter out of sight on the front desk. She made one last survey of the room, and her heart swelled. It looked utterly delightful. With candles everywhere, minilights twinkling in the windows, and Mozart filling the air, the effect was every bit as romantic as they'd promised in the ad campaign. Not to mention the mouthwatering aromas coming from the kitchen. It was promising to be a night to remember.

She smoothed the front of her dress and prepared to greet their guests.

Kaye DeVore and her husband were the first of the new group to come in.

Before they were even all the way inside, they gawked and started *oohing* and *aahing* over the inn's transformation. Kaye was looking proudly expectant in a maternity version of the little black dress. Her hair was curled becomingly about her round face, and she wore a little lipstick, but her glow came from within.

Kaye's gaze landed on Maggie. "Meg! This place looks fabulous! I can't tell you how excited I am about this weekend." She nudged her husband. "Douglas, this is Meg Anders."

He set two small travel cases on the floor beside him, wiped his palm on his trousers, and shook Maggie's hand. "This was a pretty good idea you had."

She shrugged one shoulder. "Well, if it wasn't for your wife, I never would have come up with the idea, so send your praise her way." She turned to Kaye. "You look beautiful!"

Douglas DeVore squeezed his wife's shoulders and looked down on her with an expression that told Maggie this weekend getaway had been a long time coming for the harried couple. She was glad Wren had assigned the best room in the inn to them. "Come on over to the desk, and I'll get you checked in, then Trevor can show you to your room." She stepped into the kitchen and called Trevor before going to the desk to fill out a registration form for the DeVores.

She scarcely had them signed in before two more couples came through the front door. It was starting to feel a mite crowded and overly warm in the lobby.

Trevor ducked through the archway. Maggie gave him the DeVores' keys and told him which room was theirs. "Dinner will be in about twenty minutes, but there's coffee and appetizers on the buffet, so come back to the lobby as soon as you're settled in."

A short line had formed at the front desk. Maggie greeted the next guests in line and distributed the registration forms Bart had filled out as each reservation came in. Thank goodness for his foresight, or she'd be panicking about now.

She heard Bart and Wren in the kitchen setting up the buffet.

Trevor came back and showed the next couple to their room. She'd checked in four couples, not counting the two who'd arrived earlier that afternoon. There was a brief lull, though Maggie saw another car slow down in the street outside the front windows.

She grabbed Trevor as he came back from taking the last group's luggage to their rooms. "Could you man the desk for a minute? I'm going to go see if Wren needs anything in the kitchen."

"Sure. But hurry back."

She smiled. "Don't worry. I won't leave you stranded."

Wren was bustling as only Wren could bustle. She had on a fresh cotton dress and a new quilted apron that contained scraps of Maggie's dress fabric.

"Oh, don't you look nice."

"What about me?" Bart popped out from behind the refrigerator. He was wearing a white apron, and his Santa Claus beard was groomed to perfection.

Maggie stifled a chuckle. "You too, Bart. You look lovely."

He struck a comical pose, and she let her laughter escape.

"Everything going okay out there?" Bart pointed toward the lobby.

Maggie nodded. "Just about everyone is here. Are you ready for us to escort everyone into the dining room?" Wren surveyed the colorful spread. "I think we're ready anytime."

Trevor was checking in more people at the lobby desk, and there was a small group waiting in the seating area near the fireplace. Trevor seemed to be holding his own, so Maggie went to welcome those who were waiting.

Kaye DeVore grabbed her as she slipped by the desk. "You look gorgeous tonight, Meg! It's no wonder Trevor can't keep his eyes off you!"

Maggie flushed and glanced over to be sure Trevor hadn't heard Kaye's remark.

"It's true. He's been watching you all night."

"You're sweet to say that," she whispered to Kaye. But oh, how she longed for it to be true. Blushing, and desperate to change the subject, she motioned toward the people sitting near the fireplace. "I'd better go play hostess."

"Oh, don't let me keep you." Kaye looked around the room, and Maggie followed her gaze to a cluster of rowdy men talking sports by the front door.

Kaye sighed. "I'd better go see if I can extricate my date from the little men's club over there."

She waved over her shoulder and Maggie went to speak to the guests. She licked her lips and tried to dry her clammy hands. As excited as she was that this evening had finally arrived, she was out of her element playing hostess.

She cleared her throat. "Good evening, folks. We're so glad you could come tonight." She waited for them to quiet further. "Wren has been working all week, and as you can tell from the delicious aromas coming from the kitchen"—she waved an arm toward the dining room—"dinner is served."

A little cheer went up from the guests, and Maggie relaxed. The weekend was going to be a smashing success.

*A*n hour and a half later, the meal—and the scrumptious dessert tray that had followed—were mere memories. However, a dozen or so guests had turned the evening into a party, lingering in the lobby in small groups to visit and enjoy second cups of coffee.

Bart stepped into the doorway from the kitchen, his apron skewed and decorated with splotches of marinara sauce, his large hands encased in sudsy rubber gloves. He beckoned Maggie over, and she wove her way through clusters of guests.

Bart nodded toward the beverage cart in the corner. "We're running low on coffee. Wren went up to take something for her headache, and

I don't know beans about this big coffee maker. Do you know how to work the thing?"

Maggie spread her hands. "I haven't a clue, but I'll run up and ask Wren."

He nodded and went back to his dishes.

Maggie raced up the stairs and knocked on the door to the Johannsens' apartment. "Wren?"

No response. She knocked again, louder. "Wren? Are you there?"

She heard footsteps in the apartment, and a moment later Wren opened the door.

"Are you feeling okay? Bart said you had a headache."

"Oh, nothing a couple aspirin won't cure." Wren put a hand up to her temple. "Is everything under control down there?"

Maggie gave a nervous laugh. "Mostly. We're out of coffee, and Bart and I didn't know how to work that coffee maker."

Wren smoothed her apron. "Hold down the fort for a minute. I'll be right there."

"Okay . . . thanks."

Wren did an imitation of Trevor's comical salute. Maggie laughed and closed the door. She took the stairs back down two at a time.

The lobby was still buzzing with conversation and strains of Mozart, but the chatter quieted as she crossed the lobby, as if they expected another announcement. Near the fireplace, two couples occupied the sofas, and a man was seated in the wingback chair with his back to her. She smiled, and the group resumed their conversations.

Maggie noticed one of the candles in the fireplace had tipped in its holder, and she walked over to set it aright. When she straightened, her eyes locked with the man in the wingback chair.

"Hello, Maggie. Or is it Meg?"

The blood siphoned from her face. She balled her hands into fists, clenching her fingers until the nails dug into flesh. She fought for enough air to breathe his name.

"Kevin."

His laughter chilled
her, bringing back
memories she'd almost
succeeded in burying.

Chapter Forty-Two

W hat . . . what are you doing here?"

Kevin Bryson, dressed in a white shirt and tie—his office attire—fit right in with the evening guests. His sandy hair was cut shorter than he usually wore it, but other than that, he looked instantly familiar.

He glanced at the couple on the adjacent sofa. They were engrossed in conversation together, and he turned back to Maggie, lowering his voice. "The question is, what are *you* doing here?"

"I-I want you to leave," she whispered.

He laughed, as if she'd made a terribly clever joke. His smile remained, and anyone else would have thought they were having a pleasant conversation, but she knew the hardness that came to his eyes all too well. "That's exactly what I plan to do. Go get your things."

"What do you mean?"

His eyes never wavered from hers. "Get your things. I'm taking you home . . . back to New York."

"No, Kevin. I'm not going. Please. Just leave." She clenched and unclenched her fists at her side. The buzz of conversation in the room had grown to a low roar in her ears.

Kevin's gaze made a furtive pass over the people nearby before he spoke. His tone was even, conversational. "I'm not leaving until I get what I came for."

Maggie cast frantically about the room. If she argued, he'd make a scene and ruin the whole evening. She would die before she'd let him do that to Bart and Wren.

Wren hadn't yet come downstairs, and she could hear Bart's and Trevor's voices and laughter in the kitchen as they washed dishes.

"I'll talk to you later, but I'm busy right now." Maggie knew the minute the words left her mouth that they would infuriate him. She wouldn't have dared to speak to him that way six weeks ago.

Remaining in a bent position, he eased from the wing chair to the sofa. He reached for her wrist and squeezed until she winced. His expression never changed. Anyone watching them might have thought he held great affection for her. It was a technique he'd perfected. One he could use to keep her in control when they were in public.

"Please, Kevin." She glanced to the street outside, then panned the room. No one seemed to notice anything amiss. "Come outside for a little bit. We can talk out there."

He eyed her suspiciously, then let go of her arm and unfolded himself from the sofa. "Fine." He walked to the door and held it open for her. The picture of chivalry.

But once they were outside, his nice-guy grin turned to a sneer. "What exactly are you trying to prove?"

"I'm not trying to prove anything. This has nothing to do with you." She backed down the sidewalk, trying to get out of view of the inn's front windows. Looking through the windows to the festive lights and activity inside, she wondered if anyone would notice she was gone.

It was nearly dark outside now. She back-pedaled some more, still attempting to draw him away from the inn.

He followed her, jabbing a finger at the empty air, accusing. "You walked out on me. Without saying a word. What—you couldn't tell me you wanted to leave? We couldn't talk about this like two adults?"

"I *tried* to talk to you. Many times. You wouldn't listen. And you . . . you had me so dependent on you there wasn't any way I *could* leave."

He swore and looked back toward the inn. "Seems to me you managed just fine."

"You don't understand. I-I got carjacked. Things were all messed up that day. I didn't know what to do. I was scared and I—"

"What, you couldn't call me?" His voice escalated, building to a fury she'd seen more times than she cared to count. "You had to make me come looking for you?"

When he got this way, there was no reasoning with him. She willed her own voice down an octave and measured out her words. "I didn't ask you to come here."

But he seemed not to have heard her. He paced, zigzagging the breadth of the sidewalk, kicking at pebbles and mashing the heel of his dress shoes into the concrete. He buried his hands deep in the pockets of his pants. "Is there a liquor store in this town?" He motioned to the curb. "Come on. Come with me. I need a drink. We can talk in the car."

For the first time she noticed the Honda parked at the end of the block.

"No. I have a party to go to." Her words sounded silly and incongruous. But she didn't owe him any explanations. He had no right to come here after her. "I'm going back inside." Hands trembling, she willed courage into her voice. "And you need to leave."

He didn't respond but stood in front of her looking more shocked than angry.

Taking advantage of the distraction, she started around the side of the building. Maybe if she used the back hallway entrance, no one would notice she'd been gone. She could slip into the utility room and compose herself. She envisioned Kevin standing back there, blank surprise on his face. How had she lived with that man for two years? What a fool she'd been.

"Maggie! Get back here!"

Hearing his voice behind her, she quickened her steps.

Her hand was on the warm metal of the doorknob when his fingers closed around her wrist. He pressed his body against her. "I said, let's go get a drink."

She squirmed and turned to face him, her back pressed against the door. "No. I'm going inside."

He swore again and wrenched her forearm. Hot pain shot up her arm and through her elbow. "Stop! You're hurting me."

"No kidding."

His laughter chilled her, bringing back memories she'd almost succeeded in burying. "And you don't think you hurt me when you left?"

The doorknob pressed painfully into the small of her back. She winced. "I'm sorry. I-I should have talked to you." She hated herself for groveling before him.

"Well, it's a little late for that now, isn't it?" His voice had taken on that patronizing tone she'd learned to loathe.

Her thoughts tumbled over one another, as she tried to think how she could persuade him to go. She had to get him out of here before he made a scene and ruined everything.

Forcing a calm she didn't feel into her voice, she tried another tact. "I'm sorry. Can we talk about this tomorrow? You can come back then, when things aren't so busy here and—"

"No! Stop talking." He glared at her. "You think I'm going to fall for that? Come on—" He grabbed her arm and dragged her away from the door. "Get in the car." He shoved her in the direction of where the Honda was parked.

Maggie was at a loss for how to handle him, but one thing she knew. She was *not* getting in that car with him. She started to run back toward the front entrance to the inn, but he caught up with her and grabbed her by the arms. She tried to scream, but he clamped a hand over her mouth.

"Shut up!"

She let her body go limp and sagged to the hard earth at the edge of the sidewalk. She grappled free from his hold. "Help! Trevor! Somebody!"

Music and laughter drifted from the inn. Maggie knew they hadn't heard her.

Kevin came at her again. She kicked at his legs, and when he faltered, she scrambled to her hands and knees, scuttling like a crab toward the door to the inn. He tried to tackle her, but she rolled out of his grasp and struggled to her feet.

He came after her, and she started running, blindly, the only direction she could go—away from the inn. She had to get back. Maybe she could outrun him and circle back. The man had tracked her halfway across the country. If he was willing to do that—She shuddered, not keen on exploring that train of thought.

He closed in on her and dove to tackle her again. He clipped her heels, and she stumbled, catching the heel of her sandal in her hem. The fabric ripped and her hem sagged. She cried out but kept sprinting along the grassy space between the sidewalk and the street.

The river.

The words echoed in her head the way they had when she'd fled New York. That soft breath of a voice in her ear—there, yet not there. And then that same mysterious urgency to heed its instruction.

Go to the river.

The banks of the Smoky Hill had become her special place. To walk. To think. And of course to spend time with Trevor. If she took a shortcut through the alley, it was a twelve-minute walk from the inn to the roadside park by the river. She'd timed it on several occasions when she and Trevor met there to walk. If she ran, she might be able to make it in eight. She knew that short stretch of the river—its shallow coves and overhanging branches.

She looked up. The sky had darkened to indigo now. She'd never been to the river after dark, but Kevin wouldn't know the way. She'd be safe there.

She broke into a sprint and turned down the alley. Looking over her shoulder, she discovered he wasn't following. He was standing there. Just watching her.

Gathering up her ripped skirt as she ran, she slowed to a jog, breathless and trembling. She glanced over her shoulder again. Maybe he'd given up. But she wasn't going back to find out. Not yet. She would go to the river.

She came out of the alley and turned down Pickering Street, leading north, out of town.

Headlights blinked from a side street as she passed. She slowed, waiting for the vehicle to cross Pickering. But she froze as she recognized the car.

Kevin's white Honda. And him glaring behind the wheel.

The parade of her
life started, and
slowly her confusion
cleared until she knew
it was the end.

Chapter Forty-Three

Maggie jogged behind the Honda and took off running in the opposite direction back toward the inn. She heard his brakes screech behind her and the engine rev, but she didn't take time to look. She ran for all she was worth, muscles pumping, her now-tattered skirt flailing at her legs and threatening to trip her with every step.

The Honda came at her. Kevin drove along beside her, jeering, aiming the car at her, then veering off, only to come back at her again, effectively blocking her passage to the inn. She could see the lights flickering across the street, could hear laughter inside, and intermittent strains of Mozart. But Kevin had her trapped. Gasping for air, she crossed the parking lot behind the print shop.

Go to the river.

Again she heard it. Almost audible.

And now she had no choice. She raced through the alley, then ran between the print shop and the building next door. From there she ran down an empty street.

Kevin's car had disappeared. She ran another block, winded and trembling. Soon she could make out the park ahead in the distance, dark and empty. She ran across the sandy playground a few minutes later. In the faint glow from a quarter moon, she watched the silvery flash of water making its languid course up the riverbed. But the gentle music of waves lapping at the roots of trees seemed somehow sinister tonight, like the score from a horror movie.

She slowed to a walk but made a beeline for the gnarled silhouette of an ancient cottonwood. Its massive trunk would curtain her from sight. She could wait it out there until she was sure it was safe to leave the park.

Mere inches from safety, she heard an engine rev. Then the high beams of a pair of headlights threw their spotlight upon her. She turned to stone, caught in midstride, like a marble statue.

The slam of a car door wrenched her from her paralysis. She scrambled behind the tree and skidded purposefully down the steep riverbank, praying the crackle of brittle grass and leaves wouldn't give her away.

And then he was above her, standing there on the bank, arms crossed. Patient, watching, pinning his sights on her like a hunter scoping out his prey.

Maggie slipped into the water. The silt was slick beneath her sandals. She tucked her head and dipped her face in the water, then dove beneath the river's depths. She imagined herself a mermaid, using her legs and feet as a powerful tail, taking care not to splash and give away her position. She came up for a breath and the earthy musk of mud and fish enveloped her. She dove back under, swimming deeper, feeling weightless and insignificant.

Her lungs were on fire, and she thrashed against the watery weight of her skirt. She finally broke the surface and gulped in the night air.

She stilled, forcing herself to take slow, even breaths.

A splash behind her made her look over her shoulder. But before her eyes could focus on the dark form in the water behind her, the cloying heaviness of Kevin's cologne tainted the loamy fragrance of the Smoky Hill.

He wedged her neck in the muscled crook of his arm and tightened the vice. She screamed and struggled against him, gasping for a breath that wouldn't come. Her chest burned with a hunger for air, but she got only a thimbleful, merely whetting her need for more.

She heard voices on the bank, strident, but too distant to mean anything for her. *Go to the river,* the quiet voice had said. *Go to the river.*

Had that voice led her to her death? Had her mother's demented voices finally become her own?

The parade of her life started, and slowly her confusion cleared until she knew it was the end. She saw her mother's face, laughing and happy, and Jenn as a little girl, curling up beside Maggie on the sofa. There were the Tarkans and . . . Opal Sanchez, the woman who'd given her a ride after the carjacking. Rick and Sandy, and the Blakelys. They were all there. So many caring people along the way who had helped her even when she was anything but kind in return. Kaye DeVore and Bart and Wren appeared.

And Trevor. She saw him as clear as life, sitting in the pickup that day he'd told her . . . what was it?

"If there's anything I can do, you only have to call me. I want you to believe that."

Trevor. She sucked in air and forced it from her lungs, shouting with the dregs of her strength, "Trevor! Trevor! Oh, God! Please! Help me, Lord! *Father!*"

At those words, a dam broke loose inside her. Something changed, and in an instant, she knew she would never be the same.

She heard the voices again—the *real* voices—only this time they sounded closer. She curled her legs up under her in the water and wedged her feet against Kevin's brick belly. Pushing herself up out of the water, she drew another breath. This time her lungs were satisfied.

She yelled again, her own shrill voice curdling her senses. "Trevor!"

She saw Kevin's arm above her, his white shirt sodden, gleaming against the night sky. And in an instant the sky turned to ink and everything receded into nothingness.

※ ▩ ※

*W*ater lapped at her chest. Maggie felt her body bob and sway with the river's eddies. She tried to roll over. She had to make her way to shore. But her efforts were met with resistance, and her frailty wouldn't allow her to try again.

Bits of memories from the last hours trickled back to her consciousness, and the terror of the night became reality. Kevin had come back for her. He'd followed her to Clayburn. Hunted her down and tried to kill her.

Her senses came alert, and she understood why she couldn't move. He was still there. Still had her in his grip. Maybe he thought she was dead. She slowed her breathing, made herself go limp again.

The lapping of the water lulled her. She felt at peace. Maybe she *was* dead. But no. She was being dragged through the water. But not in the vice grip he'd held her in before. Her body was numb, her muscles useless, but she felt as if she were being . . . cradled. A hand caressed her cheek.

"Meg. Meg? Can you hear me?"

Meg? Kevin wouldn't call her that. She tried to open her eyes, but her eyelids felt like cinder blocks.

"Meg? Maggie?"

"No, it's Meg," she wanted to say. Maggie didn't exist anymore. Not the old Maggie. She was a new person. She no longer belonged to the past. She tried to speak, to tell him everything. But her tongue wallowed in her mouth, thick as cotton. She heard the voice again, low and deep in her ear. And she didn't need to open her eyes to know who it was. But why had he called her by her real name? Did he know? Strong arms tightened about her, and she let herself relax against him. Trevor wouldn't let Kevin hurt her. The water lapped at them, soothing her soul. Trevor called her name again. She felt his hands smoothing the wet hair off her forehead.

"Meg? Wake up." He patted her cheeks gently.

She didn't want to wake up. She wanted only to stay here in his arms. To be safe with him.

"Meg. Maggie? Wake up!" Urgency imbued his voice. This time she heard the slap of his palm against her cheeks, and her body registered pain.

She forced a breath into her lungs and opened her eyes. Blinked. Then, with great effort, kept her eyes open. Trevor's face was inches from hers, half in shadow, a dim light reflected in the blue of his eyes.

"Trev—?" She choked on his name and fell into a coughing fit. He tipped her upright and supported her on his knee while she coughed up river water and bile. He patted her back and whispered her name until she quieted.

"Trevor," she whispered, when she could finally speak. "Kevin! He's here. He . . . he came after me. He tried to kill me."

"Shhh, you're safe. It's over, Meg. You're safe here."

She flailed her arms in the water, struggling to stand in the murky river. To see with her own eyes that he was gone.

"Are you okay?" Trevor drew her closer, carrying her ever nearer to shore.

She quit struggling and relaxed against him once again. Far in the distance, sirens split the night. After a while, she dared to ask. "Where is he?"

"He ran when he saw me come for you. The police have his car. They're looking for him now." He glanced over his shoulder, in the direction of the sirens. "Are you hurt? The ambulance is coming."

"No!" She tightened her arms around his waist. If they tried to check her into the hospital, the truth would all come out and she would lose him. "I'm fine. Really I am."

She let loose of him and struggled to her feet in the chest-deep water, desperate to prove she didn't need an ambulance.

Dizziness overcame her and she faltered.

But he caught her and drew her back to himself. "Let them check you out, okay? Just to be safe. Are you cold?"

"No. The water's warm. I-I'm fine. Really. Just a little weak."

"Wrap your arms around my neck."

She did, and he moved cautiously through the water, carrying her along on the rise and swell of the river's currents.

"Trevor? How did you know? That I'd be here?"

"Kaye said she saw you leave with someone. She heard you call him Kevin. I knew that wasn't good."

"But how did you know . . . to find me here?"

Even in the darkness, she saw his smile. "I just knew. I knew it was your special place. *Our* special place. I know you, Meg."

Her hopes wavered. "Oh, Trevor. No you don't. I'm not who you think I am. I've been so dishonest. Such a fake. You could never forgive me."

He stopped in the water. Leaned to cradle her head in his hands and place a tender kiss on her forehead. "Wren told me everything . . . Maggie."

She caught her breath and looked up, searching his face. All she saw there was love. And acceptance.

"I do know you. You're not the same person you were the day you came to Clayburn. I've watched you change and grow. You've blossomed here. Sometimes I think you're the only one who doesn't see that."

"But how can you ever trust me after all the lies? I've been so dishonest—even with myself. And selfish. I used so many people to get away from Kevin, and New York, and everything it represented to me."

He tipped her chin. Forced her to meet his gaze. "I don't see any of that when I look at you. All I see is a sweet, kind, funny, loving woman. I see a beautiful woman—inside and out—who has poured her heart and the work of her hands into helping Bart and Wren, who I know would do anything to help a friend."

The bubble of hope grew and rose up inside her, buoying her. Was it possible? Could the things Trevor said about her have become truth, even without her realizing it? Long ago, she'd latched on to Kevin because he let her feel dependent and needed. It was the opposite of the independence she thought had separated her from her mother and then from Jennifer.

But now she saw that her ideas of dependence had been warped. It was *good* to have people to depend on. To allow people to depend on you.

She raised her eyes to the starry canopy above them. The clouds had slipped away, and a heavy moon illumined them. Trevor's arms were strong beneath her. She remembered calling out to God in the water. He'd heard her! He'd sent Trevor to rescue her. But even before that, God had been with her in every detail of her journey—even using something as crazy as a carjacking to catapult her to freedom.

Her mind whirled with the truth. God's voice had led her to Clayburn. Not her mother's voice. Not voices of death, but the Voice of Life itself. It had been God who whispered, leading her west. She knew His voice. Knew *Him* now. And oh, most precious of all, He knew her. It had been Him, whispering her to the river.

His voice had saved her from drowning, brought her through the waters and safely into Trevor's arms.

"I-I've kept so many secrets." Her voice trembled.

Trevor traced her gaze to the night sky overhead. "You can't ever really keep any secrets, Meg. The only One who matters always knows."

Maggie's mind was frenzied with a new possibility. She dared to voice it now. "If you could forgive Jack . . . if you could forgive that awful day, then maybe . . . you can forgive me? Maybe God can forgive me."

"Tell me what there is to forgive, Meg?"

The way he spoke the words, Maggie knew he wasn't letting her off the hook. He was asking her to be honest with him. To confess the ways she'd wronged him. A month ago, such a request would have made her shudder. But now the kindness in his eyes, in his touch washed away all her fears.

She told him then, as the river caressed them. Everything she'd already confessed to Wren. She suspected Trevor already knew, but she needed to say the words. Needed to hear herself speak them. "Even my name was a lie," she said when she'd spilled everything out before him. "Can you forgive me?"

He drew his hand out of the water and placed it on her cheek. "I already have. I love you, Meg." He kissed her again, this time on the bridge of her nose.

She rested her head against the soggy front of his shirt, scarcely believing his words could be for her. But the tenderness in his touch told her the truth.

"Meg . . . ?"

She looked up, waiting, trailing her hand in the river, then lifting it to paint the line of his jaw with her fingertips.

"Meg Anders." He said it as if he were hearing it for the first time. "Would you mind too much if I go on calling you Meg? I don't really know who Maggie is. It's Meg I love."

The sound of her name—her new name—on his lips was like a song.

In the park, above them, headlights flashed and the red strobe of an ambulance flashed off the water. She wanted them to go away. She was fine. She'd never been so fine.

She touched a finger to his lips. "I love you, too, Trevor. So much."

He cupped her face in his strong hands and held her gaze. "Tonight you start all over. No more lies. No more secrets. Tonight is a new beginning for you. For us." He swept a wisp of damp hair away from her face and inclined his head toward the cluster of emergency vehicles that had gathered in the park. "Shall we go?"

She nodded against his chest. She was ready. It was time.

He lifted her up out of the water. She tightened her arms around his neck and let him carry her to shore.

Dear Reader

How grateful I am that God never forgets to remember His promises and always remembers to forget my sins, all because of the amazing sacrifice of Jesus Christ. How glad I am that Christ pursued me even when I didn't know what I was looking for, what I was *longing* for.

I think there is a little bit of Maggie in all of us—searching for one who sees us not as we are, but as we could be. Yet, we have a difficult time believing such a perfect love could really exist. If you haven't yet discovered His perfect love, I pray that by the time you've turned the last page of this book, you will know that it is true, and that it is meant for you. You only have to ask.

Even if you have received Christ's forgiveness, you may have a difficult time remembering to forget what is past. But when you accept Christ's gift on your behalf, *all is forgiven.* All is purified by God's "river" of grace and healing. No longer do you need to wallow in the muddy waters that try to suck you down or strangle the joy out of you. Nothing you've ever done is beyond God's forgiveness. Of that you can be assured.

Therefore, if anyone is in Christ, he is a new creation;
old things have passed away; behold, all things have become new.

2 Corinthians 5:17 NKJV

Discussion Questions

1. In *Remember to Forget*, Maggie Anderson feels trapped in her life because of an abusive, controlling boyfriend. She's unexpectedly given a chance to escape this life, but she's lived under Kevin Bryson's tyranny for so long, she scarcely knows how to handle her newfound freedom. Yet she longs for the new life she sees modeled by the people of Clayburn, Kansas.

If you think of *Remember to Forget* as an allegory—a story with layers of meaning, where characters and actions symbolize more than what is "on the surface"—in what ways does this story reveal what life is like without Christ? the longing the Holy Spirit puts within us for a relationship with God? and the transition into new life in Christ? (See 2 Corinthians 5:17.)

2. How much do you believe in "coincidence"? The Blakely family just happens to be headed where Maggie wants to go. Maggie just happens to be wearing tennis shoes and socks for the first time all summer. Wren just happens to have a bag of clothes in Maggie's size . . . and that's just for starters. There are many "coincidences" in *Remember to Forget*. Have you experienced similar circumstances—whether significant or trivial—that you believe are more than mere coincidence? Explain.

3. From the time Maggie escapes from her captor in New York, she is offered a ride several times by various people. Have you ever offered help to someone in need the way Opal Sanchez, the Henrys, the Blakelys, and Kaye DeVore did for Maggie, only to feel that your help was not appreciated? Tell the story. How did that make you feel at the time? Have you gained any other perspective since then? If so, what? Is it possible that somewhere down the road the person you helped became grateful for your help, but had no way of coming back to thank you?

Have you ever had a chance to go back and thank someone for leading you to Christ or helping you grow in your faith or develop your gifts? Did you take that opportunity? Why or why not?

4. When Maggie pours her heart out to Trevor at the bus station, she trusts him with her fears and tells him some of her needs. But she continues to harbor many secrets from him. If you've trusted God with your life, were you completely honest with Him—and with yourself—at first? Or did it take awhile to admit everything you are, were, or have done?

If you've come to the point in your faith walk where you have admitted every fault, fear, and mistake to God, what emotion accompanied that moment? Why do you think that is?

If you haven't experienced that moment of confession yet, what do you think might be holding you back?

5. When Maggie first gets to Clayburn, she finds small-town life a little overwhelming and is amazed that everyone is so close and familiar in this community. If you didn't grow up in a Christian environment, did your first encounter with Christian people—a church, Bible study, or Christian friends or neighbors—seem equally unfamiliar? Describe your feelings. If you are a believer, how might you help a new Christian feel more comfortable among the family of God?

6. Maggie gradually realizes that she has made a "crutch" of Kevin. As her attraction to Trevor grows, she feels cautious and worried that he, too, will become a crutch. How do you explain the difference between a worldly dependence on a person, and total dependence upon God, yet with encouragement and teaching from other Christians, which is completely scriptural? (See 1 Thessalonians 5:11; Hebrews 10:24–25.)

7. When Maggie decides that she wants to stay in Clayburn and "come clean" with her friends there, she puts off telling them the truth, thinking she'll first find a place of her own, pay off her bills, and straighten out her life. Have you ever responded this way to Christ's invitation—tried to clean up your act first and then come to Him? What happened as a result? What have you learned because of that experience? How do you now respond when you feel His gentle tug on your life? Give an example, large or small, of how your life has been touched or transformed.

8. Even though they are usually law-abiding citizens, the proprietors of the inn, Bart and Wren Johannsen, "bend the laws" to allow Maggie to work at the inn (paying her instead with room and board, since she doesn't have the proper identification to fill out tax forms, etc.). What do you think of their decision? How is it reflected in Scripture? (For a hint, see Romans 7:5–6 and 1 Corinthians 6:12.)

9. Business hasn't been good at Wren's Nest, but Maggie thinks up ideas to bring in new business. Soon people are coming in and recommending the inn to their friends. If you believe in Jesus, how might you "recommend" your faith to your friends? How might you bring people into "the nest"?

10. Although Wren is instrumental in helping Maggie find her new life, her own life has been far from perfect. She, and many others who

helped Maggie along the way, have experienced times of tragedy, sin, and doubt. Yet because of those times, they have great compassion and concern for those in need.

All of us are flawed. How can you help others find new life in Christ in spite of—or perhaps *because of*—your flaws? Tell about a real-life experience with this if you can.

11. When Jackson Linder shows an interest in having Maggie work for him, Trevor expresses concern and jealousy. Do you think concern and jealousy are good qualities, bad qualities, or a combination of both?

In Exodus 34:14, God says he is jealous for your affection and devotion. How does that make you feel? How might it affect your day-to-day actions?

12. After Maggie confesses her lies to Trevor, she wonders how he can possibly love her, knowing the way she was . . . not to mention everything she's done. But Trevor tells her that he doesn't even see those things when he looks at her. He tells her she's not the same person she used to be.

How does this experience between Maggie and Trevor mirror our relationship with God through Christ? (Read Psalm 103:11–13 and Romans 4:4–8.)

13. Just when Maggie has decided to forget about New York and embrace her new life in Clayburn, Kevin Bryson comes back to attempt to take her back to New York. All the while Kevin is trying to haul her toward his car and is pursuing her to harm her, Maggie is unaware that Trevor is watching over her. He is simply waiting for her to call out to him to rescue her.

Read Acts 2:20–21 and Romans 10:13. In what ways have you experienced evil pursuing you? How have you experienced God's protection in times of crisis (whether you were aware of it at the time or not until later)? Tell the story.

14. Maggie falls into the river, and Trevor rescues her there. She comes up out of the water in Trevor's arms, knowing that she is now free from Kevin's hold on her and free from the trappings of her old life. She is safe in Trevor's arms. What might this experience in the river symbolize? Have you undergone this type of experience yourself? Where the old you became the new, transformed you? If so, share what happened.

15. When Trevor tells Maggie, "I don't really know who Maggie is. It's Meg I love," how do you think she felt? (Read Revelation 2:17 and 3:5.) What does this tell you about what Christ does to you when you "come clean" with Him? What happens to your past? (See again Psalm 103:11–12 and 2 Corinthians 5:17.) What things do you need to "remember to forget" about your past life so you can move forward as a new creation—a new person with a new name, loved and accepted by Christ?

DEBORAH RANEY dreamed of writing a book since the summer she read all of Laura Ingalls Wilder's Little House books and discovered that a little Kansas farm girl could, indeed, grow up to be a writer. After a happy twenty-year detour as a stay-at-home wife and mom, Deb began her writing career. Her first novel, *A Vow to Cherish,* was awarded a Silver Angel for Excellence in Media and inspired the acclaimed World Wide Pictures film of the same title. Since then, her books have won the RITA Award, the HOLT Medallion, the National Readers' Choice Award, as well as being a finalist for the Christy Award. Deb enjoys speaking and teaching at writers' conferences across the country. She and her husband, artist Ken Raney, make their home in their native Kansas and love the small-town life that is the setting for many of Deb's novels. The Raneys enjoy gardening, teaching young married couples in their church, watching their teenage daughter's ball games, and traveling to visit three grown children and a precious little grandson who lives much too far away.

Deborah loves hearing from her readers. To e-mail her or to learn more about her books, please visit www.deborahraney.com or write to Deborah in care of Howard Books, 3117 North 7th Street, West Monroe, Louisiana 71291.